MW01711099

It is 1991 and Nathen and Authia are finally free of the curse that has haunted Nathen for over two centuries. However, their quest does not end there. It has only just begun. Nathen may be rid of his curse, but he still desperately needs to know who and what he is. Hidden somewhere deep in the Congo region of Africa are the answers. Nathen and Authia risk their lives in order to find the truth.

Meanwhile, in a valley hidden from the outside world, a tribe secretly waits for the return of their Lord. Unknown to Nathen and Authia, the High Priestess of the tribe is aware of their existence and will do everything in her power to prevent them from finding Nathen's home.

Journey to the Unknown

ISBN: 978-1-4874-1765-9
Cover art by Angela Waters

Published by eXtasy Books Inc or
Devine Destinies, an imprint of eXtasy Books Inc
Look for us online at:
www.eXtasybooks.com or www.devinedestinies.com

Journey to the Unknown
Lord of His People Book 2

By

Christine Frances

Dedication

My books will always be dedicated first and foremost to the teacher who saw in me a raw talent for writing. She cultivated my talent and made me who I am today. Though she is no longer with us, Sister Lambert will always be my mentor, my guiding light. I also dedicate my book to my sister Pat who continues to play an integral part in the writing of my books. Her unwavering support and encouragement reminds me every day to keep writing from my heart. Believe in yourself and your talent and the story will follow you.

Last, but by no means least, I must acknowledge my publisher, Devine Destinies, and especially my editor, Laura McNellis. Your support, your patience, all the knowledge that you have shared with me is appreciated far more than mere words can express. Thank you, from the bottom of my heart.

CHAPTER ONE

Congo Region, Africa, 1770

Joshawa stood outside his hut, surveying his village, his gaze taking in all that lay before him. The village was still sleeping, a privilege not afforded to Joshawa. These past few weeks Joshawa's mind was troubled for reasons that he didn't understand. As he scanned the vastness of his village, he made a mental note of two huts that needed to be re-thatched. There were over two dozen circular huts in the village, all varying sizes and all made of sapling trees and palm leaves. Hardened dirt served as the floors to these huts. A flap made of palm leaves covered the entrance to the hut. The huts encircled a large open area, and in the middle of that open area was a communal fire pit which was considerably larger than any other fire pit in the entire village. The priestesses of the village would perform special ceremonies around the fire pit, especially those that were meant to vanquish evil spirits.

His village was nestled in a clearing carved out of the rainforest. The vegetation grew thick around the village. The trees grew high, their substantial canopies protecting the village from the scorching rays of the sun. The rainforest was part of a valley hidden from the outside world. Only the people from his tribe were granted the privilege to walk the lush jungle grounds and enjoy the bounty that the valley had to offer. His tribe, christened the Jelani tribe, was as old as time itself.

He found himself lost in his thoughts of the tribe and how it was ruled by two families. One was Joshawa's family, a warrior clan, and the other was a family of priestesses. Since time began, the rule of the tribe never faltered. The Lord of the tribe ruled his people until his first-born son turned thirty. Then there was an elaborate ceremony ushering the son into manhood. For it was only when you turned thirty that the tribe truly considered someone a man. When the ceremony was completed, the new Lord would choose a priestess as his wife. Together they ruled the tribe.

Joshawa took a deep breath of the morning air. The sweet smell of the jungle filled his lungs and his mind. Then he closed his eyes and soaked in the sounds of the jungle. Birds, monkeys, the great beasts of the jungle, even the smallest insects all saying good morning to one another. He loved these sounds, for they made him feel at peace.

In the village, Joshawa knew he was considered a handsome man standing over six feet tall. That morning he had chosen to wear a loincloth made of animal skin that covered him from his waist to mid-thigh and a sleeveless vest stained a golden brown. He was very much aware of the fact that his muscular body intimidated the other men of the village. To maintain that intimidation, he wore his clothing so tight that it accentuated his body instead of covering it up.

Joshawa watched observed the people of his village as they gradually woke up and left their huts to partake in the morning meal. A meal that was being prepared over the communal fire pit. The people of the tribe didn't resemble what the outside world would classify as normal. They had shocking red hair that fell in gentle waves to their shoulders. Their faces were long and their cheekbones were unusually high. Their noses were wider than normal and their upper lips had a slight cleft. Their fingernails were long and curved. Their entire bodies were covered with a very fine, almost undistinguishable, layer of red hair.

Joshawa envied the married couples whose love was clearly displayed in their actions and how they gazed upon each other. He looked behind him, into his hut. His wife lay sleeping on their mat. Slowly, he shook his head as he gazed back out into the jungle. Love played no part of his marriage. She was beautiful. At five feet ten, Serena was of average height for the women of the Jelani tribe. Her sun-kissed complexion complemented her dazzling blue eyes. And, like all other members of her tribe, her hair was a fiery red cascading in waves to just past her shoulders.

However, he'd chosen Serena as his wife because she was the most powerful priestess ever born to the tribe. She needed to be controlled, and the only way Joshawa could think of accomplishing that was to marry her. His plan was not working so well. Serena's powers had become stronger. She had become more vocal, challenging him on a regular basis. Joshawa knew in his heart that a major confrontation was brewing and, as he walked toward the gathering hut, he acknowledged the fact that the outcome would not be good.

* * * *

Serena woke up and reached out for her husband. But, as usual, he was not there. She sat up, staring at the entrance to the hut. Anger brewed deep within her. Joshawa was distancing himself from her even more than usual. They had been married two full months and still, he had not consummated their marriage. Serena threw the blanket off her and quickly dressed in her ceremonial gown. She knew where Joshawa would be, and she was going to confront him and let him know exactly how displeased she was.

As she left the hut, five men from the scouting party ran past her, heading in the direction of the gathering hut. They were clad in animal skins that resembled large loincloths, effectively covering them from the waist to just past their buttocks. Each man carried a spear. Slung over each man's shoulder was a bow. Serena followed them, lifting her gown off the ground so that she would not trip as she kept up with the scouting party. When she arrived at the gathering hut, she took her place at her husband's side. She hoped the glare she shot Joshawa told him how much trouble he was actually in.

The gathering hut was the largest amongst all the huts in the village. The inside was bare, apart from a raised platform at the very back of the hut. A hand-woven blanket stained a bright red covered the platform, and along the outer edge were several ceremonial clay bowls. The bowls were used by the priestesses to ward off evil spirits during ceremonies and rituals. The Lord and priestess would sit on the platform and oversee whatever ceremony took place.

* * * *

The reason Joshawa was at the gathering hut was to escape his hut or, if the truth be known, to escape Serena. He was not expecting the scouting party, nor, for that matter, could he foresee the coming events that would forever alter his life.

Joshawa addressed Tamiel, the leader of the scouting party. "What is going on? Why have you returned so soon?"

"My Lord, there are strangers in our valley. Outsiders."

"How is that possible? Where did they come from?"

"They entered by the falls. There are two men and one woman."

"Are they armed?"

"Not that we can tell, my Lord."

Serena interjected. "Joshawa, you must call on Miguel. He must lead the warriors to the outsiders' camp and dispose of them."

Joshawa gave Serena a warning glance. "Tamiel, take your men and scout out these outsiders. See if you can tell why they are here." Joshawa glared directly at Serena as he addressed Tamiel. "They are not to be harmed. Understood?"

"Yes, my Lord." Tamiel bowed, then left the hut with his men. Joshawa avoided Serena's scowl as he kept a watchful eye on his men. Through the oversized opening to the hut he could see his men as they picked up some provisions, then headed back out into the jungle.

Serena shook her head. "You cannot be serious, Joshawa. These outsiders are a threat to us. They must be dealt with by the warriors."

"That is not your call, Serena. Mind your place! Unless you can produce a vision proving these outsiders are a threat, we are going to deal with them my way."

* * * *

Joshawa left Serena standing at the entrance of the gathering hut ready to burst into flames she was so angry. "Enough is enough, Joshawa. I will show you where my place is." Serena left the hut and went in search of Miguel. She finally caught up with him near the warriors' hut. It was a small hut where the warriors stored all their bows, spears, and machetes. She walked up to Miguel and crooked her finger at him. "Follow me."

Miguel was the leader of the warriors. Standing six feet tall, his fiery-red hair and deep blue eyes gave him an intimidating appearance. His long, curved fingernails were unusually sharp and proved to be an effective weapon against anyone or anything that would bring harm to him or his village.

Serena led Miguel to the priestesses' hut, where all the potions and remedies were made. It was also where the priestesses would do their conjuring. It was the second largest hut next to the gathering hut. She observed him closely as he entered the hut and scrutinized his surroundings. At the very back of the hut were several shelves, and on the shelves were clay pots stacked one against the other. At waist height was a narrow table that ran the width of the shelves. She knew no one outside the family of the priestesses knew for a fact what was contained in those clay pots. What the people of the tribe did know was that these clay pots possessed what was needed for the priestesses' incantations and sometimes, in the case of Serena, the darkest of spells.

Serena walked over to the fire pit in the centre of the hut, then sat down on the ground facing it. From her vantage point she had a full view of the entrance to the hut, which allowed her to make sure that she and Miguel were not overheard. From across the fire pit, Miguel knelt on one knee as he bowed his head.

"To whom are you loyal?"

Miguel answered without lifting his head. "To my Lord and to you, my Mistress."

"Wrong answer." Miguel's head shot up. "I ask you again, to whom are you loyal? Who are you prepared to sacrifice your life for?"

Miguel thought for a moment. "I am loyal to my Mistress." Once again, he bowed his head.

"Very good." Serena mulled over her options. She was about to cross a line, a very dangerous one. *What I am about to do could put me at great risk. No other priestess in the history of my tribe has ever defied their husband. The consequences would be devastating. But if I could discredit my husband and show him as weak and that his actions are not in the best interest of the tribe, then maybe I could turn the tables on him. Maybe I could be the first priestess to rule the tribe on my own.* The thought made Serena giddy with power. She turned her attention back to Miguel. "There are outsiders in our valley."

Again, Miguel's head shot up. "What? Why was I not informed?"

"Because, my husband decided to only send a scouting party. He wants to observe them."

Miguel stood before Serena. "But outsiders can ruin our way of life. They will bring others with them. They cannot be allowed to leave our valley."

Serena smiled ever so wickedly. "Then we are of the same mind. There is only one way to assure that we are safe. Take a small party to the outsiders' camp. When you get there, kill them. No one should remain alive."

"And what of the scouting party?"

"Make sure that you arrive before them. Make the outsiders' deaths appear as though it was an animal attack."

"And what if the scouting party comes upon us?"

"Then I pity the scouting party, for there shall be no witnesses."

Under the watchful eye of Serena, Miguel rounded up four of his most trusted men, then headed into the jungle to carry out her wishes.

Chapter Two

Joshawa went in search of Miguel. He wanted the warrior party to be prepared in case these outsiders posed a danger to the tribe. However, Miguel was nowhere to be found, and it appeared as if four of his warriors were missing. Joshawa shook his head in frustration. Serena had gone behind his back. He knew it was her. Quickly, he gathered a few of the warriors that he knew were faithful to his family and headed out into the jungle. As their powerful legs propelled them through the dense foliage, Joshawa's only hope was that he wouldn't be too late.

* * * *

Julia, Bill, and Thomas were exploring the beautiful vegetation surrounding their campsite. They were scientists from England cataloging plant life in the Congo region of Africa. It was only sheer luck that they happened upon the entrance to the valley. And what a find it had been. Julia was excited when they found plant life growing in the valley that they had never seen before. The plants they could identify seemed to be larger, more developed. Thomas was the lead scientist, and Bill was his apprentice. Julia was there to help catalog their findings. Julia was an incredible artist. Her purpose was to sketch the plant life that was to be cataloged. The detail in her sketches was incredible and allowed them the luxury of not having to disturb or destroy any of the wondrous vegetation.

They had returned to their campsite for afternoon tea when four men came upon them. The team gaped at the men who had features not unlike that of an animal. Four of them carried bows and had them pulled back, ready to attack.

One approached Thomas cautiously. "Why are you here?"

They were all taken aback. These natives spoke English.

"How did you learn to speak English?"

"I repeat, what are you doing here?"

"We study plants. Learn about them. Respect them."

"There are no plants where you come from?"

"Of course. But none as magnificent as what grows in your valley."

"That is too bad. For crossing into our valley is a crime punishable by death."

Julia gasped while the two men went white as ghosts.

* * * *

Miguel knew what he had to do. Their deaths had to appear as though they were animal attacks. Miguel stepped toward the one who spoke, raising his hand to inflict a fatal blow. He was about to strike when Joshawa walked up behind him.

"And whose orders are you obeying?"

Miguel whirled around and stood face to face with Joshawa. He lowered his arm, took a deep breath, and defiantly addressed his Lord. "I obey the orders of my Mistress, and to be honest, my Lord, I agree with her. These outsiders will only go back and bring more of them into our valley."

The outsider took a step closer. "No! If you allow us to leave, no one will ever learn of this place. I give you my word."

Miguel slowly turned to face the outsider. "I do not trust the word of an outsider." And with that, Miguel gave the order to release the arrows. Three of the arrows found their mark, and the two men died before they hit the ground. The woman turned to run but only managed a couple of steps before the last arrow hit her in the back. She stopped for only a second, then fell to the ground. Joshawa balled up his fist and hit Miguel. His fist connected underneath Miguel's chin, lifting him off his feet. Miguel landed on the ground, unconscious.

* * * *

Joshawa surveyed the remaining warriors. He let out a shrill whistle, and his warriors and the scouting party came out of the jungle.

"You have nowhere to go. Follow the high priestess, and you will be punished with no mercy. Follow me, and there will be forgiveness."

It was evident that the men knew whether they picked Joshawa or Serena, they were in trouble. They had to decide whom they wanted to anger more. The choice was easy. They laid down their bows and declared their allegiance to their Mistress. The scouting party collected their weapons while Joshawa's warriors aimed their bows at them. As Tamiel made sure there were no other weapons, he called out, "Joshawa, I think the woman still lives."

Joshawa walked over to the woman and knelt by her side. She was still breathing. The arrow appeared as though it had not done any permanent damage. He broke the shaft off so that only a small section remained protruding from her back. Then he gently lifted the women into his arms. The pale yellow dress that covered her from her neck to her toes spilled out from his arms and fell to just below his knees.

Blood from her injury dripped onto the ground at Joshawa's feet.

"Tamiel, take these men, including Miguel, and put them in the pit until I decide what to do with them. I'm bringing this woman back to our village. If anyone has an issue with that, speak now." There was silence amongst the men. "Good, after I see to her care, there will be a meeting in the gathering hut. Make sure everyone from the village attends." Joshawa turned and ran back into the jungle.

He thought the pit would be a good place to keep the traitors to his family until he could figure out their punishment. The pit was a large hole in the ground, about ten feet deep, and could hold up to ten prisoners. A heavy grate made of wood sealed the men in. It took four men to move the grate, so escape was not likely.

As Joshawa came out of the jungle, his people lined up in awe as they witnessed him carry a female outsider into their village.

* * * *

Serena, dressed only in her animal skins, arrived in time to observe Joshawa entering their hut with a woman cradled in his arms. And not just any woman. She was an outsider. Serena ran toward him, her anger building with every step she took. She entered the hut as Joshawa was gently laying the woman down onto their sleeping mat.

"What do you think you are doing?"

"Go get your mother. This woman needs medical attention."

"I will not! Get this woman out of our hut!"

Joshawa slowly stood as he glared at Serena. She could see the anger etched deeply in his face. Joshawa did not mince words. "She is here because of you. I suggest you do exactly as I say. After this woman has been treated, we are holding a meeting to decide what to do with you."

"There is nothing you can do to me, Joshawa. I am your wife, chosen by you. Nothing can break that sacred bond."

"Well, we will just see about that. Go get your mother!" As Serena turned to do as she was told, Joshawa added one more log to the fire that was already ablaze deep within Serena. "And when you return, gather your things. You will be sleeping in your family hut until this woman is ready to leave."

Serena reached into the waistband of the loincloth that covered her from her waist to her knees. She glanced back at Joshawa as she rested her hand on the leaf-covered packet. Then she thought better of it. She would have her time, and she would show Joshawa just how powerful she was.

* * * *

It was several hours later, and almost the entire village was present at the gathering hut. Joshawa had left two guards to protect the outsider, and he still had not released the men from the pit. Dressed in her ceremonial gown, Serena sat on the platform at Joshawa's side.

Joshawa stood and addressed his people. "I am saddened to say that a senseless tragedy occurred at the hands of those I should trust. Two outsiders are dead, and the third is hanging on for her life. We are meeting here not to discuss what is to happen to the outsider but rather what is to happen to my wife." There were audible gasps amongst the crowd. Serena glanced up at her husband with utter disbelief on her face. "As your Lord and ruler of this tribe, I gave a strict order that none of the outsiders were to be harmed. Serena chose to go behind my back and disobey my order. I cannot permit that kind of treachery in my village and most certainly not under my own roof. I decree that my marriage to Serena is forfeited. In time, I will choose another to rule by my side. I also decree that the men that followed her are to be banished from our village until such time that they can prove their loyalty to my family. You may bow to accept my edict or, if you disagree, stay standing and you will be heard."

Every single person in the village bowed to their Lord. Serena stood, then leaned closer and whispered into Joshawa's ear. "This is not even close to being over. Mark my words, you will pay for this." Then she silently left the hut, returning to her family's hut in disgrace.

CHAPTER THREE

Joshawa sat cross-legged on the floor of his hut, observing the outsider sleep. He was captivated by her beauty. She had honey-blonde hair that cascaded down her back almost to her waist. Her face was slightly tanned, and he knew she had the most dazzling blue eyes. The night was falling, blanketing the hut in darkness. However, Joshawa did not dare build a fire in fear of waking her. As he monitored her sleep, he tried to rationalize the desperate need he had to protect her. A woman not of his kind. It went beyond punishing Serena. There was much more to it than that. Something deep inside of him was telling him that she was important. There was a reason that the spirits spared her life and chose him as her protector.

The village was quiet. The only sounds that could be heard were those of the jungle. Joshawa stretched out on the dirt floor of the hut and stared up at the roof. He lay there listening to every breath she took until finally, sleep overcame him.

* * * *

It was the middle of the night when Julia finally woke up. She lay there, groggy, trying to make sense of her surroundings. In the pitch darkness, it was hard for her to ascertain where she was. Then the memories of the attack bombarded her as a searing pain enveloped her. She cried out in agony as she tried to sit up. One of the strange-looking men that she'd seen earlier was immediately at her side. His cat-like eyes shone in the darkened hut. Gently, he helped her lie back down onto the sleeping mat.

"Please do not move. Your injury is severe. You will need time to heal."

Julia closed her eyes and tried to take a deep breath, but the pain was too great. She opened her eyes and glanced over to the man sitting next to her. "Who are you? Where am I? What's happened to Thomas and Bill?"

"What is your name?"

"Julia. Now how about answering my questions."

"My name is Joshawa. I am Lord of this village. I am afraid your friends are dead."

Julia began to cry. Her tears ran freely down her cheeks. "This can't be happening. Am I your prisoner? What are you going to do with me?"

"You have nothing to fear from me. Once you are healed, you will be free to leave."

"And why should I trust you?"

"You have no choice." Joshawa smiled at her, then took her hand in his. "If I had wanted to harm you, I would have already done so. I give you my word. As long as I live, you will be safe." Tenderly Joshawa kissed the back of Julia's hand. "I am going to build a fire. That way you will be able to see your surroundings more clearly. I believe that will make you feel safer."

"Actually, yes, that would help. Thank you."

Within a few minutes, Joshawa had a small fire going. Julia gazed upon her protector with trepidation. His people killed her friends. How could she trust him not to kill her as well? She lay there in silence, staring at the flames that danced in the fire. Finally, sleep overcame her, and as she closed her eyes, she wondered if she would live long enough to see another day.

* * * *

The next morning Joshawa summoned Celest, the tribe healer, and Serena's mother, to the gathering hut. He didn't want Julia to overhear what Celest had to say. As he stood waiting for her, he recalled the smile that Julia had given him the night before. A smile which sparked feelings in him that he had never felt before.

"You wanted to see me, my Lord." Celest, dressed in a long robe, respectfully bowed to him. Celest was the spitting image of Serena, only an older version..

"Yes. What can you tell me about Julia? What information did the healing spirits pass on to you? Are you able to remove the arrowhead?"

"I thought we referred to her as the outsider?"

"She has a name. I suggest you use it."

"Of course, my Lord. The arrowhead is still lodged in her back. I can try to remove it, but I sense that it is quite deep. However, that is not the issue. The issue is that the medicine I need is not in great supply. I would be forced to use almost the entire amount I have on hand to keep... Julia... free of infection."

"Can you not make more?"

"Yes. But it takes time. The batch I am making now will not be ready for another two weeks. If I use our existing supply on her, then I would have nothing if one of our own is injured."

Joshawa weighed the ramifications of what he wanted to do. "Will she live with the arrowhead inside of her?"

"Only for a short time. The healing spirits tell me that the arrowhead is moving and soon it will pierce her heart."

"How soon?"

"A week, maybe two." Celest smiled. "The pain will be

excruciating."

"Then there is only one thing we can do. It is because of us that Julia is injured. I order you to remove the arrowhead."

"Are you sure, my Lord?"

"Are you questioning me?"

"No! Never, my Lord. When would you like me to remove it?"

"Now. Go prepare yourself, then meet me back at my hut."

Celest bowed to her Lord. "Yes, of course, my Lord. It will take just a few minutes."

Joshawa didn't take his eyes off Celest as she left the gathering hut. He realized that not once did she mention Serena. Not that she would question his decision. But Celest always had an opinion that she shared, whether you wanted to hear it or not. Maybe she agreed with the edict. Maybe she was waiting for a better opportunity to speak out. Joshawa was not sure which scenario would play out. What he did know was that he was going to oversee the entire procedure. He would make sure that no additional harm came to Julia.

* * * *

"You cannot be serious, Mother! You are going to help that woman... that outsider?" Serena, dressed in animal skin, paced the confines of the priestesses' hut as her mother gathered what she needed to save Julia's life.

Celest stopped for a moment and faced her daughter. "I have to save her. Our Lord demands it of me. But that does not mean that you cannot inflict harm upon her yourself. That being said, be careful, my child. Hide your anger. Your time will come." Celest left the hut, leaving Serena alone with her thoughts. She would bide her time. Joshawa would pay for his decision to humiliate her publicly.

* * * *

Celest entered Joshawa's hut to find him sitting next to Julia. As she slept, Joshawa tenderly caressed her face. Celest's mind ran wild. There was more going on than what Joshawa would have the tribe believe. "I am ready, my Lord. If you will wait outside..."

"Not happening. I am watching the entire procedure."

"Have it your way."

Celest sat next to Julia and prepared a tonic for her. While she was mixing the tonic, Joshawa gently nudged Julia awake. Slowly she opened her eyes, a small smile gracing her lips as she gazed upon Joshawa. Indignantly, Celest held the clay bowl out to Julia. "Drink this. It will help with the pain."

She handed the bowl to Julia, who looked up to Joshawa for approval. He nodded and smiled. She downed it in one gulp. Celest knew that within seconds Julia would begin to feel lightheaded. She could tell that Julia was becoming dizzy. Seconds later Julia fell back onto her pillows as she passed out. "Okay, we are ready. Turn her over, please."

Joshawa did as he was told, then stood back, not taking his eyes off of Celest as she pulled the top of Julia's dress down to her waist. She removed the corset so that Julia was naked from the waist up. For the next twenty minutes, Celest could feel Joshawa's presence monitoring her as she skillfully removed the arrowhead. Once it was out, she packed the hole that the arrowhead made with herbs. "This is the medication I spoke of. It will keep her wound clean of infection. Leave her on her stomach until she comes to."

"When will that be?"

"I do not know. I have never given the tonic to an

outsider before." Celest gathered her things and left before she could be reminded that the outsider had a name.

* * * *

Julia did not wake till the following morning. Slowly she opened her eyes to find herself on her stomach and with a splitting headache. A blanket covered her and, as the fog lifted from her mind, she realized that she was naked from the waist up. Her back felt as though someone drove a knife deep inside her body. She tried to sit up, but once again, Joshawa was there to stop her. "Please do not move. Are you all right?"

"Humm... I've a wicked headache and my back's killing me. How long have I been sleeping? Are you the one who undressed me?"

"It is already the next day. Celest removed your clothing as well as the arrowhead. You will be fine." Joshawa called out to one of the guards that Julia had seen posted at the entrance of the hut when she had arrived. "Bring me Celest."

"Yes, my Lord. Serena is here. She wishes to speak with you."

Joshawa stood, took a couple of steps, then turned to face Julia. "I will be right back. Please do not try to move until Celest gets here." Joshawa did not wait for an answer as he left the hut.

* * * *

When he went outside, he found Serena dressed in her ceremonial gown. "You have no right to wear that."

"I am a priestess. I have every right."

"What do you want, Serena?"

"A truce. We must talk. I know I was out of line, but I am

here to ask your forgiveness."

"You intentionally disobeyed my orders. How can that be forgiven? How do I know that you will not disobey me again?"

"Trust. Give me another chance."

Joshawa glanced over his shoulder at the entrance to the hut. Serena was not for him. There was something about Julia. Not unlike the jungle, she made him feel at peace. Joshawa turned to Serena. "There is no other chance. You are no longer the High Priestess."

Joshawa could see that Serena was livid. She was asking him for a second chance, and was he throwing it back in her face. "Remember this, my Lord. We are still married under our laws. You cannot change that!"

"I already have." Joshawa turned his back to Serena, returning to the hut and leaving Serena alone, embarrassed, and infuriated.

The days passed by and Joshawa barely left Julia's side. He convinced himself that it was to protect her, but deep down he knew the truth. He felt a connection with her. Something he had never felt before. No female from the tribe made him feel as she did. When he gazed upon her face, his heart ached. Her smile warmed him to his very core. Joshawa was at odds with himself. Was he falling in love with her... with an outsider? He knew that the priestesses of the village would not approve. But in Joshawa's mind, being the Lord of the village gave him every right to give his heart to whomever he pleased.

* * * *

Serena's mother routinely came by to check on Julia and to feed her information about Julia and Joshawa. Serena was livid. How dare he try to replace her with an outsider. Fuelled by her jealousy, Serena spent her days in the priestesses' hut, perfecting her spells and incantations. She could summon the spirits to do her bidding. A talent she saved for a very special ceremony. One that would see the end of Joshawa and his bloodline.

CHAPTER FOUR

While Julia healed, she was free to walk around the village and, for the most part, the villagers treated her with respect and curiosity. Julia knew that her clothing amused them. It was hot and humid in the jungle, and the villagers wore only enough animal skin to cover themselves from the waist to just below their buttocks. The women barely covered their breasts. Julia, on the other hand, wore long dresses that accentuated her breasts. In the village, only the priestesses dressed in long gowns and that was only when it was required of them. The women of the village had offered Julia their clothing, but she'd refused. She enjoyed wearing her dresses. They gave her the feeling of civility in what she thought to be a very uncivilized place. Though, as the days passed and the jungle became even hotter, she did eliminate the petticoats and the corset and eventually cut the sleeves off all her dresses. The women of the village had also offered to cut Julia's long, silky hair. Again, she'd refused the offer and instead wore her hair in a bun tied up with ribbons.

At one point, Joshawa retrieved Julia's artist satchel from her campsite. She would sit for hours drawing the people from the tribe. Her favourite subject was Joshawa himself. He gave her several parchments so she could tell the story of his people through her drawings. Julia felt honoured because Joshawa valued her parchments so much he stowed them away so future generations might see and learn from his generation.

Joshawa would entertain Julia by taking her on walks into the jungle. On one walk he took her back to her campsite so she could mourn for her friends. He had told Julia that the day after the attack, he had the bodies of her friends buried at the edge of their campsite. Julia knelt by their graves and ran her fingers through the loose dirt. Such a senseless act. She looked up at Joshawa, tears running down her cheeks. "Why? Why would your people do this?"

Joshawa knelt beside her. "My people are afraid of the unknown. To them, outsiders are a threat to our way of life."

"There have been outsiders in this valley before?"

"Yes. Once that I know of."

"And what happened to them?"

Joshawa was quiet for a moment. "They were killed."

Julia closed her eyes and said a silent prayer. When she opened them, her eyes met with Joshawa's. "And why am I still alive?"

Joshawa smiled at her. "Because you are special to me." He stood up and offered Julia his hand. She took it, and Joshawa pulled her to her feet. "We should head back."

Julia was healed, with only a scar left to commemorate the event. Joshawa had promised that once she was healed, she was free to leave. But, to her amazement, she'd never once considered returning home. She never once thought to collect on his promise to let her go. And, as the weeks flew by, Julia found herself falling in love with the Lord of the village. Sh would never return home, because she could not bear the thought of leaving Joshawa behind. And she knew he could never go with her. He would not be accepted in her world.

* * * *

Meanwhile, from a distance, Serena constantly stalked the two of them. And, as she did, the anger grew inside of her, poisoning her every thought. Even though her marriage was publicly forfeited, to her, she was still Joshawa's wife. Julia was ruining any chance she had of regaining her title in the eyes of the tribe. Julia had to be stopped, and Joshawa had to learn that he couldn't toss her aside, especially not for an outsider. Serena headed back to the priestesses' hut, where she continued practicing her spells and incantations. And she smiled to herself as her plan to regain her place as High Priestess formulated within her mind.

* * * *

Every day Joshawa took Julia out into the jungle. He said it was because he loved sharing her excitement as she explored her new surroundings. On one outing, Joshawa took Julia to a beautiful waterfall that spilled into a pond of crystal-clear water. She was amazed when he'd told her that the waterfall was the source of the village's water supply, and the pond was where they bathed.

Julia was overwhelmed with the beauty and serenity of the place. The large trees that surrounded the pond sheltered them from the sun. The ferns grew tall and wide. The smell of the jungle was intoxicating. She lay on the lush jungle floor, taking in the beauty of her surroundings. As she stared up at the clouds, she could see Joshawa walk past her, and he was naked. Quickly her hands came up, shielding her eyes. "What are you doing?"

"Going for a swim. Care to join me?"

Julia could hear Joshawa diving into the water. She sat up and cautiously opened her eyes. All she could do was smile at Joshawa, who was standing in waist-deep water, his hands on his hips. His magnificent body glistened in the sun.

Seemingly, Joshawa paid no attention to the beads of water that were running down his face. He stood there seductively smiling at her. "So? Are you going to join me?"

"That would be highly inappropriate. I am not getting naked and going swimming with you."

"Well, then I guess I will have to come and get you."

Julia laughed as she stood up. "You wouldn't dare." The words hadn't even left her lips when Joshawa began to walk out of the water. Julia quickly turned her back to him. Every fibre of her being wanted to go into the water with him, naked, holding him close. Those thoughts danced in her mind as Joshawa came up behind her and wrapped his arms around her waist. She could feel him, especially his arousal as it pressed tight against her buttocks. He turned her to face him.

"Do I carry you, or are you going to come willingly?" He smiled, and for reasons that eluded Julia, she didn't answer but instead placed her arms around his neck, then reached up and kissed him. At first, it was a tender, soft kiss. But as the passion grew, so did the kiss. Joshawa ripped open the back of her dress, causing it to fall to her hips. A gentle tug and it was on the ground. Julia wore nothing under her dress, and she could tell that her nakedness pleased Joshawa. With one hand, he pulled her tight against him. With the other, he undid the ribbons so that her hair fell in soft waves to her waist.

* * * *

Joshawa continued to kiss her, allowing his passion to consume him. His need for her deepened while he explored her delicate body, all the while knowing full well that he was about to cross a dangerous line. He made a choice as he lifted her in his arms and began walking toward the water. "If I do not go into the cool water, I will no longer be able to hold back."

"Then don't."

Joshawa stopped short. "I will only mate with you if you agree to be my wife."

"What about the tribe? They'll not accept me."

"They will if I tell them to. What is your answer?"

* * * *

"Let me down, and I'll show you." Julia took Joshawa's hand, then walked back over to her dress. There she lay down on it as she gently pulled Joshawa on top of her. Any inhibitions that Julia might have had were gone as her hands boldly explored Joshawa's naked body. She could feel the sheer size of his manhood, which frightened her.

"I will be gentle. There will be pain but only for a second. Trust me and relax."

Julia trusted Joshawa with her very soul. She allowed him to enter her, and after the pain had come and gone, she experienced a passion that took over her body and mind. A passion that she didn't want to end. They lay in each other's arms for hours. Neither wanted the lovemaking to stop. But as the sun started its descent, she knew they had to return. Together, hand in hand, they headed back to the village.

* * * *

It didn't take much for Serena to know something had gone on. When she had seen Joshawa and Julia enter the village, she'd immediately noticed the subtle differences. Julia's hair was flowing to her waist, her cheeks were flushed, and Joshawa couldn't keep his eyes off her. Serena followed them and, without waiting for an invite, barged into Joshawa's hut.

"You are still my husband, or have you forgotten that!"

"We are no longer married. You know that, Serena. I will be announcing to the tribe that Julia is going to be my wife."

"What! You must be kidding. An outsider. The tribe will never stand for it."

"Yes, they will. And you must learn to accept it as well."

"I accept nothing." Serena walked further into the hut. That was when she noticed Julia's torn dress. "Tell me you did not mate with this woman. Never mind, I will figure it out for myself." She walked up to Julia and placed a hand on her belly. What she saw caused her to roar in anger. "You would not mate with me, but you get her pregnant! This is not over, Joshawa." Serena stormed out of the hut.

* * * *

Joshawa stood there staring after Serena. She was out of control. A storm brewing to hurricane levels. And he and Julia were right in the middle of her path.

Chapter Five

The day after their return from the waterfall, Serena stood in the gathering hut, her anger growing deep within her as Joshawa proudly presented Julia as his chosen wife. That decision split the village in two. And, to add more fuel to the fire, Serena was correct, and Julia was pregnant. Those that were loyal to Joshawa accepted Julia and the child that lay secure within her womb. Those that were loyal to Serena's way of thinking made life uncomfortable for Julia. Serena pointed out to her followers that Julia had no powers. She had nothing to contribute to the tribe.

Eventually, a second, smaller gathering hut was constructed, from which Serena would spout off on how Joshawa was undermining the ways of their people. There was no way a son from an outsider would ever be allowed to rule. Nor would any priestess mate with the son of an outsider. During all the commotion, Serena was planning her revenge. Everything was falling into place. Soon, her family would rule the entire tribe, and Joshawa's family would cease to exist.

Late one evening, Serena paid an unexpected visit to her mother. She needed her help, her guidance. They say the apple doesn't fall far from the tree. To know Serena's mother as Serena did was to know how true that statement was. Celest was as evil as they came. She practiced the dark arts of medicine, learning how to raise the spirits from the dead. Learning how to perform the most intricate of curses. All her knowledge she passed on to Serena. Serena, dressed in her ceremonial gown, entered the priestesses' hut to find her mother sitting on the ground, her eyes closed, her hands resting in her lap. She was softly chanting to herself. She too was dressed in her ceremonial gown, which meant she was conjuring. A small fire smoldered in the fire pit in front of her. Celest threw a green leaf packet into the fire. Slowly it smoldered until it burst into flames, filling the hut with the smell of incense.

"Mother, are those not my packets?"

"Yes, my child. They are very powerful. But take heed. In the wrong hands, they could be deadly."

"In the wrong hands, they have no power."

"Are you certain of that?"

"It does not matter. I have come for your guidance. I need your assistance in completing my plan."

"Sit, my child." Celest motioned to a spot on the other side of the fire pit. "We will conjure together."

"Mother, I did not come here to conjure. At least not tonight. I have a plan that will destroy Joshawa and his entire family line. I have designed a curse that will live for all eternity. I want to trap Joshawa and his whore in the spirit world so they can witness the curse unfold every thirty years. I want them to suffer. I want them to feel my pain."

"Have you thought this through? In order for you to trap them as spirits, you must first design your own spirit world for them to be imprisoned in. And, in order for you to accomplish that, then you must lead the way."

"I understand, Mother. That is why I need your help. And the help of those loyal to us."

* * * *

Celest smiled at her daughter. She was so proud. Her daughter was paving the way so that she, Celest, could be the sole ruler of the tribe. So that her bloodline could rule forever. "Tell me of your plan, and I will help you in every aspect."

"I thought you would. When that whore is seven months into her pregnancy, I will curse not only Joshawa but the child as well. Then I will need you to send me to the spirit world. Once there, I will take up residency in Julia's mind. From there I can punish her in ways that I could never do in the real world. Anyone from the tribe will think she is having difficulty with the pregnancy. In the end, I will make sure that she dies giving birth to that bastard child. At that moment, I need you to kill Joshawa so that I can control his spirit. The child must be taken to the outside world, where he will live his life tormented because of his appearance. During his thirtieth year, he will die, only to have me bring him back from the spirit world to be reborn to some unsuspecting outsider. And the best part of this curse, Mother, is that Joshawa and Julia will live forever watching their son suffer so horribly and be totally incapable of helping him."

"You have given this some thought, my child."

"Yes. Will you help me see this through?"

"Of course. But tell me. Every curse can be broken. What can destroy your curse?"

Serena smirked at her mother. "It is pure genius. In order for their child to break the curse, he has to fall in love with an outsider, and that outsider must fall in love with him. Then, if by some miracle that happens, they will still have to defeat me. The curse dies when I die. And you and I both know that there is only one way to kill me."

"Yes. But be mindful, Serena. Joshawa knows of the packets. He may learn what they do."

"I will take care of that." Serena stood to leave. "Thank you, Mother. I knew you would help me." With that, Serena left the hut, leaving her mother with mixed feelings. Yes, her daughter had to die, which was dreadful, but, her death and the death of Joshawa would leave the door wide open for Celest to walk through and take control of the tribe. In just a few months she would be high priestess of the Jelani tribe.

Chapter Six

As the months passed by and Julia's belly grew, Joshawa found himself falling in love with her even more with each passing day. She was officially his wife, although she didn't join him at his side during village meetings. She would sit with the tribe members, which was her way of respecting their decision to accept her. She had given up her beloved dresses and dressed as the people of the village did. One day Joshawa would have to choose a priestess to sit at his side. But only as an advisor for the spirit world. With the upheaval in the village, Joshawa felt that it was not a good time to choose a priestess. Serena wouldn't be his choice, and that would only infuriate her further.

* * * *

Julia was seven months pregnant. Serena knew that in only two months Julia and Joshawa would be able to hold their child within their arms and present him or her to the tribe. At least, that was what they believed. Serena had been observing Julia with the patience of a saint. It was finally time. In the shroud of darkness, her mother would perform the ceremony that would kill her but, at the same time, leave her in the spirit world. Though it meant her death, Serena was anxious to begin the second part of her plan. However, that would have to wait. It was time for the first part, the actual curse. Quietly Serena followed Joshawa and Julia as they left the village for a walk. She had dressed in her animal skins so that it would be easier to follow them. Fifteen minutes later, she found them standing under a tree next to the pond.

"Well, look at the two love birds."

Joshawa instinctively moved in front of Julia. "What do you want, Serena?"

"I was collecting herbs, and I saw you. I thought I would stop by and say hello." Serena took a couple of steps closer. "I know there has been turmoil between us. But do you not think it is time to put our grievances aside? At least for the sake of the child."

"You are not to be trusted."

Serena moved closer to the couple. "Tell you what. How about I tell you the sex of your child? Let you know how healthy he or she is."

"Why would you do this, Serena?"

Serena smirked at Joshawa. "I am trying here. It would be nice to see some effort on your part."

Julia moved out from behind Joshawa. She glanced up at him as she placed her hand on his arm. "Maybe we should try to reconcile. I for one would like to know the sex of the child."

Serena didn't wait for an invitation from Joshawa. She walked right up to Julia and placed her hand on Julia's swollen belly. "Congratulations. It is a boy. And he is very healthy." Serena not only saw that the baby was a boy but also that he was the exact image of his father. Which was perfect for her curse. Julia smiled up at Joshawa, and that was when everything went wrong for them and perfect for her. Serena pulled a packet from her waistband and threw it on the ground at Joshawa's feet. It burst into flames, producing a thick, white smoke. Serena laughed as Joshawa became motionless. The spell contained within the smoke not only kept Joshawa from moving, but it also allowed him to hear and see everything Serena was doing.

As soon as the smoke totally encased him, Serena began chanting while holding on to Julia's belly. Julia tried to pull Serena's hand away, but she had no strength. Serena smiled as Julia desperately sought out Joshawa for help. Help he couldn't offer her. Serena finished her chanting and took a couple of steps back. "The effects of the smoke will die off shortly. Know that you have been cursed and your child will never see his thirtieth year. Know that you will die only to live forever under my control." Serena disappeared into the jungle, her laughter echoing amongst the trees.

* * * *

When the effects of the smoke wore off, Julia sank to the ground. "Oh my God, what have I done?"

Joshawa knelt beside her and took her into his arms. "We will find her and make her reverse the curse. I promise you." Julia and Joshawa returned to the village, and Joshawa immediately ordered the entire tribe to search for Serena. Hours went by and Julia lost all hope, for not one person could locate Serena.

* * * *

As the moon rose and darkness fell upon the village, Serena came out of hiding, and she and her mother made their way through the jungle to a spot known only by the priestesses of the village. Serena, dressed in her ceremonial gown complete with mask, knelt on her knees in the centre of a large fire pit. Celest, also dressed in her ceremonial gown, walked up to her daughter and placed a hand on her shoulder. "Are you sure this is what you want? Because there is no turning back."

"Yes, Mother. I want this more than life itself. I need to do this."

Celest smiled. A willing sacrifice so that she could rule. She should be upset, but in reality, she wasn't. Ruling the tribe was the only thing that was important. The death of her daughter was secondary. Celest placed her green leaf packets on the ground, completely encircling her daughter. Then she began reciting the incantation that would take Serena's life. She closed her eyes, stretched her arms in front of her, her palms facing Serena, her fingers spread apart. She tilted her head back so that she would be facing the heavens as she gently swayed her arms back and forth, reciting the incantation louder and louder. Slowly the packets smoldered until one by one they burst into flames. Celest stopped her incantation and stepped back. She smiled as the flames and smoke from the packets encased her daughter. When the smoke cleared, nothing remained of Serena. Only a pile of ash in the centre of the fire pit. Celest knelt at the edge of the fire pit and reached out to her.. Within a few minutes, Celest's mind came alive with Serena's thoughts.

We are successful, Mother. I am in the spirit world, and now I am able to reside in Julia's mind. From there, I will build my own world. A world to imprison those two. A world where I will have my revenge. Serena left her mother to seek out Julia. And, as her mother stood, she thought of the world that she was going to build. One free of Joshawa's bloodline.

Chapter Seven

The next morning, Julia awakened feeling drained of all her energy. As she tried to sit up, the dizziness assaulted her, forcing her to lie back down. She gently nudged Joshawa awake. "Something's wrong. I feel terribly ill."

* * * *

Joshawa glanced over at his beloved Julia. Her eyes were bloodshot and her complexion pale. He knew that something was seriously wrong. "You lay there. I will go get Celest."

"Do you think that's wise? She *is* Serena's mother."

"Yes, she is. But she is also our tribe healer. During this whole ordeal, Celest has never spoken out in favour of her daughter. Maybe she feels that Serena is in the wrong."

"If you trust her, then I'll trust her too." Joshawa stood at Julia's side as what little energy she had left her and she fell back to sleep.

Tenderly, Joshawa ran his hand along her face. She was everything to him. He couldn't lose her. He got dressed, then headed for Celest's hut. He found her not ten feet away from his own hut. "Celest? Why are you here?"

"I came to check in on Julia. How is she?"

Joshawa's gut told him that something was wrong. Should he trust her? "She is not doing well. But why do I think you already know that?"

Celest smiled at Joshawa. "May I see her?"

Without saying a word, Joshawa headed back to his hut, Celest hot on his heels. As he went to enter the hut, Celest held him back. "Maybe I should go in alone. She would probably prefer some privacy."

"Not on your life. She does not leave my sight."

"Have it your way." Celest entered the hut, followed by Joshawa.

Julia was waking up. "I hear you are not doing well, Julia." Celest sat cross-legged on the ground next to Julia and placed her hands on her upper chest, then moved them onto her forehead.

"I have no energy. I feel so weak. I can barely stay awake."

"Well then rest, my dear. I will help you." Celest closed her eyes, positioned her hands above Julia, and began to chant.

Joshawa was having none of that. "No incantations!"

"How am I supposed to help her if I cannot summon the healing spirits."

Joshawa thought for a moment. "Then summon them in a language that I understand."

Celest snorted. "These incantations are as old as the dirt we walk on. There are no translations."

"What are you not telling me?"

"I have no idea what you are talking about." Celest stood. "When you are ready for me to help Julia, well, you know where to find me."

Celest left Joshawa alone with the woman he loved and no remedies to make her feel better. Should he trust Celest? Or would she only strengthen the curse that already plagued Julia? As he stood in the hut, trying to decide what to do, one thought came to him. Serena was still missing, yet Celest did not appear worried or upset. He was right not to trust her. Somehow, she was involved. Joshawa left the hut and summoned Tamiel. "I want one guard inside and two on the outside. No one enters, especially not Celest."

"Yes, my Lord. I will summon two of your most loyal warriors."

Joshawa placed a hand on Tamiel's shoulder. "Thank you. Guard her with your life."

Joshawa headed toward Celest's hut only to find her waiting for him. "That did not take you long."

"Where is Serena? I know you know where she is."

"I can honestly say that she is not amongst the living."

"You do not seem too upset for someone who recently lost their daughter."

"Oh, I have not lost her. I know exactly where she is."

"As your Lord, I demand you to tell me where I can find her."

Celest smiled. "Come on, Joshawa. You are a smart man. I am sure you can figure it out for yourself."

Joshawa was livid. "Tell me, or you will spend the remainder of your life confined to this hut."

"You will need me for the birthing. You know that as well as I do. So, imprison me here if that is what you must do. I will see you in two months. Perhaps even sooner."

Joshawa stormed out and grabbed the first warrior he saw. Angrily he pointed at Celest's hut. "She does not leave for any reason. Nobody goes in without my knowledge. I want two men at the entrance at all times. Understood?"

The nervous warrior nodded his head and ran to do his Lord's bidding. Joshawa headed back to his hut to find Julia sitting up against several pillows. She was pale and could barely keep her eyes open. She gazed up at Joshawa and tried to smile. "Guess I'm having a bad day."

Julia's bad day turned into six weeks of pure hell. Joshawa was beside himself. It was tearing him apart having to stand by as the woman he loved wasted away day by day.

Soon it would be time for the baby to come and, even though he didn't like it, Joshawa knew he would need Celest. With much reservation, he sent one of his warriors to bring Celest to him. As she entered the hut, dressed in her ceremonial gown, Joshawa purposely stood between her and Julia.

"I warn you. Do anything to harm her and I will have your head."

"And hello to you too. I have no intention of harming her. I never did. Really, Joshawa, you have to work on your trust issues."

"How long till the baby comes?"

* * * *

Celest sat beside Julia. Serena was taking a toll on her. She was frail. Her eyes were sunken, and her complexion had a yellowish tinge to it. The chances were slim that she would even survive the birthing. "I have to check her. You may want to ask your guard to turn around."

Joshawa shot Celest a warning glance. "Come on, Joshawa. I am not going to hurt her. However, I am going to lift the blanket up to her knees whether he is watching or not. And I am quite sure that she is naked underneath this blanket." Joshawa nodded, and the guard turned his back. Celest quickly checked Julia. "She is ready. It is time to take her to the birthing hut."

The birthing hut was located outside of the village. It was remote for the purpose of giving privacy to the mother. Celest knew that Joshawa would be reluctant to take Julia to a place that was so isolated. But the hut was set up for the purpose of bringing a child into the world and healing the injured. It was where Julia needed to be. So Joshawa wrapped a blanket around Julia, then gently cradled her in his arms. "All right, Celest, but I'm bringing my men with me."

"That is your decision." And as Joshawa carried Julia out of the hut, Celest smiled to herself. It was all going according to plan.

* * * *

After a half-hour trek through the jungle, Joshawa, carrying Julia, entered the clearing that surrounded the birthing hut. It was as large as the gathering hut but with only one small entrance. The inside contained a raised platform which served as the birthing bed. It was located at the very back of the hut. Joshawa gently laid Julia on the bed. Next to the bed were several shelves that held a variety of clay pots. Underneath was a counter that ran the length of the shelves. All the medicines used to help heal the injured were made at that counter. For even though the main purpose of the birthing hut was to bring new life into the world, it was also a place of healing. A large fire pit was positioned in the centre of the hut. Its main purpose was to aid in the conjuring of the healing spirits.

* * * *

Julia was lying comfortably on the birthing bed. Joshawa was at her side. Her labour came on quickly, the contractions coming back to back. Julia's screams echoed throughout the jungle. Celest actually did her best to save Julia, but then, she had her reasons. Julia had to bond with her child. It would make the torment of witnessing him suffer all the more intense. For the next eight hours, Celest watched as Julia gave what was obviously her last bit of strength to bring her son into the world. Three hard pushes and she delivered an eight-pound-five-ounce baby boy. As Serena foresaw, the child was the spitting image of his father.

* * * *

Joshawa was so involved in Julia's well-being that he did not hear his warriors that were standing outside the hut being overtaken by Celest's men. Nor did he notice the three warriors that entered the hut. It wasn't until he heard the distinctive sound of a bow being drawn back that he whirled around to see an arrow aimed directly at Julia's head.

"And now it is time for you to know the truth." Celest bundled the baby in a blanket and handed him to Julia. She allowed Julia to hold the child for only a few minutes. Then she took him from her and handed him to one of the warriors. "You know what has to be done." Joshawa leaped up and went for the baby only to have an arrow pressed into his neck. "Not a good idea, Joshawa. Now, you either sit down and behave or I will have Julia killed."

"What are you doing with my son?"

"Perhaps you should ask Serena."

Before Joshawa could say another word, his head filled with Serena's thoughts. *Hello, my husband. I see your whore has delivered you a son. Too bad you won't be around to see him grow up.* Serena laughed. *But, my mistake, you will be able to watch. However, – you will not be alive to do so. It is important that you know the truth. Julia is dying, and I am the one who is killing her. It has been me from the very beginning.*

"Serena, why are you doing this?"

Why? You leave me for an outsider, and you wonder why.

"Where are you?"

I am a spirit living in Julia's mind. Controlling everything about her.

"Please, Serena, don't kill her. Take me. I am the one that

hurt you. Please let her live."

I like it when you beg. But it is not going to help you. You should say your goodbyes. She does not have long.

Joshawa sat on the edge of the bed, put his arms under Julia, and lifted her onto his lap. He held her tight against him as he cried uncontrollably.

"Don't cry, my love." Julia's voice was barely audible. "I will see you again. Take care of our son." Joshawa leaned down and kissed the top of Julia's head as her body went limp within his embrace. Joshawa roared in frustration, his voice deafening those that stood within earshot.

"Give her back to me! Serena, if there is any decency in you, you will bring her back!"

Oh, don't worry. You will see her soon enough. Joshawa heard the whistle of an arrow flying through the air. He felt the pain as it pierced his heart. It was over in a split second as he fell to the floor, still cradling Julia in his arms.

* * * *

Celest melded with her daughter. *Serena, are they with you?*

Yes, Mother, they are here.

Good, have your fun. Celest turned her attention to the two men standing next to her. "I am going back to my hut. Clean up this mess. It has to appear like they left of their own free will."

As Celest made her way back to the village, she revelled in the fact that Serena's devious plan succeeded. Julia and Joshawa were trapped in the spirit world Serena had created. They would be spectators for an eternity as their son lived in torment only to die and be reborn again. She would be high priestess, ruling the tribe on her own. And those who were loyal to Joshawa would wait in vain for their Lord to return.

Chapter Eight

January 1991, Congo Region, Africa

Casandra, high priestess of the Jelani tribe, had been ruling for over thirty years. Ever since the time of Serena and Celest, her family had ruled on their own with no need of a Lord. Joshawa's family had all but died out. At least that was what the tribe believed. Casandra knew differently. Serena had been communicating with all the high priestesses since the 1700s. She had become a legend amongst her family. The one priestess that was able to destroy an entire family. And not simply any family, but the family of warriors that were the Lords of the tribe. Casandra knew that Serena had kept one male alive for the sole purpose of fulfilling her curse. Up until then, it hadn't been a problem. But, with the new child, Serena was being challenged, and her adversary was proving to be a worthy combatant.

Dressed in her ornate ceremonial gown, she sat cross-legged on the floor of the hut, gazing into a pot of water that she had drawn earlier. She stood five feet, eleven inches tall. Her eyes were as blue as sapphires. She always wore her long, red hair braided even though most females in her tribe kept their hair loose. The mask which would cover the upper half of her face was lying on the ground next to her. Directly in front of her was a fire pit where six leaf-covered packets lay. These packets contained the life essence of the priestess that carried them. They also contained the potion that the priestess needed to conjure and foresee the future. Casandra was waiting on her daughter. It was time for her to mold her daughter in preparation for her becoming the next high priestess. At that time, she would choose someone to mate with for the sole purpose of producing an offspring. Unfortunately, the high priestess could not designate one family for this privilege. Even after all these years, the tribe still held hope that an offspring of Joshawa's would return. And, as long as there was hope, no other family would take the place of Joshawa's bloodline.

Tamara, Casandra's daughter, was proving to be one of the strongest priestesses since the time of Serena. Casandra was quite pleased, for she believed that Serena was losing control with the latest version of Joshawa. And if she did lose control, she would need to be stopped. No son of Joshawa could live to fulfill his destiny. Tamara was the answer. She would be the one to stop Serena.

Tamara entered the hut, dressed in a long, plain robe. Standing at only five feet, eight inches tall, she was short for the females of the village. Like all the other priestesses in her family, her eyes were a dazzling blue. She had recently turned twenty-two, though you would think, with her youthful appearance, that she was considerably younger. She joined her mother, sitting across the fire pit from her. "It is good to see you, Mother. What will we be doing today?"

"I've a surprise for you. Today we conjure Serena. She'll speak to us."

Tamara's eyes grew wide. "We are actually going to communicate with Serena? Mother, how is this possible?"

"Watch and learn, my child."

Casandra donned her mask, closed her eyes, then began chanting an incantation as she waved her arms over the fire pit. One by one the packets released a thick, grey smoke. The smoke remained contained within the fire pit, and with it came a vision. Casandra was expecting to speak with Serena, but instead, she found herself witnessing an interaction between Serena and what appeared to be a younger version of Joshawa. She knew almost immediately that it was the adult child of Joshawa's. He was angry. He was confronting her. But Serena didn't seem to be concerned. The child kept getting closer, yet Serena did nothing to protect herself. Casandra and Tamara couldn't believe what they were seeing as the child grabbed Serena. He held her tight as a figure appeared behind her. Casandra knew it was the spirit, Joshawa. He reached into Serena's robes and pulled out a green leaf packet. Casandra knew what was happening, so she ended the vision to the cries of agony as Serena was destroyed.

"What just happened, Mother?"

Casandra removed her mask, then stared directly at her daughter. "Everything you witnessed doesn't leave this hut. No one is to know that a child of Joshawa's still lives."

"But what if he comes looking for us?"

"He's half a world away from us. We're not that easy to find. Leave me, daughter. I need to think."

Casandra stared deep into the smoldering ash of the fire pit. Serena was gone. Joshawa and the whore he'd taken as his wife over two centuries ago had been released and were finally able to continue their journey to the land of their ancestors. And even though Joshawa's child was powerful, he didn't pose a threat. He was too far away to be of any consequence. Casandra sensed the presence of a fourth person. But she dismissed the feeling and smiled to herself. No, life would continue as usual. The son of Joshawa would never find his way back home.

Chapter Nine

Leading up to May 1991, Burwood, British Columbia, Canada

Burwood was a sanctuary hidden in the northern region of the Rocky Mountains. Tanya knew that it was a safe haven for the outcasts of society and had been for decades. One of these outcasts was Nathen, son of Joshawa. He was only a couple weeks old when Tanya sent him to Burwood. She had the foresight to see that he wasn't your ordinary child. Not unlike the priestesses of the Jelani tribe, Tanya was gifted. And it was through her gift that Tanya could envision what Nathen's destiny was to be. Tanya was immediately drawn to Nathen and felt that it was her responsibility to protect the small, unsuspecting child. Knowing full well what was in store for him, Tanya made sure that Charles, Burwood's founder, would raise him. Tanya's gift saw into Nathen's future and revealed to her that Nathen would be given a relatively normal upbringing, for the people of Burwood would not judge him by his appearance. They would accept him and love him as he was.

* * * *

Serena was furious beyond belief. How dare a mere outsider upset the course of her carefully laid out curse. The whole purpose of having him in the outside world was so that he would be tormented and hated for being so different. She wanted his parents to witness his suffering and the physical and mental abuse he would endure for his entire thirty years. For over two centuries, her curse ran its course without interference. But, instead of being feared and loathed, he was loved and nurtured. The people that lived with him respected him. Accepted him as a leader. He was, in a sense, a Lord in the outside world.

The anger that consumed Serena was as intense as the anger that had caused her to venture down the road of hatred and vengeance. However, she believed that her curse was impregnable, making the change of events nothing more than a mere inconvenience. Nathen was still hers to do with as she pleased. She still controlled the beast that dwelt deep inside of Nathen. A beast that taunted Nathen to become what he knew he was, an animal. She was not deterred from her course of action. She'd monitored Nathen with much satisfaction as he had grown into a man haunted by his insecurities and the desire to find out exactly who and what he was. Even with all the love and compassion the people of Burwood had to offer him, he was still alone.

Serena felt Nathen's emotions, saw his thoughts. She knew he was still hurting because, as far as he was concerned, he would never have a normal life. He would never experience the kind of love a man and woman share. To him, no woman would see past his features. It was not exactly as Serena hoped his life would play out, but it would do. She felt ever so confident in her plan. At least until the year Nathen was to turn thirty. Then all hell broke loose when two women entered his life.

* * * *

Twenty-nine years after she had arranged his passage to Burwood, Tanya came back into his life and brought with her the child that she'd raised as her niece, Authia. Authia was an attractive woman who stood five feet, six inches tall with a slight build. Her hair, which fell to her shoulders, was so dark it was almost black. She had the most beautiful dark brown eyes and tanned complexion. Authia was a younger version of Tanya. Besides their uncanny resemblance, Tanya and Authia also shared the same gift. They could bring forth a vision depicting the present and future of the person they touched. They could lay their hand on the belly of an expectant mother and know if she was having a girl or a boy. They could also meld their minds together to speak to one another or to see what the other one saw. Tanya knew of Nathen's destiny from the day he was born. On that day, she made a promise to both Nathen and to the woman that gave birth to him that she would do everything in her power to save him. Twenty-nine years later, she knew it was time. She also knew that the only way she could save him was through Authia.

* * * *

Nathen shared some of the same gifts as Authia and Tanya. So, for several months, Authia and Nathen communicated using only their ability to mind meld, and by doing so, developed a bond so strong that not even Serena could break it. It frustrated Authia that Nathen would not reveal himself to her. But, according to her aunt, that was the way it had to be. So, they continued, and with every passing day, Nathen and Authia's gift grew stronger. So strong that they felt confident in their abilities. Through their mind melds, the two of them sought out Serena in the hope of destroying her and the curse.

It was a journey plagued with many obstacles. One particular obstacle was as dangerous as Serena herself. Dext, a mountain man, proved to be a daunting adversary that plagued Authia once she moved into a cabin located not far from Burwood. He almost cost Authia her life. However, Authia and Nathen did not falter. Even when Authia lost Tanya in their fight to free Nathen, she still forged on. Their feelings for each other reached new heights when Nathen finally revealed himself to Authia and she accepted him.

* * * *

Serena's cries of anger could be heard throughout the spirit world as the first part of her curse had been circumvented. And to make matters worse for Serena, Nathen and Authia consummated their relationship. A union that resulted in a child nestled safely in Authia's womb. Serena added intense jealousy to her long list of reasons to hate Joshawa. Not only did he impregnate an outsider instead of her, but his bastard son also went and impregnated an outsider as well. Serena's anger consumed her, and she knew she had to regain control of Nathen. So, she offered him a choice. Accept his destiny to die and walk away from Authia or stand by, unable to do anything as Authia died in the most horrifying manner. Nathen left Authia, thinking he would be saving her. But that was not to be. For, after Nathen left, Serena chose to reside in Authia's mind, making her ill to the point of near death. Much to Serena's dismay, Nathen returned.

* * * *

Nathen's love for Authia was so strong he had to return to her even if it meant facing Serena's wrath. Nathen, prepared to die if he must, confronted Serena. But he was not alone. Serena, wrapped in the arrogance of her belief that she could never lose, proved herself wrong. Nathen and his father, Joshawa, joined forces and overpowered her. By working together, they were able to defeat Serena.

Nathen was content in the knowledge that Joshawa and Julia were free of the curse. They were now able to continue their journey to the afterlife. Before he left, Joshawa presented Nathen with a parchment that he had been working on for centuries. A parchment that showed Nathen the way home. Nathen was a free man able to live his life to the fullest. The first thing he did was propose to the woman he loved. The second was to plan his journey back home to his people.

* * * *

Four months after the defeat of Serena, Burwood was bustling with activity. There was a wedding to be planned, and the entire clan played a part. Authia, in her seventh month of pregnancy, had put on thirty pounds and she felt the entire weight was in her belly. She had difficulty walking and was always out of breath. She sat in bed enjoying the sunrise through the one window in her and Nathen's log cabin. Their cabin was small, comprised of only one room. When you entered the cabin, to the left of the door was a queen-size bed tucked into the corner of the room. It had a large, ornate headboard that Nathen had made himself. Along the wall, at the foot of the bed, was a large wardrobe that held all their clothing. The solitary window was situated along the same wall as the door. Underneath the window was a round table that sat four people. To the right of the door, on the adjoining wall, was a large stone fireplace that took up almost the entire wall. There was a raised hearth that you could sit on to get closer to the warmth of the fire. In front of the fireplace were two high-back armchairs. A small coffee table was positioned between the two chairs. The wooden floor was bare and glistened in the light of the fireplace. There was no stove to cook on, for all the meals were prepared in the main cabin. Fifteen minutes earlier, Nathen had gone to the main cabin to procure breakfast for both himself and Authia.

Authia shifted her weight, trying to get comfortable as their baby moved about within the confines of her womb. These days, he was constantly stretching his limbs. She could actually see the outline of his hand and foot as he pressed them tight against her belly. Nathen returned carrying two trays of food to find Authia sitting up in bed and staring at her exposed belly.

"Nathen, you've got to come see this!"

He put the trays down on the table, then joined Authia, sitting next to her on their bed. They could see the outline of their child's hand as clear as day. "This is amazing." Nathen reached out and laid his hand on top of his child's. He smiled at Authia. "You've given me such a wondrous gift."

"Oh, I think you had something to do with it as well." Authia wrapped her arms around Nathen's neck and brought him closer to her. "Every day I thank the heavens for the life we have. One free of Serena."

Nathen leaned in and kissed her ever so tenderly. "I miss making love to you."

Authia smirked. "What's stopping you?"

Nathen slowly shook his head. "I'll not make love to you in your condition. However..." He smiled seductively. "We'll make up for it after our child is born."

Authia giggled as she playfully pushed him away. "You promised me breakfast."

Nathen helped Authia out of bed, then guided her over to the table.

* * * *

As Authia devoured her meal consisting of bacon, eggs, pancakes, and juice, Nathen took a deep breath and began a conversation that he knew would lead to a subject that, at the very least, would upset Authia. "Authia, are you still unable to see the sex of our child?"

"You know it doesn't work that way. I can't see my own visions. I can only learn my destiny, my future, through people that are close to me. And so far, I've not seen any indication of what the sex of our baby is."

"It doesn't really matter. My only hope is for a healthy baby and a safe delivery."

Authia smiled at Nathen. "Then you and I are on the same page."

Nathen decided that it was as good a time as any to plunge into the conversation he was dreading. "I was thinking why don't we wait until after the baby is born to be married?"

Authia's fork stopped midway between her plate and her mouth. "No. You know the significance of being married in May." Authia placed her fork back on her plate. "You turn thirty in May. You were supposed to die in May. Getting married in May, to me, is a way of saying *we won!*"

"I know, my love." Nathen hesitated for a moment. "You know that freighter that Charles lined up for us? The one that's going to take us to Africa."

"Yes, what of it?"

"We're planning to leave in August after the baby was born."

"Yes. What are you getting at, Nathen?"

"The freighter is leaving in two weeks and then it's going into dry dock for repairs. It'll be months before it's on the ocean again."

"But that's the only freighter we have available to us." Finally, what Nathen was trying to tell her became obvious.

"You want to leave now. You don't want to wait. Are you thinking of leaving without me?"

"Authia, I don't know when the freighter will be available to us again, if ever. And you can't travel in your condition."

Authia shook her head as she pushed her plate away. "Don't you dare try to tell me what I can and can't do. If we leave in two weeks, with all the stops the freighter has to make, it'll be two months before we reach Africa. I'll be having this baby on the freighter." Authia thought for a second. "You know, that's probably why I can't get a vision from anyone concerning the sex of our baby. No one from Burwood will see our baby. I'm not meant to have the baby here."

"No, you'll not have the baby on the freighter. It's not safe. I won't allow it."

"You won't allow it! When are you going to learn that you can't control me? We need to discuss this with an open mind."

"It's too dangerous. It's bad enough that I fear for your safety. But we can't bring our child into the unknown. We don't know what awaits us on the other side of that waterfall."

* * * *

Authia thought for a moment. There had to be a way to keep their baby safe. Then she remembered the parchment. "Nathen, the parchment speaks of a misplaced soul that found her way into the outside world. She's our connection to your tribe. She could also be the answer to our problem."

"That parchment is centuries old. Whomever that misplaced soul is, she's long gone by now."

"Okay, first of all, I don't believe that parchment is as old as you think. I've been studying it, closely. The inks are different, Nathen. I believe Joshawa has been working on that parchment during his entire incarceration."

"I don't understand."

"Over time, things change. Like landmarks and people. It would make sense that Joshawa changed the parchment over the years so that it would be accurate for today. Otherwise, why would Joshawa even give us the parchment? If it were centuries old, it would be of no use to us. Hear me out. What if that misplaced soul is still in that village waiting for your return? What if we take Tammy with us? She's a nurse. She can help when I'm ready to have our child. Then she and our child can stay in that village protected by that misplaced soul. Tammy has done nothing but talk about our trip to Africa. I'm sure she would love to come with us."

"You're counting very heavily on that parchment being accurate."

"After everything we've been through these past months, I'm willing to go on a little faith."

"Are you willing to risk your life and that of our child's?"

"As I see it, we have two options. Stay here, never being able to leave Burwood. Or, venture out and possibly find your people. Nathen, it's a chance to be with your own people. I think it's worth the risk."

Nathen stood, then went to kneel before Authia. His eyes were filled with concern, filled with fear of what was yet to come. "You and this child are my life. I would give anything to keep you both safe. Charles once asked me that if you were willing to risk everything to save my life, then why would I not help you. Once again, you're risking everything for me." Nathen placed his hands on the sides of Authia's belly and tenderly kissed it. His eyes met hers. "If you're adamant about leaving for Africa with me, now, then that's what we'll do."

So, the journey into the unknown commenced.

* * * *

Tamara sensed the premonition of impending upheaval. She knew of the fourth person, though she would not reveal that to her mother. The son of Joshawa, the fourth person, and her mother were about to have their lives intermingle on a level that none of them could have foreseen. It would be that unknown person that held the key. Tamara knew that she would be an integral part of the triangle. A triangle filled with hate, dishonesty, and revenge.

Chapter Ten

Nathen wanted to keep the love of his life happy, so he agreed to hold the wedding before they left for Africa. It was two days before the wedding, and he found himself standing in the middle of the courtyard as he took in all the splendour of his valley. A valley that had been his home for his entire life. A valley he had to leave in order to find out who he was. Nathen was lost in his thoughts. He barely noticed several people going about their day, as the exquisitely decorated arbour was set up not fifteen feet away from him. All he could think about was that less than a year ago, he stood in this very spot believing that he would never share his life with a woman. That no woman could ever love him. But that had changed, for not only did he have a woman to love, but he had a woman that loved him in return. And she was gifting him with a child. The greatest gift a woman could give a man. Nathen's thoughts returned to the present and to the project of the day. Preparing for his wedding day. And the people of Burwood were going to make it a wondrous event.

* * * *

Within the hallowed walls of the sanctuary that Charles had built, life was blissful. Burwood had grown to seventy-two people strong. The valley in which it lay was breathtakingly beautiful. Totally encircling the valley were the majestic Rocky Mountains. They rose so high that the peaks were hidden amongst the clouds. A crystal-clear stream wound its way through the valley. And outside the large wooden gates, the redwood trees and evergreens grew tall and strong. It was nature's way of protecting Burwood, hiding it from the outside world.

Charles designed the log cabins that the people of Burwood lived in to be efficient. They cooked on wood stoves and heated their homes with wood burning fireplaces. The cabins were constructed to accommodate the family, nothing more. They consisted of only one room, with a drape separating the sleeping area from the rest of the cabin. He made sure the Burwood clan did not miss the conveniences that they had given up. The only modern conveniences that Charles allowed the clan were a couple of generators and a short-wave radio. Besides the cabins that housed the living quarters, there were two other cabins. One served as a medical building, and the other was a large cabin used as the main meeting hall. It was a gathering place where all the meals were prepared. Charles and his people would share their daily meals in that cabin or celebrate special events. The union of Nathen and Authia was an event that held a special place in Charles' heart. The two people he loved most in life would exchange vows in the courtyard, then partake of the meal and festivities in the main cabin.

* * * *

In nine days Authia and Nathen would be on their way to Africa. They had not yet asked Tammy to join them. They had their reservations, knowing the trip would be dangerous. But the bottom line was that they needed her help. So, they headed for the medical cabin, knowing she would be there. The cabin itself was made up of two rooms.

One was a waiting room with half a dozen chairs, and the other was a combination of a regular doctor's examination room and an operating room. Edward performed everyday exams to minor surgeries all in the one room. Authia loved the room, for it reminded her of Edward's office in Gainsbourgh. Warm and inviting, much like the man himself.

When Authia and Nathen walked in, they found Tammy unpacking supplies that had been delivered earlier on that day. Authia had heard her story from John and Charles when Authia first moved there. Tammy was twenty-nine years old, five feet, four inches tall with honey-blonde hair and hazel eyes. She had a slight build, weighing only one hundred and five pounds. She had taken her nursing in Vancouver, which was where she'd met John. Burwood's former resident physician. Back then, Tammy was at a crossroads in her life. Her drinking and drug use were jeopardizing not only her job but also her life. She had no one to turn to. Tammy grew up in foster care, going from one house to another. When she told John her story, he introduced her to Charles who, in turn, invited her to move to Burwood. Tammy seemed to embrace Burwood and everything it stood for. With the help of Edward, Burwood's current resident physician, Tammy straightened her life out and became Edward's assistant. Now they were going to ask her to leave all that she had come to love.

As Tammy put the last box of medical supplies away, she turned and appeared surprised to see Nathen and Authia standing there. "Oh, I didn't hear you come in. Are you seeing Dr. Simmons today, Authia?"

"No. Actually, we're here to see you."

"Me? What can I help you with?"

Authia motioned toward the chairs that were in front of Edward's desk. "Why don't we sit down." The three of them sat, with Nathen sitting in Edward's chair and Tammy and Authia occupying the chairs in front of the desk. "Nathen and I have a favour to ask of you. A very large favour. But before we ask, I want you to know that if the answer is no, there'll be no hard feelings. I don't want you to feel obligated in any way to say yes."

"Well, you certainly have my curiosity aroused. What's the favour?"

"You know that Nathen and I are leaving a week after the wedding for Africa?"

"Yes. I think it's so exciting." She focused her attention on Nathen. "To think that you might find your family is amazing."

Nathen smiled at Tammy. "It is exciting, Tammy, but I'm afraid for Authia. Especially in her condition. The favour we need to ask is if you'd accompany us."

Tammy's jaw dropped. "Come to Africa with you? Yes! I'd love to!"

Nathen shook his head. "It's not that simple. It's going to be very dangerous. I can't guarantee your safety. Tammy, we'll need your medical knowledge to help when it comes time to deliver the baby. Then, when we reach the African village, we need you to stay there with our child while Authia and I go in search of my home."

Tammy smiled at both Nathen and Authia. "It can't be any more dangerous than the life I'd lived before I came here. My answer is yes. I would love to come to Africa with you."

Authia jumped out of her chair and threw her arms around Tammy. "Thank you so much. This means everything to us." She stood back, tears forming in the corner of her eyes. "I can't even begin to tell you how important this is to Nathen and me."

"Not a problem. Though I think Dr. Simmons is going to

be a little jealous that you didn't ask him."

Authia smiled, knowing Tammy was right. "Speaking of Edward, where is he?"

"With Charles at the main cabin."

"Nathen, we should go talk to him. Let him know that we've asked Tammy to accompany us." Authia gave Tammy another hug. "Thank you so much."

"You're very welcome. And don't worry. I'll make sure we have all the medical supplies that we'll need."

Authia and Nathen left the medical cabin, relieved that Tammy agreed to accompany them. But, at the same time, they also felt very selfish with their decision. They were putting Tammy's life on the line because they needed her. In reality, they should be going on their own. And if Authia were not pregnant, they probably would be. But the baby changed everything. Authia and Nathen had discussed that they would do anything to keep their baby safe. Which apparently included jeopardizing the life of another.

Charles, Authia's father, and Edward were having lunch in the main cabin. The minute Authia entered the cabin, the tantalizing odour of the noonday meal assaulted her. She grinned at Nathen, who tenderly kissed her on her forehead. "Go ahead and sit down. I'll bring you some lunch."

Authia joined Charles and Edward at their table and pulled out a chair. "Mind if I join you?"

"Of course not. How are you feeling today?" Edward changed seats so he could sit next to her. Authia was very appreciative that he was so protective of her. He had been ever since he'd met her so many months ago. Edward was an amazing doctor with the warmest bedside manner. He was in his early sixties. His thick, greying hair was the crowning glory of his five-foot, eleven-inch, medium build. As Authia got comfortable in her chair, Edward wrapped his arms around her and gave her an affectionate hug.

"I feel fat. But other than that, I'm doing good."

"You look amazing. And you don't look fat." Charles tried to sound as if he were scolding her, but his sparkling hazel eyes gave him away. He was a little taller than Edward, standing at nearly six feet. His greying hair, tanned complexion, and almost perfect physique gave him that rugged, attractive appearance.

* * * *

Charles had only recently discovered that Authia was his daughter, and he was doing his best to make up for the lost time. But how do you make up for twenty-nine years of not being in your daughter's life? And now his daughter and his son, for he'd always thought of Nathen as his son, were leaving. Possibly never to return. The thought of losing them to Africa broke his heart. However, he would not reveal his true feelings to them. The journey was far too important to them. So, instead, he would support Authia and Nathen in their quest to find Nathen's origins.

Nathen joined them at the table, bringing a tray of food for both himself and Authia. "Have you heard anything from Morris?" Morris was the captain of the freighter that would be taking Nathen and Authia to Africa.

Charles shook his head. "No. But that doesn't mean anything. They're not scheduled to dock till tomorrow. I'll probably hear from him then."

"Good, because we have to tell him that we are bringing one extra person."

Both Charles and Edward queried in unison. "Who?"

Nathen glanced at Authia, then turned his attention to Charles and Edward. "We've asked Tammy to accompany us. I want her there to take care of Authia. I'm sorry,

Edward, that we didn't discuss this with you earlier."

"That's all right. Does she understand how dangerous this venture could be?"

"Yes. At least I hope she does. I'll admit I'm putting Authia's needs ahead of hers. But I give you my word, I'll do everything in my power to protect not only Authia and our child but Tammy as well."

"That's a lot to take on, Nathen." Charles placed a hand on Nathen's arm. "Just promise me that you'll be safe. That you won't take any unnecessary risks."

* * * *

Nathen didn't have an answer for Charles, nor could he make any more promises. He knew that the minute they crossed behind the falls, every step they took would be a risk. How perilous a risk would depend on what they found. That was why, in the back of Nathen's mind, he was formulating a plan that would keep Authia in the village, and he alone would cross into the unknown.

CHAPTER ELEVEN

The Jelani Tribe, Africa

Casandra sat on the raised platform at the back of the gathering hut. She surveyed her people as they all bowed before her. "You may sit, for I have an edict to proclaim." They all sat on the ground, curious as to what the new edict would be. No one had spoken of a new edict since the time of Joshawa.

"First I'll ask as I do at every gathering. Has anyone seen or heard from Joshawa's bloodline?" There was no answer. "Has anyone seen or heard from Dena?" Once again, there was no answer. "Fine, then I believe that now's the time to finally put to rest the bloodline of Joshawa. It's evident that the bloodline of Joshawa has died out. We need to move on and select a family, a strong family, from which the priestesses may choose a mate. A mate that's worthy of taking his place at our side and assist in the rule of the tribe."

There was murmuring amongst the crowd. It was obvious that she didn't want a family to take over as Lord of the tribe but rather as an advisor. She was unwilling to relinquish her position as ruler of the tribe. A position that her family had held for the past two centuries. Before Casandra could ask, Tadeo stood. Tadeo was a warrior standing just shy of six feet. Casandra stared him down. "You wish to be heard?"

"Yes, my Mistress."

"Then speak. But be forewarned. I'll not tolerate

treachery."

"There's no treachery in my heart, my Mistress. I was wondering if maybe we need to expand our search to the outer limits of our valley. That's where Dena ventured to. She was adamant that she would find Joshawa's descendants there."

"Tell me, Tadeo. What if we do find Joshawa's descendants? Joshawa left of his own free will. He turned his back on his own people to be with an outsider. Is that who you want as our Lord?"

"It's written that any descendant of Joshawa's will be given the opportunity to explain themselves. Are you not curious as to what happened to them? As to what happened to Dena?"

Casandra did not answer right away. Tadeo opened her eyes to the fact that, even after all these years, there were still people that were loyal to Joshawa's bloodline. She had to think. Somehow, she had to squash the hope that still lived in the hearts of Joshawa's loyal followers.

"I'm very curious but also disheartened. It saddens me that Joshawa would leave our village. Turn his back on his own people for the sake of an outsider." Casandra stood. "I'll speak to the spirits and see if they can give us any direction as to whether or not the bloodline remains. In the meantime, I want it to be known that I'm preparing my daughter, Tamara, to be our next high priestess. Bow before me if you agree, or stand and be heard." Casandra was delighted as each and every one of her people bowed to her as their high priestess.

Casandra returned to her hut, frustrated that her plan to finally kill off any and all hope of Joshawa returning blew up in her face. After all these years, Joshawa's memory lingered. Still lived on in the hearts of these naive, foolish people. If the truth ever came out, she would be banished or, even worse, put to death. And Dena, that misguided child. She didn't go to the outer limits. She went to the outside world, naively thinking that she would find the son of Joshawa. Even though Casandra found it highly unlikely that the son of Joshawa would find his way home, she was not taking any chances. There were four warriors permanently stationed at the falls. No matter who or what came through that opening, they would be captured and brought forth for punishment.

It was a risky game that she was playing, but still, Casandra didn't worry, for only herself and her daughter knew the truth. Her daughter was such a gentle soul with exceptionally strong powers. Casandra needed to harness those powers and use them to her advantage. The biggest problem facing her would be convincing Tamara to think as she did.

"Is there something I can help you with, Mother?"

Casandra whirled around to find her daughter standing at the entrance to the hut. "How'd you know?"

"I could sense that you were thinking of me. Though I could not hear what you were saying."

Casandra was taken aback with the knowledge of Tamara's new ability. If Tamara ever learned to read Casandra's mind, the consequences would be devastating. "Well, now that you're here, and since the morning is still young, why don't we start your training. Come, daughter, and sit with me." Casandra motioned to a spot on the ground in front of the fire pit. She went to retrieve a clay pot from the shelves, then sat on the ground across the fire pit from her daughter. Carefully, Casandra removed six leaf-covered packets from the clay pot and gently laid them in the fire pit. "The first and most important thing you must learn is how to create your essence."

"I am sorry, Mother. I do not understand."

Casandra gestured to the packets lying in the fire pit. "For centuries, your ancestors have used these packets to contain their essence. Each packet works only for the priestess whose essence it contains. They are useless to any other priestess."

"Is that not how Serena died. Her packet was used against her. How could that have happened?"

"Because she was in spirit form. As a spirit, you have no essence. A priestess' packet works by reacting to the essence contained within the priestess. It must be the exact same essence. In Serena's case, because she was dead, she had no essence. The packets that existed when she died lost their essence as well. That made them very dangerous because without the priestess' essence they could be used by anyone. Somehow Joshawa figured that out and used Serena's packet against her. With or without the essence, the power of the packet is contained to a very small area. The more packets you use, the larger the area. That's why only Serena perished. Joshawa's son stood too far back to be affected by the packet. You must know that as a priestess, we transfer the majority of our essence into just one packet. From then on, we use the original packet to make more. We use these packets in our spells, incantations and, when needed, to defend ourselves. We protect the original packet with our lives, for whoever controls the original packet controls the priestess. In time, you'll learn how to create your own packet. But for now, we'll meditate." Casandra laid her arms on her thighs, tilted her head back so that she faced the roof of the hut, closed her eyes, and began her meditation.

* * * *

Tamara was still taking in everything her mother had told her. She also closed her eyes, but her mind was filled with thoughts of Joshawa and his child. She relived the final moments of Serena's life. There was something different. Something she had not seen before. The fourth person on that fateful day, it was a woman, hiding in the background. Tamara focused on the woman and found her mind to be open. Tamara could meld with her. She could actually seek her out. She tried to speak with her, but the intrusion frightened the woman and she ended the meld. In those few moments that Tamara was with her, she learned that someone other than her family had the gift to meld with someone's mind. And that woman had a name. Authia!

Chapter Twelve

Burwood, British Columbia

Authia woke up and reached out for Nathen. But he wasn't there. She closed her eyes and smiled. There was a reason Nathen wasn't asleep by her side. It was their wedding day. Nathen had spent the night in Charles' cabin, keeping to the tradition of not seeing the bride on the day of the wedding. At least not until she was walking down the aisle. Authia threw the covers off her, rolled to her side, and with much difficulty, she managed to sit up with her legs over the edge of the bed. She stared down at her enormous belly, which was doing its best to hide what little lap she had left.

Tenderly she ran her hands along the sides of her belly. She couldn't even begin to explain how wonderful it felt to be pregnant with Nathen's child. Not so very long ago, Nathen did everything in his power to prevent her from seeing him. Now, she could curl up in his arms every night. She could gaze into his emerald eyes, feel his lips against hers. How far they had come in such a short time. Authia was about to get out of bed when she felt it. Someone was playing the mind game. It was very faint but definitely there. It was a female presence. Authia panicked. What if Serena was back? Authia blocked the meld. Her mind was racing. It couldn't be Serena. She'd witnessed her die. She would have to check into it another day. Nothing was going to ruin her wedding day.

Authia got out of bed, and as she reached for her housecoat, there was a knock on the door. Quickly, Authia wrapped the oversized housecoat around her belly as the door opened.

Tammy came in first, followed by Cheryl, who was carrying Authia's wedding dress. "Good, you're up." Tammy opened the drapes, allowing the sunlight to stream in and brighten up the room. "I'm going to do a breakfast run. Anything in particular that you want?"

"Whatever you bring me. This kid will eat anything."

Tammy left for the main cabin while Cheryl hung the dress up on a hook by the bed. The dress was sleeveless and used to have a square neckline. But that reminded Authia too much of a dress she wore not that long ago. Of a time when she was hunted down by a mountain man and was nearly killed. The only good that came out of that experience was that it prompted Nathen to finally reveal himself to her. Needless to say, Cheryl changed the neckline to something closer to a princess style. The dress was fitted but only to under Authia's breasts. Then it was finished off with a beautiful sash that tied in a bow at the back. The rest of dress flowed elegantly to the floor, effectively downplaying the size of Authia's swollen belly.

Authia hugged Cheryl. "You've done an amazing job! The dress is so beautiful!"

"Well, you deserve it. Both you and Nathen deserve this day." Authia had known Cheryl since her run-in with Dext, the mountain man that had attacked her. Cheryl had taken care of her ever since. She was only forty years old and already a widow. She was an attractive woman of average height and build, with long, blond hair that she always wore in a ponytail.

"Life's so perfect, Cheryl. I have a man who loves me deeply, and I'm about to have his child. What more could I ask for?"

"I might be out of line here, but do you honestly think this trip to Africa is wise?"

"Yes, I do. Nathen needs to discover who he is. I believe with all my heart that his tribe still exists. And we *are* going to find it."

The conversation was cut short when Tammy returned with three breakfast trays. "This is too funny." She placed the trays down on the table. "I ran into Nathen, and he's so nervous. The guy can fight a spirit who's trying to kill him, but a simple wedding has him shaking in his boots."

Authia shook her head. Her poor Nathen. The girls sat down and, as they ate their meals, they discussed the plans for the day.

* * * *

Nathen nervously paced the confines of Charles' cabin. The wedding was at three, and it was only nine in the morning.

"You know you're going to wear a hole in the floor if you keep that up."

"The wedding is six hours away, and I still haven't written my vows."

"Don't worry. You'll know what to say when the time comes. Now, how about we go get something to eat."

"I couldn't eat. My stomach's in knots."

"Nathen, as your best man, I'm telling you, we're going to get something to eat."

Nathen reluctantly followed Charles to the main cabin. On the way there, they met up with Edward, Nathen's one groomsman.

"Well, my shirt is ironed, thanks to Cheryl. Jeans are laid out. I'm ready to go."

Nathen and Authia decided that they didn't want a

formal wedding. With the exception of the wedding dress, everything else was casual. The men would be dressed in jeans and white dress shirts. Tammy and Cheryl would be in jean skirts that fell to their knees and sleeveless tops made with white lace and a silk lining. One of Burwood's residents, Alex, was a justice of the peace. He would officiate the wedding. All of Burwood would be attending. As Nathen walked past the centre courtyard, he marvelled at the beauty that surrounded him. The arbour was set up, and large pots of spring flowers lined the aisle Authia would walk down. The chairs were placed in a semi-circle so everyone could have a good view.

When they entered the main cabin, it was a flurry of activity. The kitchen area was jam-packed with men and women preparing for the feast that would be enjoyed later that evening. Nathen stood in awe as two men carried the three-tiered cake into the walk-in fridge. In the far corner of the cabin, a six-piece band was practicing for their performance that night. Nathen was beside himself with joy. He was actually getting married. Tears welled up in his eyes. Nathen gave his head a shake, then joined everyone at the serving table. All of a sudden, he was very hungry.

* * * *

The girls stayed in Nathen and Authia's cabin. After breakfast, Tammy gave Authia a manicure and pedicure while Cheryl was trying to decide on how Authia should wear her hair.

"You know, Authia, I think you should wear it down like you always do. I've been to so many weddings where the bride doesn't look like herself. Between the makeup that she doesn't normally wear and the fancy hairdo, it's a wonder that the groom actually recognizes her."

"You're right. I'm going to go out there looking like I normally do. I have one problem, though. Nathen and I decided to write our own vows, but now I'm wondering if that was really a good idea. Everything I want to tell him, he already knows."

Tammy put her arm around Authia's shoulders. "When you get out there, you'll know exactly what you want to say."

"Are you saying I shouldn't write anything down. You want me to wing it?"

Both Cheryl and Tammy answered. "Yes!"

* * * *

It was two thirty, and the people of Burwood were taking their seats. Nathen was talking to Alex while Charles and Edward went about making sure all the last-minute details were done. They wheeled the piano from the main cabin to the courtyard so that Authia could walk down the aisle to the traditional wedding march. Charles had two jobs that afternoon. Not only was he Nathen's best man, but he was also going to give the bride away. Everything was ready, and at five to three, Charles went to get his daughter. When she opened the door, and Charles saw her in her dress, wildflowers in her hair and in the bouquet she carried, he broke down in tears.

Authia wrapped her arms around him. "Now don't you start crying. If you do, then I'm going to start, and it will ruin what little makeup I have on."

Charles stepped back, overwhelmed by the moment. "You look totally amazing. You're so beautiful."

"Thank you."

Charles offered Authia his arm. "Shall we go?"

Authia linked her arm in his. "Yes. I'm so ready for this."

* * * *

Cheryl led the procession down the aisle, followed by Tammy. When they reached the arbour, the wedding march began to play, and Authia and Charles began their walk down the aisle. Authia gazed upon her husband-to-be. His white shirt accentuated his muscular frame. His jeans were so tight they left nothing to the imagination. Like most girls, Authia had dreams of marrying her handsome prince. A prince that loved her unconditionally. Finally, her dreams had become a reality. Her prince, the man she loved, waited for her, ready to become her husband.

* * * *

Nathen could not believe how beautiful Authia was . He couldn't take his eyes off her. The wedding march finished as Charles and Authia joined the wedding party. Nathen shook Charles' hand, then took Authia's hand in his. As Charles took his place next to Nathen, both Authia and Nathen faced Alex. The ceremony was beautiful and had many of the guests in tears. Nathen, however, was oblivious to his surroundings and everything that was being said. All he could do was drink in the beauty of the woman standing next to him. The woman who was going to be his wife. Charles gave him a gentle nudge as Alex asked that Nathen and Authia face each other and exchange vows. Authia gave her bouquet to Tammy, then turned to face Nathen. They held each other's hands and gazed deep into each other's eyes.

"Authia, I tried to write my vows to you, but I couldn't find the words that could even come close to describing my feelings for you. So, I've decided to let my heart lead the way. Before you came along, I was so alone. I was empty. I had all but given up on ever finding love. No one could ever love this face, love me for who and what I am." The tears welled up in Nathen's eyes. Slowly they trickled down his cheeks. He took a moment to compose himself. "And then you filled my mind, my soul, my very being. I've loved you from the beginning. You took this child and helped me become a man. I can't promise you riches or a life in the outside world. What I can promise you is that I'll love and adore you. I'll always be there to protect you, to care for you, to be that man that you dreamt about."

Authia gently wiped away his tears. "And it's this tenderness that I fell in love with. I never knew what true love was till I met you. Nathen, you're my world. I can't ever imagine my life without you in it. I don't need riches or a life in the outside world. All I need, all I'll ever need, is you. I promise, from the bottom of my heart, to love you and be the woman from your dreams as you are the man from mine. I'll be there for you, at your side, always and forever."

Nathen and Authia exchanged rings. Then Alex spoke the words Nathen never thought he would ever hear. "And I now pronounce you husband and wife. You may kiss the bride."

CHAPTER THIRTEEN

Seventy people stood and clapped as Nathen wrapped his arms around Authia and tenderly kissed her. When the kiss ended, Nathen whispered into her ear, "All I want to do is to pick you up into my arms, take you to our cabin, and then make mad, passionate love to you all through the night." Then he melded with her. *And I will do just that, after the baby comes.* Nathen took Authia's hand in his, and the two made their way to the main cabin while being showered with rice and confetti. When the doors opened and Authia walked inside, the ambience that surrounded her took her breath away.

Every table had a white linen table cloth on it. The tables were decorated with candles of varying sizes and vases containing the same beautiful wildflowers that adorned Authia's bouquet. The back of all the chairs had white satin sashes tied to them. An exquisite three-tiered wedding cake sat in the centre of the serving table. Knowing Authia's love for waterfalls and streams, Nathen had designed and built a water feature located on the wall that Authia would be facing as she sat at the head table. The water gently cascaded down from the ceiling to a pond that was eight feet wide, three feet high, and four feet across. Candles floated in the pond as well as sat on shelves jutting out from the waterfall.

Tears filled Authia's eyes as she turned to face Nathen. "How'd you do that?"

Nathen leaned down and kissed her. "To see you smile, to make you happy, anything is possible."

Dinner was served at five and what a presentation it was. The cooks had made all of Authia's favourite dishes. Which, in her condition, was endless. In the first six months of her pregnancy, Authia had been quite picky as to what she could and couldn't eat. But in the last trimester, Authia could eat anything. She was like a child in a candy store as the servers brought her ham, meatballs, chicken breasts stuffed with cheese and broccoli, scalloped potatoes, and the list went on. For dessert, besides the cake, there was only one thing on the menu. Authia's absolute favourite. Cheesecake smothered in chocolate.

After the meal and during coffee, only two speeches were heard. One from Charles, then one from Authia and Nathen. Charles stood at the podium, gazing out at his people. "Earlier today Nathen was panicking because he didn't have a speech ready for his vows. I told him that when the time came, he would know what to say." Charles took his speech and ripped it in half. "I'm going to follow my own advice and speak from the heart. But before I begin, I have to say, Nathen, how you managed to build that water feature without Authia knowing is beyond me."

There was laughter from the crowd as Nathen responded. "Why do you think I was bringing all her meals to the cabin for the last couple of days."

"And here I thought you were being romantic." Authia turned her attention to the water feature, then back to Nathen. "Incredibly romantic." She leaned closer and kissed him. The crowd cheered as Authia whispered, "I love you."

"Okay, from the heart, I love you two more than I can say. Authia, your mother did an incredible job raising you. Nathen, I can't thank her enough for bringing you into my life. I'm so very proud of both of you. Proud to be your father. I'm so happy that you two found each other and brought our family together. In all honesty, I wish I could go to Africa with you and remain a part of your life. But I know that's not meant to be. However, even though we'll be separated, you'll always be a part of me and I a part of you. I wish you all the happiness and love that any two people could have and share. Nathen, I hope that you find what you're looking for. Authia, I can't even begin to tell you how happy I am that you came into my life. I want the two of you always to remember that you have a family here that loves and cares for you. And, when you do find your people, Nathen, I'll be on the first freighter to Africa to come visit you." Charles raised his glass. "To Authia and Nathen." Everyone in the room raised their glass and toasted the happy couple.

* * * *

It was eight P.M., and Captain Morris was guiding his freighter, the Free Spirit, into his assigned dock. He was surprised to see several shipping containers loaded on the pier. For a moment, he thought he had the wrong dock slip, but no, he was where he was supposed to be. He glanced at his first mate, a man everyone called Hansen. "As soon as we dock, keep the men on the freighter. I'm going to locate the harbour master and find out what's going on. This pier should be empty."

Hansen nodded in agreement and keyed the microphone to the P.A. system. "Okay, we're getting ready to dock. All hands on deck. Once we are docked, no one's to leave the freighter until the captain gives the green light."

Captain Morris went on deck and surveyed his eighteen men went about their duties. As soon as the gangway was in place, Captain Morris went in search of the harbour master. It didn't take long to find him since he was already on his way to see Captain Morris.

Morris thought to himself about how he must come across to the harbour master. He knew he was on the short side standing five feet, eight inches tall. He was of medium build with tattoos completely covering both his arms. He liked to keep his head shaved bald, believing it gave him an intimidating appearance. He was only forty years old, but his face weathered by time and the elements made him look much older. Captain Morris was not someone you would choose to mess with. He had a reputation of holding his own in any confrontation.

He hadn't even walked ten feet past the gangway when he ran into Jack, the harbour master. Jack was six feet tall with a stocky build, but that didn't intimidate Morris. "What's going on, Jack? Why's my pier loaded with shipping containers?"

"Well, to begin with, it's my pier. And it's loaded with containers because they're being loaded onto your freighter tomorrow."

"What? My men are supposed to have the week off. We're not scheduled to leave until next Saturday."

"Look, Morris, five of those containers have to be at your first port of call by Wednesday."

"Wednesday! That would mean I'd have to leave no later than Monday morning."

"Sorry, but your freighter's the only one I have available that can make the schedule. I have a crew lined up to load the containers tomorrow morning."

"My men aren't going to be happy. What time are they going to start loading?"

"Eight A.M."

Morris shook his head. "That doesn't give my men any time with their families."

Jack just shrugged, then turned and headed back to his office, leaving Morris the unfortunate task of informing his men.

When Morris returned to the Free Spirit, Hansen was waiting for him. Hansen was five-ten with pitch-black hair, brown eyes, and the physique of a man who had been working the freighters since he was a child. At thirty-one, he proved himself to be an invaluable first mate. "You don't look happy. What's going on?"

"Apparently, we're leaving Monday before sunrise. Those containers are being loaded first thing tomorrow morning."

"Oh shit! The men aren't going to be happy."

"Go tell them. I have a call I have to make." Morris ignored the puzzlement on Hansen's face as he headed for the bridge.

Morris sat in his chair, keyed the microphone, and made his call to Charles. "This is Morris calling Charles. Charles, are you there?"

* * * *

The party was in full swing. One of the children ran up to Charles and proceeded to pull on his pant leg. Charles smiled at the small five-year-old. He bent down and picked her up in his arms. "And what can I do for you?"

"The radio's calling your name."

"Which radio?"

"The one in the kitchen."

It took Charles a second, but he finally realized what the child was referring to. He put her down and headed to the kitchen. As he entered the kitchen, he could hear garbled sounds coming from the radio. Quickly, he picked the mic up. "This is Charles."

"Charles, this is Morris. Can you hear me? What's all that noise?"

Charles could barely make out what Morris was saying.

"One moment, Morris." Charles scanned the crowd and called out, "Harry, cut the music."

The music stopped, to the vocal disapproval of the crowd. Charles keyed the mic. "Okay, Morris, I can hear you now."

"Got bad news, Charles. Apparently, I'm shipping out Monday before sunrise. If Nathen and Authia still plan to come, they're going to have to be here by tomorrow night."

Charles scanned the crowd for Nathen. When he couldn't find him, he sent Harry to search for him. "They'll make it. There's going to be a third person. Will that be a problem?"

"Not on my end. Their quarters will be tight. Look, Charles, I'm going to have to bring my first mate into our little circle. There's no way I can pull this off without him finding out."

"Do what you have to do. They'll be on the pier by midnight. Charles signing off."

As Charles replaced the mic, Nathen and Authia approached him. Nathen's expression was that of concern. "What's going on, Charles? Why has the music stopped?"

Charles motioned for Harry to resume the music , then took Nathen and Authia aside. "Morris just called. He's leaving early. You're going to have to be at the pier by midnight tomorrow."

Authia and Nathen looked at each other. Authia placed a hand on Nathen's arm. "We can do it. We're just going to have to say our goodbyes sooner than later." Authia tenderly smiled at Nathen. "It's going to be okay. Let's finish our party."

* * * *

So, the time had come, and the journey was about to begin. Nathen could not keep his eyes off Authia as she laughed and danced the night away. He wanted to find his people.

To discover who he was. But at what cost. Was he prepared to lose what he had for the possibility of the unknown? Nathen returned to the dance floor, and as he held Authia in his arms, he knew that she would never venture past the falls.

* * * *

Tamara sat in her hut, practicing her meditation. But no matter how hard she tried to concentrate, her mind always went in search for the woman named Authia. She was going behind her mother's back, and by doing so, she risked being the recipient of her mother's anger. But it was something she knew she had to do. As Tamara calmed her mind, she heard music, strange music. Then a vision came to her. A vision of a large vessel.

CHAPTER FOURTEEN

The sun rose on the last day that Nathen and Authia would be in Burwood. Nathen woke to find Authia still asleep curled up next to him. Lovingly he kissed the top of her head, then stared up at the ceiling. Only last night he had celebrated the biggest day of his life. He and Authia should be heading to the cabin in the woods for their honeymoon. But instead, Nathen was dragging her halfway across the world on the slightest chance that they might find his people. And what if they did exist? How would he and Authia be received? If Serena was any example of what his people were like, he was sending Authia to her death. But what if they were more like Joshawa? If that was the case, both he and Authia would be accepted. Nathen closed his eyes and took a deep breath. As he opened his eyes, his gaze fell upon his wife, the mother of his child. What was he doing? Why not stay at Burwood? If they wanted, they could live in the cabin in the woods. Authia and Tanya had rented it when they'd first come to the Burwood area. But after Serena died and their life became normal, Authia bought it outright. Thcy would be happy there. They could raise their children there. If they went to Africa, there were no guarantees. Nathen was torn between staying where he knew it was safe and forging on to the unknown. Should he discuss his concerns with Authia? He knew where she stood on the subject. Nathen wondered how he was to deal with the most difficult and the most crucial decision he'd ever had to make? Quietly Nathen got out of bed, dressed, left a note for Authia, then headed out to Charles' cabin. He needed a sounding board, and even though he knew Charles would be all for them staying, he also knew that he would be open-minded.

* * * *

Charles was pouring himself some coffee when someone knocked on his door. He was surprised to see Nathen standing there. "Good morning, Nathen. Where's Authia?" Charles stepped aside so Nathen could enter the cabin.

"She's still in bed, sleeping."

"And why are you here instead of being curled up next to your new wife?"

Nathen sat in one of the two overstuffed chairs that faced the fireplace. "I need your guidance. I'm so confused as to what to do. Stay here in Burwood and raise my family or drag Authia to some place that I don't even know for a fact exists."

Charles handed Nathen a cup of coffee, poured himself a cup, then sat in the matching chair. "That's a tough one. On the one hand, you have Burwood. A place you know, a place that's safe. And, on the other hand, you have the unknown. You have the possibility of discovering who you are. Something you've wanted to know since you were a child. You've been tormented your entire life because you don't know who or what you are. You have an opportunity to figure it out. However, the path you need to follow to gain this knowledge is somewhat obscure. Nathen, if you were on your own, we wouldn't be having this conversation. You'd be halfway to that freighter by now. The problem is that you're not on your own. I'm going to hate myself for saying this, but I think you should go."

"Really? And risk Authia's life?"

"You see, son, that's the point. It's Authia's life. It should be, it has to be, her decision. You can't make that decision for her."

"He's right, Nathen, it is my decision." Both Nathen and Charles turned around to find Authia standing in the doorway. "Sorry for the intrusion. I was going to leave, but I overheard my name being mentioned." Authia went to Nathen, who immediately got up and offered her his chair. She sat down, then held out her hands for him to take. Nathen sat on the edge of the hearth and took her hands in his. "Nathen, this is not an easy decision for either one of us to make. To be honest, I'm scared. Scared of losing you, scared of what we might find. But this is a journey we have to make, together. If you don't go, you'll regret it for the rest of your life. If you go without me, then you'll spend the entire journey wondering how I'm doing. How your child is doing. You need to be focused, and the only way that will happen is if I'm at your side."

Nathen stared deep into Authia's eyes. Charles knew at that moment that Nathen saw the truth in what she was saying. Nathen smiled at Authia. "You're right. You're both right. I guess I just needed to hear it." Nathen stood up and extended his hand to Authia. "Come, we have some packing to do."

* * * *

Morris stood on the bridge, monitoring the crane operator as he loaded the freighter with shipping containers. He'd checked out all the ports of call and had calculated that it would be a month and a half to two months before they reached Africa. A long time for Nathen to stay cooped up in his cabin. Hansen entered the bridge, carrying two mugs of coffee.

"Alen has ordered the supplies we'll need for the kitchen. They should be here by three this afternoon." Morris didn't say anything. He accepted the coffee, took a sip, then stared out the window to the open sea. "Okay, do you want to tell me what's going on. You've been acting strange all morning."

Morris sat down in his chair as he made the decision to bring Hansen in on his little secret "What I'm about to tell you doesn't leave this room."

"Okay?"

"You know the passenger from cabin three."

"Right. Some woman heading for Africa."

"Actually, we have three people in that cabin. The woman, her husband, and I'm not sure who the third person is."

"So, we have three. What's the issue?"

"I grew up with the man. His name is Nathen. You couldn't ask for a better friend. Problem is, he's different. He looks different than we do. So different that he'll only leave his cabin at night and only if there's no one on the decks."

"What's wrong with him?"

"Nothing really. He just looks different. Hansen, I need him to be safe. Will you help me keep him safe?"

"Of course, you know I've got your back. I'll make sure he and the other two passengers are kept safe. When are they boarding?"

"Midnight tonight."

"I'll greet them with you. Help them get settled."

"Thanks, Hansen. Oh, by the way, the woman's pregnant. She'll probably be having the kid on the ship."

"Holy crap! Anything else I need to know?"

"That about does it. Once the containers are on board, tell the men they can take off. I want them back at zero four hundred. Not a second later."

"Mind if I stay on board with you? If there are three people staying in the cabin, I'll have to move a cot in there. Get the cabin ready for three people. I'd rather do it before they come aboard. I'm going to the supply room now and make sure we have what we need to accommodate the third person." Hansen didn't wait for a reply. It was more of a statement than a question. Morris finished his coffee, then went to check on the containers.

* * * *

Nathen and Authia were in their cabin, packing, which was not an easy task. They were only taking two backpacks apiece and one small suitcase that contained the medical supplies and clothing for the baby. The next decision was what route to take to the vehicle. One way was a two-hour hike down the mountainside, which led to an old abandoned logging road. Or, the four-mile hike to the cabin, which led to another section of the same logging road. Due to Authia's condition, Nathen chose the four-mile hike. Trying to play mountain goat with the first option was not something Nathen was willing to attempt. They would leave early so that Authia could take as many breaks as she needed. Then they would remain at the cabin in the woods until it was time to leave.

Tammy arrived at their cabin, and the three of them went through the backpacks and suitcase, reassuring themselves that they had everything they needed. Once they were finished, they decided it was time for their last meal in the main cabin. Nathen and Authia walked hand in hand, with Tammy at their side. The courtyard was strangely quiet.

"What's going on, Nathen? Where is everybody?"

Nathen shook his head. "I have no idea. Charles never mentioned anything when I was with him earlier."

They didn't need an explanation from Charles because as soon as Nathen opened the door to the cabin, every single resident of Burwood gave the couple a standing ovation. The banner that read *Congratulations* the night before now read *Bon Voyage.* Nathen and Authia, still holding hands, walked to the centre of the cabin. Nathen could feel his eyes glistening. However, Authia was all-out crying. Charles walked up to them, gave Nathen and Authia a huge hug, then held his hand up to silence the crowd.

"Just so you know, I didn't tell you to leave because I knew this was happening. I truly believe deep in my heart that the two of you need to make this journey. Everyone here has come together to give you this gift." Charles handed Nathen a large envelope. Inside the envelope were two smaller envelopes. One contained U.S. currency and the other contained currency which Nathen believed to be the currency they would need for Africa.

Nathen shook his head and attempted to hand the envelope back to Charles. "We can't accept this. It's too much. There has to be thousands of dollars here."

Charles refused to take the envelope back. "Eight thousand United States dollars and a few thousand francs. It was all the francs we could get our hands on. Morris says that francs will be the currency for the area you're going to. He also tells me that he can get you anything you need during the voyage with U.S. currency. You'll need to buy more francs when you get to Africa. Morris can arrange that for you as well."

Nathen scanned the group of people that, to him, were family. "Your generosity is overwhelming. Just this morning I was debating as to whether or not we stay. I'd be proud to raise my family amongst people as kind and generous as you. However, it was pointed out to me..." Nathen smiled at Authia , then turned back to face the crowd. "That if I don't pursue this endeavour to find my origins that I may regret it for the rest of my life. I know, in my heart, that I would regret the decision to stay. So, after breakfast, Authia, Tammy, and I are heading to the cabin. There, we'll wait until eight tonight, at which point we'll begin our odyssey. We may never be back, so I want to take this time to thank each and every one of you. You've treated me with respect and kindness my entire life. And for that, I'm eternally grateful. Judging from the enticing odour coming from the kitchen, I'd have to say breakfast is ready. I'd be honoured if you'd all partake in one last meal with us."

* * * *

Breakfast lasted almost to noon. By the time everyone said their personal goodbyes it was time to head out to the cabin. Authia had not walked the path since she'd come to Burwood back in December. With the coming of spring, the trees were budding. Wildflowers were poking their heads above the ground, and the aroma of the new season filled the air. The walk was breathtaking. It took them over three hours to make the four-mile hike.

When Authia entered the yard to her cabin, she had to stop for a moment and take it all in. A porch ran the entire width of the cabin. A swing hung from the roof of the porch next to the front door. Dozens of flowering shrubs and wildflowers were planted in rock gardens in front of the cabin. Authia closed her eyes and allowed the aura of the cabin and the yard to surround her completely. There were so many memories. Good times, bad times, and also some pretty scary times. But in the end, the good times won out, and Authia smiled as these memories flooded her mind.

To Authia, leaving Burwood behind meant a new chapter

was evolving in Nathen's and her life. And with the new chapter would come the chance to make new memories. Unfortunately, Authia knew only too well that these memories may not be ones she'd wish to keep. She could sense that the new chapter would prove to be challenging and extremely dangerous. It would be filled with uncertainty, upheaval, sorcery, and the persistence of two people determined to find the answers.

Chapter Fifteen

Authia opened the door to the cabin to find it in immaculate condition. Of course, she knew she would find it that way. It was no different than the very first time she opened the door to the cabin back in the fall. To her left was the kitchen. The kitchen counter ran almost the entire length of the wall except for a doorway at the very far right which led to a storage room. There was a small wood stove, fridge, and sink along the same wall. The cabinets were all made from pine and open with no doors to cover them. In the middle of the kitchen was an old wooden table with four chairs. Along the back wall were three doors that led to two bedrooms and a very small bathroom located between the bedrooms. To Authia's right was the sitting room. A stone fireplace almost covered the entire wall. A love seat faced the fireplace, with a rocking chair on one side of it and an oversized upholstered armchair on the other side. To Authia, she was home. As she gazed about the room, she knew her decision to purchase the cabin was the right one.

Authia had discovered months ago that Burwood, or rather Charles, had an attachment to the cabin and, over the years, he'd felt the need to maintain it. After Authia had purchased the cabin, Burwood continued to keep it clean and in excellent condition. While Authia was living at Burwood, she made the cabin available to couples so they could escape to it for a few days of seclusion and romance. At one time, she'd even imagined her and Nathen living in the cabin, but when Joshawa had given Nathen the parchment, when he'd shown Nathen that there was more to his life, all her plans had changed.

Authia headed straight for her favourite chair. It was the oversized upholstered armchair that she had spent many a night curled up in. Unfortunately, due to her rather large size, the armchair was no longer comfortable. She opted for the love seat and let her feet rest on the coffee table. Nathen dropped the backpacks at the door. He had ended up carrying his and Authia's about midway through the hike to the cabin. If she had allowed him, he would have carried her as well. But Authia drew the line at the backpacks. Tammy went into the kitchen and drew a glass of water from the tap for Authia. Nathen keyed the mic to the two-way radio and called for Edward. Edward had left for the town of Gainsbourgh the night before. He wanted to get everything ready for the trip to Vancouver and a night on the docks.

"Edward, are you there? This is Nathen."

"Yes, Nathen, I'm here. Are you at the cabin?"

"Yes. We're ready whenever you are."

"How about Authia? How's she doing?"

Authia was standing next to Nathen as she helped herself to another glass of water. Nathen passed the mic to her. "I'm fine, Edward. When do you think you'll be here?"

"I thought I'd leave soon. You need to eat before we leave for Vancouver."

Authia smiled. "You are always taking care of me. See you in a couple of hours."

Authia handed the mic back to Nathen, then returned to the love seat to get comfortable. After a brief conversation with Edward, Nathen joined Authia. He sat beside her, putting his arm around her shoulders. "You need to get some sleep. I'll wake you when Edward arrives."

"I'm not very tired." Authia cuddled close to Nathen, resting her head on his chest. "I'm just going to rest for a few minutes." Within five minutes, Authia was fast asleep.

* * * *

Tammy, who was curled up in the armchair, laughed. "You sure called that."

"She was exhausted after the long walk. She just didn't realize it. Tammy, now that she's sleeping, we have to talk."

"That sounds serious."

"It is. I can't, under any circumstance, have Authia accompany me past the waterfalls."

"Good luck with that. She's adamant on going."

"I know she is. When we reach Africa, I want you to make sure that she doesn't follow me."

"Are you kidding me! There's nothing I can say that would stop her."

"You wouldn't need to say anything. Just return to Vancouver with Morris. That would leave Authia no choice but to stay behind with our child. She'll not risk the child's life for the sake of joining me on this journey."

* * * *

Tammy was conflicted. She considered both Authia and Nathen her friends. What Nathen was asking her to do would mean she would have to betray one of them. She decided to pacify Nathen for the time being and make her decision when the time came. "Okay, but I'm not happy about it. You're asking me to betray Authia's trust."

"Yes, I know. But is her life not worth it?"

"Yes, of course."

The two sat in silence as they waited for Edward.

* * * *

Meanwhile, Authia's subconscious mind registered all that transpired. *Has it been so long that you've forgotten, Nathen? Forgotten that I can see and hear your thoughts even in my sleep.* She did not speak directly to Nathen, for she too was developing her own plan. A plan that would ensure the two of them would continue on the quest.

Edward arrived at five thirty, bringing with him all the fixings for a fabulous dinner. Charles and Cheryl arrived shortly after. Authia was giddy with delight. Her entire family was there for their last meal together. Supper consisted of barbecue steaks, corn on the cob, freshly baked bread, and baked potatoes. The mood was carefree as they recalled all the events that led up to the decision to find Nathen's origins. Bad or good, the group found the positive in all that happened. At eight P.M., reality hit home, and it was time for the three travellers to get ready to head out. They all dressed in dark clothing. They wanted to blend in with the darkness of the pier. Nathen wore his old coat that he'd worn before to conceal his features from Authia. It was long, with the bottom edge of the coat covering his knees. The hood, when raised, effectively concealed his face. The three were ready, and all that was left was to say goodbye.

Edward led the group to a path that took them from the yard of the cabin to a clearing where Authia usually parked her truck. But instead of the truck, there was a black panelled van. Authia looked questioningly at Edward. "Where's my truck?"

"At Marvin's. I thought the van would better suit our purposes for tonight. He let me borrow it."

"Well, be sure to thank him for me." Marvin was a soft-spoken car salesman who owned his own car lot and was a good friend of Edward's. Authia had purchased her truck from him a few months earlier.

Tammy sat up front with Edward as Authia and Nathen

climbed into the back of the van. It was not the most comfortable arrangement, but it was the best way to conceal Nathen from the outside world.

Authia drew a deep breath as the first leg of their journey began. She knew that they risked so much all based on the belief that an age-old parchment was not only accurate but true. For all they knew, it could all be a bedtime story. But, if that were the case, then where had Joshawa, Serena, and Nathen come from? They also took the chance that the tribe did exist at one time but, after all these years, there was nothing left but the memory of a spirit that died centuries ago. Authia had her doubts, not that she would admit them to Nathen. She feared the unknown. She feared the possibility that she would lose Nathen. She questioned whether or not they should stay at Burwood. But the reality was that they had made a commitment to each other, and whether Nathen liked it or not, they would continue on the quest, the two of them. If Authia only knew what waited for them. If only her gift could foresee her own future. Then maybe they would both still be in Burwood. Maybe the quest would be nothing more than a dream.

* * * *

Secluded in her family hut, Tamara was practicing her meditation. Only she was not seeking out her forebears as she had been instructed to but instead a faceless apparition she had come to know as Authia. Tamara closed her eyes and focused on the memory of Authia. Reaching out for any sign of her. Then slowly Authia appeared. She was frightened and conflicted. But most importantly she was searching for something. Tamara strained to focus deeper. Authia was searching for the family of her loved one. Tamara tried to focus even deeper but, as before, the meld ended and she was left with a vision of a man, cloaked, his features hidden from her.

* * * *

Authia lay in Nathen's arms, trying desperately to get comfortable. Then she came to her. Tenderly seeking out who Authia was. Authia allowed her to penetrate her mind so that she could learn more about her. But the presence was not allowing the meld to flow both ways, so Authia ended the meld in the fear that she may learn too much. Who could be melding with her and should she tell Nathen? The presence had a distinctive signature. A signature that reminded Authia of Serena. No, she wouldn't tell Nathen. At least not until she discovered who and what the presence was.

CHAPTER SIXTEEN

It was eleven o'clock as Edward pulled the nondescript van up to the harbour master's office. As Morris had promised, the lights were all out. Nobody occupied the office after eight in the evening. Edward parked the van facing out toward the pier. That way he could see if anyone approached them. The area was dimly lit. With only enough light to see their way along the pier but not enough to reveal what lay in the shadows of the shipping containers and freighters lined up along the pier. According to Morris, they were to meet him at dock twenty-six, five freighters north of the office, precisely at midnight. They had an hour to kill. An hour for their nerves to take control of their worst fears.

* * * *

Tammy and Edward seemed to handle the wait quite calmly. But for Nathen, it was a totally different story. He knew what the risk was if they got discovered. Each minute that went by seemed to be a lifetime to him.

At eleven thirty Nathen had enough. "It is time. We're going to leave now."

Edward turned to face Nathen. "But you still have a half hour."

"I'd feel more confident if I could see the freighter. There are plenty of containers on the pier that we can hide behind." Nathen opened the side door to the van, jumped out, then reached back in to help Authia. He grabbed the four backpacks as Tammy reached in and grabbed her backpacks along with the suitcase.

* * * *

Authia's gaze met Edward's. "I guess this is goodbye." Tears freely ran down her cheeks. Edward got out of the van and went directly to Authia. They hugged for the last time. And as they hugged, Authia whispered into Edward's ear, "I'm going to miss you so much."

Edward sat back in the van and kept an eye on Nathen, Authia, and Tammy as they walked out onto the pier. They went as far as dock twenty-five, then disappeared behind a pile of containers. Edward felt so empty. She was truly gone. For the second time, he lost someone who meant everything to him. Reluctantly he drove away, constantly checking his rear-view mirror in case they changed their mind. But, as he drove past the second block, he knew his time with Authia was over.

* * * *

Authia and Tammy hid in the shadows of the containers. Nathen chose to stand at the very edge of one of the larger containers. From his vantage point, he could see dock twenty-six and the freighter that was going to be their home for the next two months. How ironic that thirty years ago Nathen had been on this very dock, cradled in the loving arms of Tanya. Waiting to be taken to his new home, to be taken to Burwood. As a grown man, he stood waiting to be taken to a place that could explain his origins to him. A place that was a lifetime away from Burwood.

It was eleven forty-five, and the chill of the night air caused Authia to shiver. She drew her jacket closer around her, trying to ward off the cold. Nathen immediately went to take his coat off. Authia smiled at him and shook her head. Nathen couldn't remove his coat. At least not until they were safe inside their cabin.

Nathen sat next to Authia and wrapped his arms around her instead. "Tammy, keep a watch out. Morris will be on the gangway when it's safe to approach the freighter."

Tammy did as she was told, and for the next fifteen minutes, she kept an eye on the freighter while Nathen tried to keep Authia warm. Exactly at midnight, Tammy said, "Nathen, there are two men on the pier."

"Two?" Nathen stood and went to Tammy's side. Cautiously he peered around the container. "Morris said he'd be alone."

Authia stepped out of the shadows. "Come with me, Tammy. Nathen, you wait here until we're certain it's safe."

Nathen wanted to argue. He should be the one making sure it was safe, not Authia. However, he knew she was right, so he reluctantly stayed hidden in the shadows while Authia and Tammy approached the two men.

* * * *

Authia would have been lying if she said she wasn't scared. But showing fear would only hinder her situation. She had to approach these men with confidence. Take control of the encounter. Very calmly she addressed the two men standing in front of her. "I understand one of you is Captain Morris?"

Morris extended his hand, which Authia accepted. "I'm Morris, and this is my first mate, Hansen."

Hansen kept his hands in his pockets. "Good evening."

"I'm Authia, and this is Tammy. Before we go any further, I want to make sure it's safe for Nathen to come aboard."

"Nathen has nothing to fear here. Hansen and I'll make sure you're safe during your entire voyage. Tell Nathen that it's safe to come out. We're the only ones on board."

"Nathen tells me that we can trust you. Do I have your word on that?"

"Nathen's like a brother to me. You have my word."

Authia turned and melded with Nathen. *It's safe. The second man is Captain Morris' first mate.*

* * * *

Cautiously, Nathen left the darkness of the shadows and walked toward the group only to have Morris meet him halfway. He threw his arms around Nathen. "Man, you got big! Good to see you, old friend!"

Nathen returned the hug. "You haven't changed a bit."

"Come with me, Nathen. I want you to meet Hansen. He's a good man. And take that damn hood off."

Nathen left his hood on, approaching Hansen with wariness. He didn't know Hansen, and even though Morris vouched for him, Nathen was always leery of strangers. Hansen extended his hand to Nathen. "My captain says to keep you safe. That's exactly what I intend to do."

Nathen hesitantly extended his hand. Hansen accepted it and took no notice of it. He didn't acknowledge the length of the fingernails or the fine layer of hair that covered Nathen's hand. "If you're not comfortable removing your hood, then that's fine with me. Just let me know what you need, and I'll make sure that you get it. Where are your bags?"

"They're still behind the shipping containers." Nathen turned to retrieve the bags.

"Let me help you." Hansen joined him.

When they were out of earshot of the others, Hansen spoke to Nathen. "My mother was in a fire. Scarred her up pretty bad. I don't know what your problem is, but believe me, looks don't mean anything to me. I judge a man by his actions." Hansen stopped to face Nathen. "If you're a friend of the captain's, then that must mean you're a decent guy. And that's good enough for me."

Hansen bent down and picked up three of the backpacks. Nathen took the other three and the suitcase. He took a couple of steps, then stopped and put the bags down. "The same goes for me. If Morris trusts you, then that's good enough for me." With that, Nathen removed his hood, picked up the bags, and continued walking back to the gangway.

Hansen smiled as he walked toward the Free Spirit. "I don't know what all the fuss is about. I've seen worse. Follow me, I'll take you to your cabin."

Nathen, Authia, and Tammy followed Hansen while Morris returned to the bridge. As he climbed the metal stairs leading to the bridge, he called down to Nathen. "Once you're settled in, come see me. My crew won't be back till zero four hundred. We've got some time to visit."

* * * *

The cabin was quite compact. To the left of the door, there was a double bed pushed into the corner tight against the wall. A cot had been placed at the end of the bed, leaving only two feet between the cot and the adjoining wall. Against the wall in front of the door was an eight-drawer dresser standing about waist-high. Above that, there was a small porthole. To the right of the door was a table with two chairs and a love seat. Next to the love seat, there was a door that led to a washroom. The shower was so tiny that Authia had her doubts as to whether she would fit or not. Hansen and Nathen placed the bags on the bed.

"Nathen, if you want to see the captain, I'd go now. Do

you girls need anything? How about you follow me and I'll show you where the galley is and the quickest way to get to the upper deck."

Authia could see that Nathen was hesitant to leave, but she insisted he go. After he'd left, Authia and Tammy were shown how to get to the upper deck, then where the galley was. The cook, Alen, was there to greet them. Authia was surprised that someone was on board, but Hansen assured her that Alen rarely left the galley. He lived to cook, spending all his time either in the galley or his sleeping quarters, which were right next door. He seldom ventured beyond his domain.

"Alen, I want you to meet our passengers. Authia, Tammy, this is Alen."

"I was told that there'd be a pregnant lady coming on board, so I put this together for you to take to your room." It was a platter of fresh fruit, vegetables, and cheeses. "If there's anything particular that you want to eat, just let me know. I'll fix you anything you like."

"Thank you, Alen, but I'm sure whatever you make will be fine. And this platter's amazing. Thank you so much."

"No problem. And if you don't feel up to coming to the galley, just let me know and I'll have your meals sent to your cabin."

Authia smiled at Alen. "You're too kind. I appreciate that."

* * * *

Tammy went to take the platter from Authia. "It's late. Authia, you need your rest."

The girls said good night to Alen and Hansen, then headed back to their room. When they finally found their way, they were greeted by Nathen, who had returned minutes before and was already in bed. He threw the covers back and smiled at Authia. "I saved a spot for you."

"So I see." Authia was too tired even to remove her street clothes. She kicked off her shoes, then curled up in bed next to Nathen. Within minutes, she was fast asleep.

Tammy placed the platter on the table, went into the bathroom to change into her pajamas, then crawled under the covers on the cot. "Nathen, you still awake?"

"Yes."

"It's real now, isn't it? I mean, there's no turning back. We're really going to Africa."

"Do you regret coming?"

"Not in the least. Good night, Nathen."

"Good night, Tammy."

* * * *

Nathen pulled Authia closer to him. If what he was doing was the right thing to do, why did he have a nagging feeling that something was terribly wrong? Why did he have such a disturbing premonition of doom? Slowly he closed his eyes. Tammy was wrong. They still had one chance to turn back.

* * * *

Tamara entered her mother's hut. "You wanted to see me, Mother?"

Casandra studied her daughter thoughtfully. "To whom are you loyal?"

"I do not understand the question."

"It's very simple. To whom are you loyal?"

"To you, Mother. Why would you ask?"

"I've had a vision. Dena's alive and in the outside world. She waits for the return of Joshawa's son."

Tamara chose her next question carefully. "I thought you said he could not find us?"

"The son of Joshawa mustn't find his way home. We need to stop Dena."

"How do you suggest we do that?"

"If you are loyal to me, then you'll join me, and together we can destroy her."

"But, Mother, she is one of us. She is your sister."

"She's a traitor to our family. To our destiny to rule this tribe. I'll not permit her to bring that bastard child of Joshawa's to our village."

"Then you do believe he will come?"

"Sit." Casandra motioned for Tamara to sit across from her at the fire pit. She placed her leaf-covered packets in the fire pit, then sat down herself. "We'll perform the death incantation. Are you prepared?"

"Yes, Mother." Tamara knew it took at least two skilled priestesses to perform the incantation. However, her mother did not have the option of asking one of the other three priestesses. Tamara made a choice that very moment that would forever affect the life of the tribe. As she pretended to join her mother in the incantation, her mind sought out Dena and warned her. *Protect yourself. My mother means to kill you. Joshawa's son is on his way.*

Chapter Seventeen

When Authia woke up the next morning, she could feel the gentle rocking of the freighter as it glided through the ocean waves. The hum of the engines vibrated throughout the ship. Authia found the rocking of the ship and the sound of the engines soothing. Both Nathen and Tammy were still sleeping. Quietly, yet awkwardly, Authia got out of bed and stood by the dresser, gazing out the one small porthole in the cabin. All she could see for miles around was the ocean. Nathen and Tammy were still asleep, so Authia decided to leave them sleep while she went on deck for some fresh air. Quickly she changed into an oversized t-shirt and maternity pants, left a note, then tried to remember Hansen's instructions on how to get to the upper deck.

When she finally reached her destination, she ran into three of the crew working on various duties. Almost immediately Hansen was at her side. "Good morning, miss."

"Good morning, Hansen, and please, call me Authia. And actually, it's not miss anymore. Nathen and I were just married. I'm Mrs. Roberts now." Nathen and Authia decided that in memory of Tanya they would take her last name as their own.

"The captain would like to see you if you'd come this way." Hansen stepped aside so Authia could pass him. He turned to see his men all gawking at Authia. Authia grinned when Hansen scowled at his men, which resulted in all three of them going back to work.

She made her way along the deck, and the spray from the sea gently fell on her face as the sun warmed it. It was a beautiful day, and Authia felt disappointed that Nathen wouldn't be able to share moments like these with her. Carefully Authia climbed the stairs to the bridge, where Morris was waiting for her. She found him at the wheel, gazing out to the open ocean. He glanced up as she entered the bridge. "Did you sleep well?"

Authia chuckled. "As well as can be expected with someone kicking at you all night." She rubbed her belly to emphasize it was the baby and not Nathen.

Morris allowed Hansen to take the wheel , then offered Authia his chair. "I want you to let Nathen know that, if he wishes, he can spend his daytime hours here on the bridge with me. We're high enough up that the men can't see inside and Hansen's the only one who comes up here."

Authia smiled at Morris as she made herself comfortable in his chair. "That would be terrific. I'll be sure to tell him. You know, I can't thank you enough for helping us. There's no way we could've made this happen without you."

* * * *

Morris paused for a moment as he allowed the memories of Burwood to come alive in his mind. "I was a bit of an asshole when I was growing up. Angry, mad at the world. When I was in my late teens, Charles was ready to boot my ass out of Burwood. But then this baby came to live with us. When I first laid eyes him, I realized that my life wasn't so bad. As Nathen grew, he became a big part of my life. He changed me." Morris gently shook his head and smiled as the memories of Nathen as a child flooded his mind. "He showed me how to like myself. Be content with who I was. I should've been his mentor, but instead, he was mine. I owe

Nathen my life. This trip is the least I could do."

"Well, no matter what the reasons are. We appreciate it. Are you taking on any more passengers? I understand you have two more cabins."

"I was going to talk to you about that. We were supposed to have the cabins full this trip, but I decided to cancel them."

"You didn't need to do that on our behalf."

"Yeah, I did. It's safer for Nathen this way. Tammy can move to her own cabin whenever she's ready. Just let Hansen know."

"Your generosity is overwhelming." Authia stood to leave and as she did she placed her hand on Morris' arm. The tender smile she gave Morris warmed him to his very core. "Nathen has a true friend in you. And for that, I'm eternally grateful." Authia's stomach made slight rumbling noises. She placed her hands on her belly and giggled. "If you don't mind, I'm going to get something to eat. This baby's hungry."

Morris smiled at Authia. "Go ahead and enjoy. Tell Nathen I expect him on the bridge at some point today."

* * * *

Authia left to find the kitchen. From there she fixed two trays with enough food for three people, then took them back to the room. Nathen and Tammy were awake when Authia returned. "I have breakfast for everybody."

Tammy walked out of the bathroom with a towel wrapped around her. "You just missed Hansen. He brought us a pot of coffee."

Authia placed the trays on the table. "Perfect. I was going to have to go back for that."

Nathen, dressed only in his jeans, wrapped his arms

around Authia and gave her a good morning kiss. "How did you sleep, my love."

"Quite well considering this kid of yours was running a marathon. I have news. Tammy, you're going to get your own cabin." Authia sat on the couch next to the table, helping herself to some breakfast.

"Really, how'd you manage that?"

"I didn't. Morris chose not to take on any more passengers." Authia glanced up at Nathen. "He really likes you. His only concern is that you're safe. By the way, he wants you to join him on the bridge at some point today."

"That's impossible. I can't be seen by the crew."

"You can go there the same way I did. There's hardly any crew. And you can't be seen on the bridge from the deck. So, you're good. Just wear your coat until you get to the bridge."

Over the next couple of hours, Tammy moved to her own cabin, Nathen went to visit Morris, and Authia chose to remain behind. She wanted to review the parchment. Her entire plan hinged on finding the misplaced soul.

* * * *

Darkness surrounded the freighter. The moon, hidden behind a cloudy sky, shone no light on what was a very eerie night. Nathen took advantage of the darkness, and he and Authia stood at the railing at the stern of the ship. The waters were still, and it felt as though the freighter was floating along the sea. Authia turned to face Nathen, resting her back against the railing. She put her arms around his neck and brought him closer. "You know, I think this is the first time we've been alone since we left Burwood."

"You're right." Nathen leaned in and passionately kissed Authia. "If you only knew how badly I ache for you."

"Oh, believe me, I know." Authia glanced down at

Nathen's manhood, which was clearly evident in his tight jeans. "You look like you could use a cold shower."

Nathen chuckled as he wrapped his arms around Authia. "I don't believe that would help. Ready for bed? I know I am."

Nathen and Authia returned to their room. Authia was asleep within minutes of curling up next to Nathen. However, sleep did not come so easily to Nathen. He kept rethinking the parchment, thinking of what was waiting for them in the village. A misplaced soul ready to guide them. Guide them to what? Nathen could handle himself in the forest. He could live off the land if he had to. But in the jungle, Nathen would be lost. He was out of his element. The responsibility of keeping Authia safe weighed heavy on him. He couldn't live with himself if anything happened to her. The only answer was for her not to cross beyond the falls. As Nathen slowly drifted off to sleep, a distant voice came to him. Soft and soothing. He tried to concentrate but could not make out what the voice was trying to say to him. Nathen fell into a deep sleep as someone tried so desperately to meld with him.

* * * *

Dena, one of the priestesses of the Jelani tribe, foresaw the coming of Joshawa's son. She had known that it was her responsibility to go to the outsiders' village. A village of people who grew up on the stories of the Lion people—her people—who lived beyond the falls. The outsiders feared her people and she knew why.

The village where Dena would be waiting was only thirty people strong. No one from the village dared go beyond the falls, for they believed they would anger the gods if they did. Once, three young men from the village tried, and only one returned. His stories of the valley and the people that lived there cemented the fear of the village, and no one had ever tried since. Then one day, from out of the falls, Dena had come. Three men from the village had been fishing in the pool that formed from the waterfall. Dena had examined the men from her hiding place at the edge of the falls, amused at how short they were. They appeared to be several inches shorter than the men from her village. They were dressed in ragged blue jeans cut off at the knee and buttoned shirts that had the sleeves cut off. Their hair was jet black and matted as though they hadn't brushed it for quite a while. Their origins seemed to be white, though their skin was quite dark, most likely from spending a considerable amount of time in the sun.

They'd stood knee deep in the water, spears raised, ready to strike at any fish that should swim by them. When she came upon them, they dropped their spears, then, while remaining in the water, knelt on one knee, bowing to her.

"Please get up. I need you to take me to your village."

One of the men had raised his head and boldly asked, "Do you mean us harm?"

"No. Of course not. I need your help. You and your entire village. Will you please take me there? It's very important that I speak with your elders."

The men retrieved their spears, then did as they were requested and took Dena to their village. When she walked into the clearing, everyone from the village gathered around her. They seemed stunned at seeing an actual person from the Lion tribe.

Dena had stood in the centre of the clearing, uncertain of how these people were reacting to her. Was it fear, awe, or plain curiosity?

Sam, one of the men that had led her to the village, came up to her. "Come with me. The elders of the village wish to speak to you."

Dena had followed him to a hut that was not unlike her own. Inside, there were two men and a woman sitting on the ground next to each other. Their faces were weathered, their hair grey. The brown robes they wore hung on their frail bodies. Dena had approached and bowed before them. "I come out of the greatest respect for your village. I need your help in bringing our Lord back home to our village."

The woman had spoken. "I am called Sensay. So tell me, why would your Lord leave?"

"We're uncertain of the true facts. But some of us believe that he was forced to leave. And now his son makes the journey back."

"If he's returning, why do you need our help?"

"Because it has been two centuries since his family has walked our grounds. Our Lord's son requires guidance. He needs to be shown the way home. I need for you to allow me to stay with you. To wait here until he arrives."

"How do you know he'll come here?"

Dena had smiled. "I was given a vision."

CHAPTER EIGHTEEN

Things were not going so well for Casandra. A son of Joshawa's existed. Her sister was in the outside world searching for him. Did she know something Casandra didn't? How could the son possibly know of her village, of where to search? And to make matters worse, Casandra couldn't produce the death incantation. Tamara was too weak. She needed one of the skilled priestesses. But they would not help her. Not to kill one of their own. Casandra needed a new plan. She needed to gain control of her daughter so that she could use Tamara to do her bidding. There was only one way. Tamara had to release her essence into a packet. Then Casandra had to gain control of that packet. Tamara would have to do as she was told. Even though she was Casandra's daughter, Casandra knew there was too much at stake. If it came down to it, Tamara would be forced to obey or suffer the same death as Serena.

* * * *

They had been on the Free Spirit for a little over a month. The three of them were surprised and felt rather fortunate that no one suffered from sea sickness. The further south they ventured, the hotter it became. Authia, well into her eighth month of pregnancy, was having difficulty dealing with the heat. The fans they had in their room helped somewhat. But when the days were extremely hot, Authia would pay a visit to the walk-in refrigerator to cool down.

Her clothing barely fit her. Her belly stuck out of most of her t-shirts, and her pants were terribly uncomfortable. Even Nathen's shirts were tight on her. As the weeks went by, her wardrobe was reduced to the two maternity dresses that Cheryl had given her.

* * * *

Tammy was keeping a close eye on Authia. Her cervix was thinning, which meant it would not be long before the baby came. Tammy thought a lot about the delivery. She wondered if Nathen's tribe delivered babies the same way. Nathen was not that much different from anyone else. However, Tammy remembered the stories of Nathen's rapid development when he was first brought to Burwood as a baby. She kept telling herself that there would be no difference, but deep down she was worried. Worried that she would not be able to deliver the baby. Worried that if things were different and she didn't know what to do, either the baby or Authia or maybe both might die during the birthing. Tammy was grateful that at each port of call Morris had a doctor come aboard and give Authia a thorough checkup. She hoped that when Authia went into labour, they would be at a port where a doctor could be made available to them. But then the more she thought about it, the more she realized that it would never happen. There was no way of knowing who the child would resemble, Nathen or Authia. Therefore, there would be no way that they would trust a stranger to deliver their baby. Not to mention that Nathen would want to be by Authia's side the entire time. There was no way around it. Tammy would be delivering the baby on her own.

* * * *

Nathen was spending his time in solitude, sitting in the cabin, plotting their journey for when they docked at Cabinda. Cabinda was a shipping port in Angola, Africa. Hansen managed to get his hands on a modern-day map of the area outlined on the parchment. To Nathen's astonishment, the parchment was amazingly accurate. Maybe Authia was right, and Joshawa had been altering the parchment as the years had gone by. All Nathen knew was that he could place the map on top of the parchment and the landmarks and towns matched up perfectly. When they arrived at Cabinda, they would disembark at night. Morris would have a truck with a canvas-covered back waiting for them. They were going to be docked at the pier for two weeks for repairs, so Hansen volunteered to drive them as far as the road would take them. From there they would have to rely on the parchment, a compass, and a whole lot of luck. According to the parchment, the village they had to find was eight hundred miles southeast from Cabinda. Nathen was hoping most of that distance could be travelled by truck.

* * * *

It was one in the afternoon, and Tammy and Authia were on the upper deck, lounging on two deck chairs that had been provided for them. The sea was rough, sending sprays of water over the railing and soaking the girls each time. With the ninety-plus temperature, they didn't mind and actually giggled like schoolgirls every time a spray of water hit them.

At one point, Hansen came by with cold beverages for the girls. He appeared amused to see them lying there, soaked to the skin, their hair dripping wet. "I brought you some ice tea. Authia, don't stay out in the sun too long. The heat tends to catch up to you real fast."

"I won't. I'll go back to the cabin as soon as I finish my ice tea." Authia couldn't help but notice that Hansen couldn't keep his eyes off of Tammy the entire time they were speaking.

"I'm heading back to the bridge. Let me know if you need anything." Authia kept an eye on Tammy as Hansen left and, apparently, she couldn't keep her eyes off him either. "Something going on that I should know about?"

"What?"

"Don't give me what. What's going on between you and Hansen?"

"I have no idea. I think he likes me, but man is he shy!"

"You might just have to make the first move."

"Perhaps, but for now I'm going to move you out of that deck chair and into your cabin."

"Tell you what. I'll leave, but you stay here. I bet you dessert that Hansen comes back before you finish your ice tea."

"That's a bet. You're on."

* * * *

Tammy lay back on her deck chair, hoping that Authia was right. Not five minutes later, Hansen showed up. "Good. I see Authia took my advice."

"Yes, she did. I've been meaning to ask you. Is Hansen your first or last name?"

Tammy waited for a reply, but Hansen only stood there staring at her.

"It's not important. Just trying to strike up a conversation."

"Last name."

"Okay, what's your first name."

"William, Bill. But everybody calls me Hansen. I've got to head back to the bridge." As Hansen turned, a spray of water came crashing over the railing, totally drenching him. Tammy tried not to laugh, too loud. "That's been happening to us the whole time we've been here. It is quite refreshing, don't you think?"

Hansen didn't answer but turned and headed for the bridge. Tammy smiled as he left, thinking to herself that she lost her dessert and she didn't mind one little bit.

* * * *

Authia entered her cabin to find Nathen dressed only in his underwear, scrutinizing all the notes he was making. "Let me guess, you're a little warm."

"Yes, Tammy's not here, so I am taking liberties." Nathen glanced up from the parchment and grinned. "Did you go for a swim?"

Authia chuckled. "It's a little rough on deck." She went to stand by Nathen's side. "You know, by the time we reach Africa, you're going to have both those maps memorized. We won't need them."

"Maybe so, but we're taking them anyway. How are you feeling?"

"Tired, a little overheated. I'm going to lay down for a while."

Nathen couldn't keep his eyes off Authia as she pulled her dress over her head, then removed her panties. "Looks like I'm not the only one taking liberties."

Authia smirked. "What? You don't want to see me naked?"

Nathen smirked at Authia as he locked the cabin door. Then he took her in his arms and drew her tight against his body. "Very much so." He leaned down and kissed her while his hands explored her ample breasts.

"Someone wants to play."

"You have no idea." Nathen helped Authia to bed, then removed his underwear and crawled in next to her. He pulled her naked body close to his. Gently he ran his hand across her swollen belly. He could feel his baby moving within the confines of Authia's womb. From there he tenderly explored her breasts, then reached up and placed his hand along the side of her face. "I am going to explode my need for you is so deep." Nathen and Authia had not made love for the past six months. To Nathen, it felt like forever.

"Then let me help you." With one hand, Authia brought Nathen toward her, then kissed him, her tongue playfully seeking out his. Her other hand was exploring his bulging manhood, holding it seductively as she stroked it.

Nathen pulled away from her kiss. "I'm too close. I'll not be able to hold back."

"Then don't."

That was all the encouragement Nathen needed. He kissed Authia as if it were their last kiss, at the same time pressing his manhood tight against her hand. It didn't take much to release six months of pent-up desire sending Nathen over the edge. His heart was racing to the point that he thought it would burst from his chest. Nathen lay back on the bed, his body trembling from the release. As soon as he regained his composure, he faced Authia and drew her into his arms. "I promise that when you're ready, I'll take you to the heavens and back again as often as your body can handle."

"I'm going to hold you to that. In the meantime, just cuddle me while I sleep."

Nathen accommodated his beautiful wife, and the two of them fell into a contented sleep.

* * * *

Dena sat cross-legged on the ground of the hut provided to her by the elders of the village. She closed her eyes and reached out to Tamara. *Tamara, are you free to speak?*

Yes, Mother is not here. How are you?

Fine. I'm in the village, and they're going to help us. I'm trying to meld with Joshawa's son, but it's not working for some reason.

I have reached out to Authia. I believe she hears me, but she is frightened. I have to work on calming her.

You do realize that if Casandra finds out what you're up to, I won't be the only one she's trying to kill.

I know. But I also know that things are not as they should be. My mother's need for power has poisoned her heart and her thoughts. I fear for what she is capable of. The son of Joshawa is close. He needs to bring peace to our village. Watch for him. Bring him home, Dena.

Chapter Nineteen

Nathen, Hansen, and Morris all stood on the bridge, staring out to the open sea. Only two more ports before they arrived at their destination. Nathen was anxious beyond belief. Anxious that they were getting closer to the second leg of their journey and anxious that Authia had not yet had their baby. He eyed the deck where the girls were sunning themselves. It had been some time since he and Authia had melded. *You're so beautiful.*

Authia looked up toward the bridge. Nathen knew she couldn't see into the bridge, but she knew he was there. She smiled as she answered him. *Thank you. But I feel more like a beached whale.*

Well, you certainly don't resemble one.

Nathen, who was grinning as he looked down at the girls, piqued Morris's curiosity. "You see something funny that we're missing?"

Nathen glanced at the two men. "I was telling Authia how beautiful she was." That response drew a puzzled expression from both men. "Authia and I can join our minds and speak to each other. You could say that's how we met." Before Nathen could continue his explanation, he suddenly sensed that Authia was in distress. He quickly looked back out the window to see Authia standing in a puddle of water, Tammy at her side. *It's time, Nathen. Our baby is coming!*

Nathen threw his coat on, raised his hood, then ran down the stairs to the deck. Carefully he scooped Authia up into his arms. Tammy led the way as Nathen carried Authia back to their cabin and gently laid her on their bed. A minute later, Hansen came running into the room. "What do you need? What can I do?"

Tammy was placing pillows under Authia's shoulders to raise her up a bit. "Just some clean towels and a large basin. Oh yes, and a plastic sheet if you don't want the mattress ruined."

"Don't worry about the mattress. I'll be right back with the towels and the basin."

Tammy helped Authia remove her dress and panties. Then she tucked her into bed, making sure she was warm.

Nathen was taking everything in. "It's really happening!"

"Well, not yet. Her water broke, but the contractions haven't started. At least not the ones that count." Tammy turned to face Authia. "Okay, I want you to assume the position so I can check you."

Authia pulled the blankets up to her hips, then raised her knees and spread her legs as Tammy put on a pair of surgical gloves. Nathen sat on the bed next to Authia, tenderly holding her hand in his. "You're two centimetres dilated. You've a little way to go yet."

Nathen was covering Authia back up with the blankets when Hansen returned. "Here are your towels and basin." He placed them down on the table. "I'm going to be parked on a chair outside that door. If you need anything, just let me know." He was about to leave when Tammy stopped him.

"It could be hours. You don't need to sit out there all that time."

Hansen looked at Tammy with an expression of sincerity. "Yes, I do. It's my job to keep everyone here safe. I'll sit there for as long as it takes." He left the room with Tammy staring after him, a small smile gracing her lips.

"He's a keeper," Authia commented as she tried to shift her weight to get comfortable on the bed.

"Yes, he is. Nathen, can you help me with this dresser, please." With Nathen's help, Tammy moved the dresser from under the porthole to against the wall at the end of the bed. After clearing it off, she laid a couple of clean towels down, then proceeded to set up everything she needed to deliver the baby. Nathen was dumbfounded as Tammy placed what appeared to be a large pair of tongs on the dresser.

"What on earth are those for?"

"Sometimes the baby needs a little help. Don't worry, they won't hurt the baby."

Nathen picked them up and held them in his hands as he examined them closer. He directed his attention to Authia and shook his head. "What you're prepared to go through is astonishing."

"Prepared! Not even close. Remember, this is my first child. I've no idea what to be prepared for."

Nathen smiled at Authia. "Well, neither do I, so we'll face this together."

"Okay, you two. You're making it sound more intense than it needs to be. Authia, I'm going to set up an IV drip. It'll keep you hydrated and, if need be, I'll be able to administer pain medication through it." Tammy held up the bag and glanced around the room. "Humm, didn't think as to where I was going to hang this. Let's put Hansen to the test." She opened the door to find Hansen sitting exactly where he said he would be. "I have a slight problem. I need to hang this IV bag. Do you have any suggestions?"

"Yeah. The medical room has an IV pole."

"You're kidding."

"No. I'll go get it."

Tammy turned to Authia and Nathen. "Problem solved."

"So, Tammy, I probably should have been asking this question a long time ago, but what exactly am I in for?"

Tammy thought for a moment. "Okay, I'll tell you what's happening as it's happening."

"Why not just tell me everything, start to finish?"

"Well, for one thing, there's no way of telling exactly what you'll experience. Women handle labour and delivery differently. And, secondly, you guys freaked out over the forceps. You're just going to have to wing this. You're in the first stages. You've been probably feeling some mild pain in your lower abdomen."

"Yes. I thought it was the baby." Authia made a face. "There it is again."

"When was the last one?"

"Not sure. Ten, maybe fifteen minutes ago."

Tammy removed her watch from her wrist and handed it to Nathen. "Okay, Nathen, your job is to time the contractions."

There was a knock on the door, and when Tammy went to answer it, she found Hansen with the IV pole, a large thermos of coffee, and three mugs. "IV pole's for Authia, coffee's for us." Hansen poured himself a cup, then went back in the hallway.

Tammy laid out everything she required to set up the intravenous. Skillfully, she placed the tiny intravenous tube into the back of Authia's hand. Within a few minutes, she had it set with a steady drip keeping Authia hydrated. "Now remember. This is only to hydrate you. If the pain becomes too unbearable, I can administer some medication to ease the pain. However, that being said, you should know that any medication of any type will not be good for the baby."

"So basically, I should just suck it up."

"We'll decide that when the time comes. How are those contractions coming, Nathen?"

"Fifteen minutes apart."

Tammy went to sit on the love seat. "And now we wait. Once the contractions are coming every couple of minutes, I'll check you again."

Authia lay back on her pillows and sighed. "How bad can it be. Women have babies all the time."

Tammy laughed. "Have you never talked to anyone who has had a baby?"

"Sure. But not about the labour or delivery. It's usually about how big the baby is or why his head looks like a misshapen potato."

"You're too funny."

For the next two hours, Nathen held Authia's hand as her contractions came closer and more severe. When they were steady at two minutes apart, Tammy checked her progress. "You're five centimetres dilated. The contractions are going to come closer and harder. You have to remember to breathe. Believe me, it helps."

Tammy no sooner spoke those words when a contraction took hold of Authia, causing her to scream out in agony. One minute later, another contraction filled her face with pain. They were coming back to back, and Authia's screams of agony echoed throughout the freighter.

Nathen felt useless. He could sense her pain, and he knew when the contractions were coming, but he could do nothing to comfort her. He had never seen anyone experience the intensity of pain that Authia was going through. "I promise never to put you through this again." He delicately moved aside the hair that had fallen onto Authia's face.

Twenty minutes later, Authia was given a reprieve as the contractions seemed to subside. She fell back onto her pillows. Her face was pale and drenched in sweat. Her breathing laboured. "Sorry about the hand." Authia had Nathen's hand in a death grip the entire time.

"Don't be sorry. You do whatever you have to do to help

manage the pain."

"And by the way, fat chance that this will be our only child." Authia smiled up at Nathen.

"You want to go through this again?"

"I was thinking it would be your turn next time."

Tammy laughed. "If only."

Authia turned to Tammy. "How far am I now?"

Tammy quickly checked her. "You're seven centimetres and it doesn't feel like the baby has entered the birth canal yet."

* * * *

"All that for two centimetres." Authia closed her eyes, then immediately opened them. "Oh my God, they're starting again." The contraction was a bad one. No matter how much she concentrated on her breathing, the pain was still excruciating. Authia was plagued with another five hours of merciless contractions. She was spent. Her energy was gone. Beads of sweat ran down her face. However, she refused the medication that would ease her pain, several times.

Then, in the tenth hour, she felt the uncontrollable urge to push. Tammy immediately checked her. "Your kid has black hair. It's time, Authia."

It took only four pushes to deliver a beautiful eight-pound, eight-and-a-half-ounce baby boy. Authia, totally exhausted, fell back on her pillows as Tammy suctioned the child's nose and mouth. A healthy cry assured everyone of the child's well-being. Authia and Nathen eagerly waited as Tammy cleaned their son, wrapping him in a soft towel when she was finished. She carried him to Authia and placed him on her chest. "Here's your son. You did good, Authia." Authia wrapped her arms around her son, brought him under the blanket, and held him close. The joy that enveloped Authia was overpowering. She looked up at Nathen, tears in her eyes.

"Why do you cry, my love?"

"I can't help it. I'm so unbelievably happy."

The child was a combination of both his parents. He had Authia's dark hair, which fell to his shoulders in gentle waves. He also had her dark brown eyes. The rest of him was all Nathen. He had his father's high cheekbones, the bridge of his nose was wider than usual, and there was the small cleft in his upper lip. For a newborn, he was very alert. It was as if he was completely aware of his surroundings. The proud parents lovingly gazed upon their son. Twenty minutes later, when she was finished cleaning and suturing Authia, Tammy asked them that all-important question. "What are you going to name him?"

Authia checked with Nathen, who nodded in approval. "We're naming him Joshawa Charles Roberts. Can you take him, Nathen? I just want to try to sit up." Nathen cautiously took his son from Authia. Lovingly, he cradled him as Authia pushed herself up to a sitting position.

* * * *

Nathen felt as if his heart were going to explode. He not only had a beautiful wife who dearly loved him, but he also had a child, a son. Never in his wildest dreams did he believe such a day would ever be a reality.

Tammy helped Authia put on a clean nightgown, then led her to the love seat so she could clean up the bed. Nathen sat beside her and carefully passed Joshawa to his mother. Tammy just stood next to the love seat, totally captivated by the new family. "You guys have no idea how relieved I am that everything went so well."

Nathen smiled at Tammy. "We had complete confidence

in you."

"Thank you. Hey, mind if I invite Hansen in? I'm sure he's dying to see the baby."

"Of course not."

Tammy went into the hallway only to find Hansen pacing the confined area. "It's a boy. Do you want to come in and see?"

"Yes!" Hansen entered the room and walked over to Authia. He looked upon Joshawa's face. It appeared to everyone as if the child smiled at Hansen. As if the child knew that Hansen was a good man. "He's amazing." Hansen extended a hand to Nathen. "Congrats! I'm going to go tell Morris." As he turned to leave, he noticed the blood-soaked mattress.

Tammy followed his gaze. "I told you it was going to be a mess."

"No worries. You'll have a clean one within the hour."

A few minutes later, they could hear the announcement of their son's arrival over the P.A. system, followed by the cheers of the crew.

Nathen's family was complete. Within the next two days, they would be in Cabinda ready to for the next leg of their journey. As Nathen watched Authia breastfeed his son, he knew that she could never accompany him beyond the falls.

* * * *

Authia glanced up at Nathen and smiled, all the while thinking, *Good luck with that, Nathen. You'll never be able to stop me.*

* * * *

Tamara sat in her mother's hut, observing her as she r tried to conjure a vision telling her where the son of Joshawa was.

The smoke in the fire pit dissipated, but the only shared vision was that of a newborn child. Casandra verbally dismissed it and didn't take the vision further. Evidently, as far as she was concerned, the vision was showing her Joshawa's son as a baby. But Tamara knew better. As Casandra angrily walked away, Tamara smiled knowing that the bloodline of Joshawa continued with the introduction of yet another son.

Chapter Twenty

It was midnight by the time Morris guided the Free Spirit into the docking berth at the Cabinda pier. Hansen and Nathen were at his side. Hansen had suggested that Authia, who was cradling her newborn son, and Tammy stand on the upper deck keeping close to the railing. That way they weren't in the way of the crew and Hansen could keep an eye on them. He felt protective of them, especially Tammy.

Once the gangway was in place and the crew had finished docking the freighter, some of them called it a night and returned to their bunks while others ventured out in search of whiskey and women. The full moon lit up the pier, revealing the truck that Morris had arranged for parked close to their berth. After Hansen made sure the freighter was secure, he went to check out the truck. He also wanted to confirm that the supplies they'd ordered were stowed in the back of the vehicle. As he approached the rear of the vehicle, two men emerged from around the front.

* * * *

Tammy turned to Authia. "I didn't know there was going to be anybody else with us."

"There wasn't supposed to be." Authia passed Joshawa to Tammy. "Here, take Joshawa. I'm going to check this out."

Nathen's thoughts came alive in Authia's mind. *Stay where you are. Let Hansen find out who these men are.* Authia stopped at the top of the gangway. Curiously she watched as

Hansen spoke to the two men. They were dressed in cut-off jeans and sleeveless buttoned shirts and their hair was matted, giving them a dishevelled appearance. After a couple of minutes, Hansen signalled for Authia to join them. Authia cautiously approached the men, wondering what they could possibly want. Maybe Morris arranged for them? Though she thought that he would have mentioned something. When she stood not three feet away from them, both men bowed to her. Authia, surprised by their actions, turned her attention to Hansen, who just shrugged. "They're looking for Nathen. All I told them was that you're his wife."

"Please, there's no need to bow."

The two men stood and gazed in awe at Authia. "Hansen, who are these men?"

"They're from the village we are trying to get to. They're our guides."

"How on earth did the village know we were coming?"

One of the two men spoke up. "I am Sam, and this is Tomas. She told our elders that it came to her in a vision."

Authia shook her head. "Okay, so who is *she?*"

Sam and Tomas exchanged puzzled glances, as if Authia should know who they were speaking about. "She's one of the Lion people that live beyond the falls. She came to us seeking our help to find the Lord of her tribe. She had a vision that he would arrive on a large vessel with his mate. We came here from the village and have been waiting many days for you. Is he here with you?"

Authia could not believe what she was hearing. How did they know so much? *Are these men going to help us? Or do they have more sinister motives?* She knew of only one way to discover if these two men spoke the truth. "May I hold your hands?"

Sam held out his hands to Authia, who gently grasped

them within her own. She closed her eyes and saw for herself a village located high in the mountains. Off in the distance was the waterfall that the parchment spoke of. She opened her eyes and gazed deep into Sam's eyes. "I see no deceit here. You've travelled far for the sake of a people that are a mystery to you." Authia let go of Sam's hands. The misplaced soul from the parchment was real. *Nathen's tribe exists!* Authia turned so that she was facing the bridge of the Free Spirit. *Nathen, it's all real. Someone from your tribe is waiting at the village for you. These men are here to guide us to her. I think it's safe for you to come out now.* Authia turned back to the two men. "Yes, he is here."

* * * *

Nathen stared out into the darkness of the night, in shock at what he was hearing. His tribe still existed, and they were seeking him out. Without saying a word to Morris, he grabbed his coat that was hanging over the chair and put it on. Instinctively, he raised the hood as he left the bridge. The two villagers nervously sized him up as he approached them. He was tall and intimidating and, to make him even more imposing, his face was concealed. Nathen stood by Authia's side. The two men's nervousness didn't go unnoticed. Nathen wondered if they feared him. Or were they just nervous about meeting him? The unspoken awkwardness was broken when one of the men took a step forward and addressed Nathen. "Are you the Lord that the Lion woman seeks?"

"Yes. My name is Nathen, son of Joshawa."

"Why do you hide your face? Show me that you're one of the Lion people."

Nathen slowly pulled back his hood. Wide-eyed, the men immediately bowed to Nathen.

"Why do you bow to me?"

"You're one of the Lion people. The gods created you. They protect you. They would be angered if we did not honour you."

"There's no need. I'm an ordinary man that would be eternally grateful to you if you would show us how to get to your village."

The men seemed completely bewildered by his comment. "You're special. You live in the Valley of the Gods. It's our duty to take you to our village."

* * * *

Hansen stood by taking everything in. He wasn't totally convinced that these two men were honest. Their story was absurd, to say the least. Yet, Authia and Nathen seemed to be taking everything they said as the gospel truth. And what was all that hand holding about? Nathen mentioned that he and Authia shared a special gift. Was what he witnessed part of it? "So how far is this village?"

Sam eyed Hansen as if deciding whether or not to answer him. "We take the road as far as it will take us. Then it's a two-day journey to our village."

Hansen walked to the truck and opened the back flap. The supplies were there as promised. "We're going to need more supplies. I'm going to go talk to Morris."

* * * *

Hansen left Authia and Nathen on the dock, talking to the two villagers. He stopped for a moment as he passed Tammy, who was still on the upper deck. "You could probably go down. They seem to be harmless."

"Who are they?"

"Apparently, they're from the village you're going to."

Hansen looked back down at the docks. "Frankly I think it's all bullshit, but what do I know." He returned his gaze to Tammy. "Go on, head down. They may need you to put what these men are saying into perspective." With that, Hansen turned and left for the bridge.

Tammy smiled as she watched Hansen leave. "If you only knew." Then she headed down the gangway to join the others on the dock.

* * * *

Hansen entered the bridge and shook his head at Morris. "You won't believe what's going on down there. Those two men are completely whacked."

"Why, what're they saying?"

"Something about Nathen being the Lord of a village of Lion people." Hansen chuckled. "Created by the gods."

"I wouldn't be so quick to discount these men. Nathen filled me in as to what they've been through these past few months. Those men sound like they're right on the money."

"You're kidding me!" Hansen walked to the window and scrutinized the group standing on the dock. "Look, Morris, I'm not that comfortable with Nathen being alone with those two men." He turned to face his captain. "Ship's heading to dry dock. You don't really need me. I'd like to go with them. Help Nathen protect Tammy, Authia, and the baby. I'll come right back as soon as I see them safely to this village."

"I knew you were going to want to go with them. Go ahead. Catch up with me in Vancouver. Just promise me you'll take care of yourself."

"Don't worry, I will."

The two men shook hands. Then Hansen left the bridge.

Hansen and Nathen loaded the truck with their bags and

medical supplies. Then Hansen and Tammy raided the galley for extra food. To their surprise, they found a case of formula for Joshawa. "My mother couldn't breastfeed me, so I thought I'd have that on board. Just in case."

Hansen and Tammy turned to find Alen standing in the doorway to the pantry. "So, what are you guys doing here?"

Hansen nodded. "Is that all the formula you have?"

"No. There are two more cases in the back. You haven't answered my question. What are you doing here?"

"Look, Alen, these people have a place they have to be. It's going to be a long hike, and they need supplies. Especially for the baby. Just replenish whatever I take."

"You're the boss." Alen thought for a second. "That is if Morris knows what you're up to?"

"He knows. You wouldn't happen to have any small empty crates that we could pack all this stuff in?"

"Yeah. In the hold. I'll go get them."

He and Tammy carried the three boxes of formula and all the crates of food out to the truck. An hour later, everything was packed away and it was time to leave.

* * * *

Morris had joined everyone on the dock. He went to Hansen and extended his hand. Hansen shook his head. "A handshake just isn't going to cut it." He embraced Morris as tears welled up in his eyes. "You've been good to me. I want to thank you, Morris, for everything you've done for me in the past years. For trusting in me. I promise I'll return as soon as I can."

"You've earned it. Take care of yourself. I want you back." Morris turned to Nathen. "I'm glad I could help you out. I hope you find what you are looking for, Nathen."

"So do I. I'm very grateful for all your help. I owe you

one."

Morris smiled. "No, it was me that owed you. Take care of your family and keep an eye on Hansen for me." Morris wrapped his arms around Nathen, then stood back and shook his hand. "If you ever need me, you know where to find me."

Morris was about to leave, then changed his mind. He turned around and watched as Hansen joined the others at the truck. He had an ominous feeling that it would be the last time he would see Hansen—or any of the others, for that matter.

* * * *

Nathen, Authia, Joshawa, and Tomas all took their place in the back of the truck. As Hansen climbed behind the wheel, he took a last look at the Free Spirit. It had been his home for over a decade and, after all that time, he was willing to walk away from it. Tammy got into the truck and sat in the middle, and Sam climbed in next to her. Hansen sat behind the wheel and looked over to Tammy. She smiled at him, and with that smile, Hansen knew she was worth it. He handed the modern-day map to her. "Can you navigate?"

"Of course." Tammy opened the map, then folded it so it only showed the area that they needed.

Hansen stared out at the road in front of him. "All right, Sam. Where're we going?"

Sam pointed to a spot on the map. "That's where we need to be. We follow the dirt road from there." Sam had pointed to a place west of where they were. Right on the edge of Cabinda.

* * * *

Dena sat cross-legged in her hut. Her eyes were shut, and her hands were resting on her knees. She sought out Joshawa's son. She could sense that he was close, which was confirmed by Tamara, who knew he was in Africa. And, according to Tamara, he'd arrived with his mate and his newborn son. That was why Dena had sent the two tribesmen in search of him. To find him and bring him to her. Dena cleared her mind. She reached out to her Lord in the hope that she could communicate with him.

* * * *

At the same time, Tamara sat in her own hut, focusing her mind on Authia. She and Dena desperately needed to reach at least one of them to warn them of the danger. And also to prepare them for what lie ahead.

Chapter Twenty-One

Nathen sat with his back against the side of the truck, his massive arms wrapped around Authia and his child. Not the most comfortable ride. However, it would keep Nathen out of sight, which, as always, was their objective. He grew increasingly uncomfortable as Tomas continued to stare at him. "Why do you stare?"

"Never did I think that I'd meet a Lion person. Now, not only is there one in my village, but I've been given the honour to guide the Lord of these people to my village."

"And we are grateful that you came all this way to help us."

"It's my pleasure, my Lord."

"Please, call me Nathen."

Tomas looked surprised. "That would be wrong. It'd be disrespectful."

Nathen smiled at Tomas and shook his head. He gazed down at Authia and his son, both of whom had fallen asleep in his arms. Sleep that eluded him. It didn't take long for Tomas to nod off as well, leaving Nathen alone with his thoughts. As he sat there, the nagging ache in the pit of his stomach plagued him, warning him of the danger. If only he knew what that danger was. Nathen stared off into the darkness of his confined space. There was an argument playing out in his mind as to whether or not he should return to Burwood. Whether or not he should stop his foolish venture before someone he loved got hurt. He still had time. The Free Spirit had not left the pier yet. As he seriously considered requesting that Hansen turn the truck around, a faint voice came to him. A delicate, female voice. Nathen strained to hear the whispers that were spoken to him. He closed his eyes and listened. Then the two minds collided and the woman's thoughts became one with his.

Please hear me, my Lord.

Who are you?

* * * *

Dena's eyes flew open. He heard her! *My Lord, I know you're troubled, but you mustn't waiver. You and your mate must meet me at the village.*

Why must we?

Because your bloodline has suffered an unspeakable injustice and only the two of you can right this wrong. Only the two of you can bring peace back to our people.

I intend to be the only one crossing past the falls.

No! My Lord, it must be the two of you. Your mate plays an integral part of any chance of success that you may have.

I can't, won't, endanger her life.

Sometimes you have to chance losing the ones you love in order for justice to be done.

* * * *

Nathen was suddenly quiet, for he'd heard words similar to those once before. It appeared as if once again, he faced a fight that might take those precious to him. *You still haven't told me who you are.*

My name is Dena, and I'm one of the priestesses of our village. I'm a descendant of Serena.

And why should I trust any descendant of Serena's?

We're not all like her. As we speak, another priestess seeks out your mate to help with your arrival to our village. I know you have many questions, but you must trust me and save your questions for when we meet. Trust the men I sent you. They will protect you with their lives. Hurry, my Lord. Time is short. With that, Dena left and Nathen was at odds with himself more than ever.

* * * *

As Authia slept, a woman reached out to her unconscious mind. She called to Authia in the hopes that she would hear her. Even in her sleep, Authia could sense how troubled Nathen's mind was. And she could sense that he wasn't alone. Someone was playing the mind game with him. Was it the same person she'd felt earlier? Or was there yet another new person who had joined the quest? As if to answer Authia, the woman's voice penetrated the very depths of Authia's mind. Her thoughts came alive and Authia could hear them as clearly as her own.

You can hear me. I can sense it. You must be strong, my Mistress. You and you alone will be the one to restore our Lord's bloodline. You have already started by presenting our Lord with a son. You must accompany our Lord to our village. It will be dangerous, but it is the only way.

Who are you?

I am the priestess Tamara, daughter of the high priestess Casandra. I come from the bloodline of Serena.

If you're a descendant of Serena, how do I know I can trust you?

I will prove it to you. And with that, Tamara was gone.

Authia slowly woke up, her mind digesting all that she'd heard. A descendant of Serena's trying to help her. Did she not know that it was because of her and Nathen that Serena was dead? She looked up to Nathen. "You hear her too. Tamara spoke to you also?"

"No. The woman who spoke to me was called Dena. She waits at the village for us."

"There are two? Who's Dena?"

"Apparently, a descendant of Serena's."

"So's Tamara. This doesn't make any sense. Why would descendants of Serena be helping us?" Authia's attention was diverted as Joshawa began to squirm in her arms. It was time for another feeding. Authia and Nathen changed spots so that Nathen could shield Authia from Tomas' view. Though it really wasn't necessary since he was still sound asleep. Authia positioned Joshawa on her right breast, and as he began to suckle, Authia returned her gaze to Nathen. "You and I have a lot to discuss. Starting with the fact that you don't want me to continue past the falls." Nathen tried to speak, but Authia cut him off. "I don't know what lies ahead for us. But hopefully, there'll be answers once we arrive at the village. Then you and I, together, will decide our course of action."

* * * *

Nathen knew not to continue the conversation. Instead, he sat quietly watching as Authia fed Joshawa. However, he wasn't focused on his son. His mind was already in the village. Both he and Authia had been warned about the dangers ahead. He'd thought the battle was over with the death of Serena. But it appeared as if it had only just begun.

The group had travelled all night and into the next day. As the day progressed, the heat soared, causing the back of the truck to feel like a sauna. Authia stripped down as far as she dared with Tomas there. Nathen stripped down to his boxers. The heat did not seem to be bothering Tomas at all. He undid his shirt buttons, but that was the extent of his undressing.

* * * *

In the cab of the truck, there was no air-conditioning. They had the windows rolled down, trying to capture what little breeze they could. Their clothes clung to them, and the smell of sweat permeated the air around them. Tammy was studying the map and was a little concerned because, according to the map, the road they were on seemed to disappear not five miles from their position. "Hansen, we might be running out of road."

Hansen took a quick look at the map. "Sam, do we walk from here?"

Sam just stared straight ahead and shook his head. "No. There's still more road."

"Not according to this map."

Sam turned to face Tammy. "Maybe you're using the wrong map."

Tammy looked dumbfounded at Sam, then remembered the parchment. It was rolled up sitting next to her. Carefully she unrolled it and, sure enough, there was evidence of a road past the five-mile mark. "Doesn't look like much of a road."

"It's a path made by migrating animals. We'll follow it for a few miles, and then we walk."

A few minutes later, they came to the end of the paved road and the start of the path that Sam referred to. It was narrow and badly rutted. Hansen and Tammy got out and went to the back of the truck. Hansen pulled the tailgate down and opened the flap. "Thought you might want to get out and stretch your legs. Nathen, you want to come see this?"

Tomas exited the vehicle, followed by Nathen, who took the time to put his jeans back on. Authia stayed put. It was way too hot to get dressed. Instead, she remained in the back of the truck with Joshawa, who was sleeping contently in her arms. Tammy joined her while the four men went to check out the path that lay before them.

* * * *

Hansen shook his head as he surveyed the makeshift road. "I don't know, Nathen, it's going to be rough."

Nathen directed his question to Sam. "How far do we have to go on this road?"

"Half a day. Then we walk."

Nathen turned to Hansen. "Whether we walk it or drive it, it's going to be rough. From here on in, the women ride up front. I'll ride in back with our guides."

"Okay. You're the boss."

"Take it slow. We need this truck in one piece."

The group took a short break. Then Authia and Joshawa joined Tammy and Hansen in the cab of the truck. Cautiously they started their journey down the path. Most of the time Hansen couldn't get the truck out of first gear. The path was so rough that he didn't dare travel any faster. The further down the path they went, the thicker the jungle became until they could no longer see more than a foot past the edge of the road. The day progressed into the evening, and as nightfall was to overcome the day, the travellers reached their destination. Sam banged on the side of the truck to let Hansen know to stop. Everyone got out and looked around at their surroundings. There was nothing but jungle as far as the eye could see.

Sam got out of the truck and walked over to the south side of the path. "We'll stay the night here where it's safe."

Hansen and Nathen joined him. "Where do we go from here, Sam?"

Sam pointed in a southerly direction. "My village is this

way. If we leave early in the morning, we should reach it by noon the next day. Tomas and I will take turns tonight. We'll keep watch over you while you sleep."

Hansen retrieved the sleeping bags and laid them out on the ground close to the fire that Sam was building. Night fell upon them, shrouding the jungle in a disturbing darkness. The sounds of animals vibrated all around them. Then, as the fire burst into flames, the jungle grew quiet. The group ate a quick meal of pork and beans, then called it a night.

* * * *

Once again, Nathen couldn't sleep. Every nerve in his body was shouting at him. Warning him of the danger that lurked in the shadows. Giving him every reason to turn back.

Not on your life. Authia melded with Nathen. *You are not giving up this easy. Let's go to the village and hear what Dena has to say. As I said before, we'll decide then. Go to sleep, Nathen. You won't be able to protect your family if you're exhausted.*

Nathen knew that Authia was right. He needed his energy if he was going to venture into the jungle and face whatever danger awaited them. Slowly he fell asleep. Dreaming of a village of Lion people. Dreaming of being their captives—

* * * *

Dena felt Nathen's hesitation. His fear of the unknown. Cautiously she melded with Tamara. *He's frightened. Frightened for his family.*

Our Mistress is focused. However, she does not trust us. I must prove to her that we are loyal to our Lord.

And how will you accomplish this?

First, you must win their trust. Then I will commit the ultimate sacrifice to prove our loyalty.

What do you have in mind?

I cannot share with you. But you will know when the time comes. Prepare. Our Lord is near.

Chapter Twenty-Two

The early morning came alive with the sounds of the jungle. Snuggled in her sleeping bag, Tammy woke up to find Nathen already awake. "What the hell's that noise?"

Nathen smirked. "It's the sounds of the jungle. All the creatures are saying good morning to each other. I've heard these sounds many times in my dreams. I feel at peace when I hear them."

"Well, can you tell them to take it down an octave or two. Like, do they all have to talk at the same time?" Tammy rolled onto her side and came face to face with Hansen. He woke up that very moment, his face turning beet red.

"Sorry! I must have rolled over in my sleep."

"No need to apologize." Tammy gave Hansen her most dazzling smile. "I'm not complaining."

Hansen quickly got up and started rolling up his sleeping bag. "I'm going to go see what our guides are up to."

Tammy chuckled as Hansen went in search of their guides. "He's too funny. But I do have to find a way to break him of the shyness."

Authia was still lying in her sleeping bag, Nathen sitting next to her, Joshawa cradled tenderly in his arms. Lazily she stretched her arms above her head. "Well, if anyone can do it, you can." Authia sat up and wrapped her arms around Nathen's neck, giving him an affectionate good morning kiss. One that he passionately returned.

"All right, you two... get a room."

Nathen smiled at Tammy, then stared deep into Authia's

eyes. "I would love to."

Authia looked seductively at Nathen. "Maybe, when we reach the village, they'll have a hut we can use."

"Oh, you two are impossible!"

Tammy got up and went in search of Hansen only to find him behind the truck, arguing with Sam and Tomas. "We've two litters and four men. We can carry everything."

"No! We can only use one carrying plank. You must choose what you want to bring."

Nathen left Joshawa with Authia and went to see what all the fuss was about. "What's going on?"

"My Lord. We can only bring one carrying plank. We need two men. One up front to cut a path. One in back to protect. I'm sorry, my Lord, but if you want the supplies, then you and that man must carry one of the planks."

"Hansen... my name is Hansen!"

"Why do we need a man to protect? Protect from what?"

"The jungle, my Lord. The jungle has great beauty, but also it's very dangerous."

"Do as he says, Hansen. Let's sort through what we can leave behind."

An hour later, they were ready to leave. To the group's astonishment, their guides had hidden two machetes and two spears in the undergrowth.

* * * *

Hansen could not believe that they could actually find the exact spot where they'd come out of the jungle. As he scanned the dense vegetation, he couldn't see any landmarks. The jungle seemed to go on forever. Even the path their guides had taken to leave the jungle was barely discernible.

All members of the group strapped a backpack to their

back. Then Sam took the lead, hacking at the dense foliage that blocked their way. He was followed by Authia, who was carrying Joshawa in a bunting that was strapped to the front of her. After Authia was Tammy. Then Nathen and Hanson, who were carrying the litter. Tomas took up the rear, his spear and machete ready to fend off whatever might come out of the jungle to harm them.

* * * *

The foliage was so thick it made the going slow and tedious. Authia spent her time soaking in the beauty of the jungle. She was mesmerized by the brilliant colours of the flowers and wild birds that flew from tree top to tree top. The sounds of the jungle echoed within the large canopies that reached high above their heads.

* * * *

Nathen scrutinized his surroundings. Ever since childhood, he'd always feared the unknown. Avoided it when he could. But that had all changed when he'd met Authia. He'd learned to overcome his fears. But with all the uncertainty that surrounded him, his fears became real again. Everything was foreign to him. He was out of his element. *How can I protect my family if I'm unaware of what the danger is or where it's coming from?*

They walked for what seemed to be hours before Sam stopped for a break. Authia took advantage of the downtime and fed Joshawa. Tammy prepared some lunch for the group from the supplies they brought with them. It wasn't much. Smoked sausages served cold with crackers and water. Sam smiled and promised a more filling supper.

Their break lasted long enough for Authia to feed Joshawa. Then they were on their way again. The next leg of their journey to the village was filled with bug bites and sweltering heat. Sweat dripped down their faces, stinging their eyes, as they trudged through the jungle. Five hours later, they came upon a clearing in the dense foliage. Sam and Tomas said they had cleared the area on their way to find Nathen in preparation for their return. Close by was a freshwater pond that Sam assured them was safe to bathe in.

* * * *

Authia and Tammy stripped down to their panties and dove into the cool water. Authia welcomed the respite from the intense heat of the jungle. Both she and Tammy stood in chest-high water. The dense canopy of the large trees that surrounded the pond sheltered them from the scorching rays of the sun. Authia dove under the water and swam next to a group of fish. Quickly she surfaced and called out to Tammy. Then the two girls dove under the water, totally captivated by the large schools of fish that swam around them. As they resurfaced, they saw Nathen heading toward them, carrying Joshawa. He undressed his son as Authia came out of the water to get Joshawa. As he passed Joshawa to Authia, he leaned in and kissed her cheek. Authia winked at Nathen, which earned her a playful slap on her backside as she turned to go back to the pond. Tammy was trying to hide her nakedness from Nathen by going deeper into the water so that only her head and shoulders were exposed. Authia giggled to herself, for in the crystal-clear waters, Tammy wasn't concealing much.

* * * *

Nathen returned to the clearing to help set up camp and to give the women some privacy. From the camp, he could hear the girls' laughter. Nathen wanted so much to join Authia, but that type of privacy was a luxury they did not have. Nathen watched as Hansen kept looking back in the direction of the pond. It didn't take much to realize that Hansen was falling for Tammy. Nathen busied himself setting up a campfire, at the same time wondering what it would take for Hansen to man up and admit his feelings for Tammy. Nathen glanced over his shoulder and smirked at Hansen, who was shaking his head in frustration as he went to the litter to unpack the sleeping bags. In no time at all the camp was set up, with the sleeping bags laid out so they circled the fire pit. Inside the pit was a roaring fire on which they could cook their dinner.

* * * *

Tomas went in search of dinner while the rest of the men had their turn in the cool waters of the pond. Tammy and Authia were sitting by the fire, Joshawa fast asleep in Tammy's arms. A short time later, Tomas returned with a medium-sized animal skewered on a pole. It was skinned, gutted, and ready to cook. He placed it over the fire, securing the pole on the makeshift supports that Sam had made earlier. Tammy took one look and shook her head. "What the hell is that? You know what... I don't want to know." She glanced at Authia. "They're probably going to tell us it tastes like chicken."

* * * *

After a filling meal, which remarkably did taste like chicken, everyone settled down on their respective sleeping bags. Tammy made sure that Hansen's bag was right up against hers. Which he either didn't notice or was pretending that he didn't notice. Nathen smiled at the two of them and shook his head. He went over to his and Authia's sleeping bags, then zipped them together. They crawled in, cradling Joshawa between them. As Nathen lay in his sleeping bag, he moved closer to Authia and kissed her ever so tenderly. "Thank you."

"Thank you for what?"

"For this. For traipsing halfway around the world for me."

"You'd do the same for me."

"I'd give my life for you." Again, Nathen kissed her.

"Just think, Nathen, tomorrow you're going to meet one of your own people. And she's going to help us find your tribe."

"I don't think it's a matter of finding the tribe. She knows exactly where it is. Whatever happened all those years ago... I believe that the evil is still there. It's going to be dangerous, Authia. That's why I don't want you to come with me. My father was punished for falling in love with an outsider. What's going to happen to you if I bring you to the tribe?"

"According to Dena and Tamara, I have to go with you. Apparently, I play a very important part in whatever it is that we're walking into. When we get to the village, Dena will explain it all to us. Nathen, you have to realize that what happened to your father took place a long time ago. A lot could've changed since then. You know, we're probably making a mountain out of a molehill. Now go to sleep."

Nathen closed his eyes. It wasn't a mountain. It was a volcano ready to erupt all around them.

Morning came, and Nathen woke to the jungle sounds he loved so much. He lay there listening to all the different animals and birds conversing to each other. Authia was already up and had fed Joshawa. The guides were drinking freshly made coffee, and Tammy and Hansen were still asleep. In the night, while he slept, Hansen had moved even closer to Tammy, placing a protective arm around her. *This should be interesting.* Nathen got up and went to the fire.

He sat on the ground next to the fire and accepted the coffee that Sam passed him. "So how long till we reach your village, Sam?"

"We'll be there by noon. We should start packing up as soon as you're ready, my Lord."

Nathen turned to check on Tammy and Hansen. Tammy was awake but just lying there and staring at Hansen, who was still sleeping. Coffee in hand, Nathen got up and walked over to them. Gently he kicked at Hansen's feet. "Okay, you two. We're getting ready to leave."

Hansen woke up, realized where his arm was, and quickly removed it. He was up and on his feet before Tammy could say anything. She just shook her head and giggled at him.

* * * *

Authia smiled as she watched the two of them wake up. Hansen, obviously embarrassed, went to the fire to get some coffee while Tammy went to the pond to freshen up. Afterward, Tammy joined Authia while the men packed everything up. "So, are you nervous, Authia?"

"Nervous about what?

"Meeting Dena. Of Nathen finding his own people."

"Not in the least. For whatever reason, I'm not afraid. I mean, after Serena, how bad could it get."

"This coming from the woman who said *How bad can it be. Women have babies all the time.*"

"Thanks for that memory. But I'm still not afraid. We went in blind with Serena. Now we have two priestesses to guide us. It's going to be okay."

Authia secured Joshawa to her chest, all the while thinking, praying really, that everything would be fine. That they were walking into a utopia of kindness and acceptance. Authia kept telling herself that, but, deep down, she had an uneasy feeling that life wasn't going to be so simple.

The last leg of their journey was the most strenuous. The terrain they travelled was uneven, and they felt as though they were heading in a constant upward direction. The higher they climbed, the thinner the air became. Authia was feeling lightheaded and started developing a slight headache. Tammy and Hansen complained of the same symptoms. However, none of the symptoms plagued Nathen. Authia marvelled at how he was able to adjust to the changing altitude, as if his body was already conditioned, ready to accept the changes. And the higher they climbed, the denser the jungle became. It was as if it were closing in around them. Sam was making little headway with his machete. After four long hours, they finally made their way into a large clearing. Authia walked over to the edge and peered down upon the jungle, and the view was breathtaking. They were so high up that for miles around, all they could see was the canopy of the jungle. Inside the clearing, there appeared to be approximately fifteen huts made of saplings and palm leaves. They were all of varying sizes. And in the distance, through a narrow band of jungle, Authia saw the waterfall that was their gateway to Nathen's people.

The people of the village surrounded the group, anxious to meet the Lord of the Lion people. With the greatest respect, the entire village bowed to Nathen.

* * * *

Nathen was overwhelmed and had no idea how to react. He was no more special than the people that bowed before him. He was about to tell them as much when Sam came up to him. "The elders wish to speak to you and your mate." Sam pointed to Tammy and Hansen. "They must remain behind." Nathen took Authia's hand in his and followed Sam. The curious villagers followed Nathen and Authia as they approached the main hut that housed the elders. Neither Nathen nor Authia were prepared for what was waiting for them. Standing in front of the hut was Dena, priestess of the Jelani tribe. She was dressed in a long, flowing ceremonial gown, minus the mask. As Nathen approached, Dena bowed. "I am here to serve you, my Lord. I'm loyal to you and to your mate."

Nathen was face to face with a taller version of Serena. Only she was of flesh and blood and not a spirit living in a spirit world. Dena was nearly six feet tall and could have easily passed as Serena's twin sister. The only difference was that Dena's eyes were as green as Nathen's, and Serena's had been a sapphire blue. "How many of us are there?"

"Your tribe is sixty-two people strong. You look exactly as your father did."

"My father has been dead for over two centuries. How do you know what he looks like?"

"There are parchments, secret parchments, which contain the likeness of Lord Joshawa. We've kept them safe so that when the time came, we would know what the true descendant of Joshawa's should look like. You are that man. I know you have many questions. The elders of this village have prepared a hut for you and for your companions. They wish to speak with you. Afterward, you need to rest. We'll talk soon."

"I'd like to talk now."

"We must wait for Tamara. We'll talk, soon. In the

meantime." Dena motioned to the hut that housed the elders. "Go... speak with them. I'll wait for you here."

Nathen and Authia, who was still cradling Joshawa, entered the hut. They found two men and a woman sitting cross-legged on the ground in front of a fire pit. Their long, brown cotton robes were faded, thin, and stained with sweat.

* * * *

The smell of incense permeated the room. Since their run-in with Serena, Authia associated incense with danger and death. But she did not sense a negative aura from the room. The two men had their eyes closed, their arms resting on their lap. However, the woman looked at Nathen and shook her head. "So, you're the Lord that the woman from the Lion people seeks. It's an honour to have you in our village. But I must ask you, my Lord. Are we safe? Or have you brought with you the wrath of the gods that protect your home?"

"These gods that you speak of are not even aware of my existence. My bloodline has been absent from my home for two centuries. I would not be surprised if the gods have forgotten about me altogether."

"You have much to learn, Lord of the Lion People. The gods haven't forgotten you. They prepare for your return. However, I can't see past the veil that shrouds your valley."

Authia shifted Joshawa's weight to her other arm. "You have the gift of sight?"

"Yes, as you do."

Authia's jaw dropped. "How do you know of my gift?"

"I know of many things. You, both of you, are strong. I sense that a change is coming. And the two of you are in the centre of it. It'll take all your energy, your strength, to fight for what's yours. Now go and rest. A hut has been prepared for you." The woman closed her eyes, effectively ending the conversation.

Sam led Authia and Nathen to a hut that contained a fire pit and sleeping mats. Next to their hut was one for Tammy and Hansen. True to her word, Dena returned and joined Nathen and Authia in their hut. She walked up to Authia, who was cradling Joshawa in her arms. "May I hold him?"

Authia was leery of handing Joshawa over to her. Then she had an idea. "May I touch your hair?"

Dena appeared surprised but agreed. Authia passed Joshawa to Nathen, then reached up and held a few strands of Dena's hair. At first, the vision came in a flurry of colours, bombarding Authia's mind. Then, as she focused on Dena, the vision became clear, and she learned all there was to know about the priestess. She also learned of the evil waiting for them at the village. An evil related to Dena. "You're a good person. But tell me, who or what is Casandra?"

Dena's eyes went wide. "How could you know of Casandra?"

"I know of her because you know her. I can read you. See your thoughts, sense your feelings."

"Then you're truly the one that will conquer Casandra. For only a priestess can take her place."

"I'm not a priestess. That being said, I do have a gift."

"A wondrous gift. Come, sit by the fire. I've much to tell you and show you. But first, I would like to hold your son."

Nathen passed Joshawa to Dena. She held him tight against her chest, reached into the folds of her gown, and pulled out a leaf-covered packet. Authia immediately grasped Dena's wrist with her right hand. "You're going to hand that to me, carefully. Don't you dare drop it." Authia extended her left hand toward Dena, palm facing upward. Dena did as she was told and placed the packet on Authia's hand. Authia handed the packet to Nathen, then took

Joshawa from Dena.

"I don't understand. Why do you fear me?"

"I don't fear you. But I've seen what these packets can do. You're not going to use it on my son or anyone else for that matter."

"Unlike Casandra, my packets do not contain evil. I was just going to produce a vision that we all could see. A vision of the child's future."

"How do I know that I can trust you?"

"You saw into my very soul. Did you see evil lurking in the shadows of my mind?"

"No. Actually, there was only good and sacrifice. A sacrifice you've made in order to help us." Authia hesitated for a moment, then passed Joshawa back to Dena. She took the packet from Nathen and returned it to Dena. "I'll trust you."

* * * *

Nathen looked on in disbelief. But he had the greatest confidence in his wife and her gift, so he remained quiet. Dena placed the packet on Joshawa's forehead. She closed her eyes and started chanting softly as she slowly rocked back and forth. As promised, visions appeared all around them. Joshawa did not pass beyond the falls. He remained in the village where he was safe and untouched by the evil that ruled Nathen's people. But the vision would go no further, and Dena ended her chanting.

Authia was confused. "What does this mean? Why is there no vision of him as an adult?"

"Because, my Mistress, his future hasn't been written yet. It can follow different paths. His future depends on your success." Dena handed Joshawa back to Authia. "Come sit with me, and I'll tell you a story."

Chapter Twenty-Three

Casandra sat on the platform at the back of the gathering hut. By her side was her daughter, Tamara. The camp was unsettled. Talk of Dena finding the lost Lord ran rampant throughout the village. Casandra had to squash the rumour, but she had to be careful. A son of Joshawa did exist, and if by some miracle he did find his way home, Casandra had to appear excited by his return. She'd welcome him to the tribe. Her true feelings must be hidden behind a mask of deception. Then and only then would she be in a position to discredit the son of Joshawa.

"Once again, I ask my people, has anyone seen or heard from any descendant of Joshawa?" The tribe remained quiet. "Has anyone seen or heard from Dena?" Again, no response.

"I've news for my people. I've seen Joshawa's son in a vision." Tamara's head shot up as she stared wide-eyed at her mother. "Dena's waiting for him beyond the falls. She means to bring him home to us. My vision did not predict when or even if he'll make it to our valley. But if he does, he'll be given the opportunity to explain his father's indiscretion. At that time, the tribe will decide his fate." With that, Casandra left the gathering hut, followed closely by Tamara.

* * * *

As they entered the priestesses' hut, Tamara spoke up. "Mother, you did not tell me that you had a vision of

Joshawa's son."

"That's because I haven't received a vision. Like you, I only know that he exists. Where he is now is beyond my knowledge. However, I trust that if you have a vision, you'll share it with me."

"Of course. Why would I not?"

"You and Dena are close. I know for a fact that she waits for her Lord to return. I only hope that you don't share the same sentiments."

"Mother, I know nothing of the return of the Lord. I have seen what you have seen. Nothing more, nothing less."

Casandra smiled. "Good. We must prepare. Sit with me, and we'll try to conjure a vision predicting the future of our tribe." Tamara sat by the fire pit, but Casandra remained standing behind her.

There were no packets in the fire pit. "Mother, where are the packets? How will we be able to conjure a vision without a host to obtain our vision from?"

"I intend to use you. Your talents are strong. Through you, I might see what's in store for my future."

Tamara took a deep breath as her mother placed her hand on the top of her head. It was time to see just how strong she was as she desperately tried to hide her thoughts from her mother.

* * * *

Authia took Joshawa to Tammy and Hansen's hut. "Would you mind watching him while we talk to Dena?"

"Not at all." Tammy took Joshawa from Authia. "Hansen, you and I could play house." Hansen turned red and looked away from the two women. "Do you want me to bring him to you when he gets hungry?"

"No. Try the formula on him. He's going to have to start

getting used to it."

"Okay. But when you're ready to quit breastfeeding altogether, let me know. I brought a couple of pills that will dry you up right away."

"Does it matter?"

"Only if you don't mind pain, leaking so badly that you soak whatever shirt and bra that you're wearing, and, of course, not being able to stand anything or anyone touching your breasts."

"Okay... I get the picture." Authia turned to leave, then looked over her shoulder. "I don't know how long we're going to be."

"No worries."

Authia joined Nathen and Dena, who were already sitting on the ground around the fire pit. Dena placed three leaf-covered packets within the confines of the fire pit. "I know you've been through much at Serena's hand. And I'm not sure how much you know."

Authia interjected. "Coles Notes version. Serena was royally pissed off at Joshawa, which resulted in her cursing him as well as Nathen. I'm assuming it was because Joshawa fell in love with an outsider and got her pregnant."

"Joshawa was our Lord, and he chose Serena as his wife. His companion to rule the tribe. It's written that he chose her to try to control her, but she was a force that couldn't be controlled. One day, outsiders, two men and a woman, entered our valley. That has only happened one other time in our history. Joshawa sent a scouting party to learn about these outsiders. However, Serena went behind his back and had them killed. The woman, Julia, survived. That very day, Joshawa publicly ended his marriage with Serena. Soon after, he chose Julia as his wife. That's when all the trouble started.

"It was common knowledge that Celest, Serena's mother,

wanted control of the tribe. But the only way that would happen is if Joshawa chose her to rule at his side, which she knew wouldn't happen. At the same time, Julia was pregnant. If she had a son, then he would be next in line to rule once he reached his thirtieth year. Celest knew that the time of her family ruling together with their Lord was coming to an end. Serena was angry beyond reasoning with. According to the parchments, she cursed Joshawa, then disappeared.

"At the same time of her disappearance, Julia became very ill. Our family believes that Serena possessed Julia's mind. She was powerful enough and knew of the dark spells, which she learned from Celest. Serena could've easily cast a spell and possessed Julia. But we had no proof. Then, when Julia was ready to have her baby, she, the baby, and Joshawa disappeared. Celest, who was just as evil as Serena, convinced our people that our Lord ran away with Julia. That he turned his back on his people. She convinced the tribe to allow the family of the priestesses to rule until such time that a descendant of Joshawa returns. Upon his return, he has the opportunity to defend his bloodline. And that's how it has been ever since."

* * * *

Nathen took in all that Dena had to tell him. It filled in many of the blanks he'd had while combating Serena. "Your family was right. Serena killed herself, then killed my mother and father. I was sent off to live what life Serena granted me only to die and be reborn time and time again. She kept my parents in some sort of spirit world that she devised."

"You have to come back with me and tell your people the truth."

"Why would they believe me. It'll be my word against

whoever is ruling now."

"That would be Casandra, my sister. Her mind is full of hatred and greed. She'll not be willing to step down. You'll have to fight for the right to rule your people."

"How do I fight a priestess. It didn't work so well for my father."

"Did you not destroy Serena?"

"Yes, but it was just her. We were not fighting an entire tribe."

"And you won't be this time either." Dena closed her eyes and waved her hands over the packets while chanting an incantation. Slowly the packets started to smoke, and within the smoke came a vision of Dena's village. Dena opened her eyes and sadly gazed upon the vision. "Casandra does have some followers but so do you, my Lord. And when they see you and learn that our Mistress has powers, not unlike my own, then your followers will stand behind you. Look into the smoke... see your people. They need you... they need both of you."

Materializing in front of Nathen and Authia was an entire village of people who resembled Nathen. The aura that emanated from the vision was that of unhappiness and fear. A dark evil shrouded the entire village. "What you're asking is for me to risk my life and that of Authia's based on the chance that we may win. We've fought this fight before. We fought for the right to live. Now you ask us to fight for the right to rule. Why's it so important that a son of Joshawa's rules this tribe?"

"I could see in your eyes that you felt it. Only evil rules now, as it has since the disappearance of our Lord. The tribe is sick. It needs to be healed, and the only way for that to happen is if you destroy the evil. You need to defeat Casandra."

"And how are we to accomplish this?"

"By proving to your people who you are and revealing the deception that has plagued our tribe since the time of Joshawa."

"You still haven't answered my question. How are we to accomplish this with only you on our side?"

"Not true, my Lord. You also have Tamara. The next high priestess. Daughter of Casandra. And your loyal follower."

* * * *

Casandra placed her hand on Tamara's head, closed her eyes, and recited the incantation—of knowledge. It was an excruciating ten minutes as Casandra delved deeper and deeper into Tamara's subconscious. If she didn't know better, she would have sworn that Tamara was blocking her. Finally, she removed her hand and stood back. Tamara turned and innocently looked up at her mother. "Did you find what you were seeking, Mother?"

"No. But I did sense that you were holding back."

"Why would I hold back? I must learn from you, Mother, if I am going to rule this tribe as you would wish me to."

Casandra was quiet as she sized up her child. She wondered if Tamara was hiding something. But then she dismissed that thought. Tamara was not that clever. She was naive, like a babe in the jungle. Casandra knew that she had to start molding her. Getting her ready for the slightest chance that the Lord did return.

CHAPTER TWENTY-FOUR

Night time fell, blanketing the outsiders' village in darkness. Authia returned to Tammy and Hansen's hut to retrieve Joshawa. Joshawa was asleep, cradled in Hansen's arms. They were sitting in front of the fire that Hansen had started earlier. "Well, that's a nice picture." Hansen just smiled as he gazed down at the small child. "I've come to relieve you. How did he take the formula?"

"Great." Tammy motioned toward the fire pit. "They brought you supper. Only they didn't want to disturb you, so they left it here. Actually, since you and Nathen have some privacy now, I thought I'd take Joshawa for the night. You can have a little alone time before your great adventure."

"Are you sure?"

"Yes. Go. Have fun!"

"Okay. I'm out of here before you change your mind."

Authia left the hut carrying only the plates of food. Hansen looked up at Tammy. "That was very nice of you."

* * * *

Tammy smiled at Hansen. He'd accomplished what he'd come to do. Making sure that everyone arrived safely. *Does that mean he's going to leave?* Tammy didn't want him to go. She'd never met a man quite like him. He was compassionate, and his loyalty was unwavering. She knew he liked her. But did he like her enough to stay?

"You're staring at me."

"Oh... sorry." She sat down on the mat next to Hansen. "You look like a natural holding Joshawa."

"I'm the eldest of eight kids. I've held my fair share of babies."

"Eight. That's a big family." Tammy was stalling. How was she going to approach the subject of him staying? Like she approached everything else in her life... head on. "So, what happens now? Are you staying or are you leaving?"

* * * *

Hansen thought for a moment. This could be the opportunity he was waiting for. An excuse to let Tammy know how he felt. "What do you think I should do?"

"Oh, for love of... of course I want you to stay. But what do you want to do?"

"I guess I'm staying, then." Hansen leaned closer to Tammy and gently kissed her. "I've wanted to do that for a long time."

"So have I!" Tammy threw her arms around Hansen's neck, boldly kissing him. He allowed her tongue to taunt and tease his. Slowly, sensuously, she ended the kiss.

Hansen just sat there staring at her, wide-eyed. "Wow! I like your kiss better."

"Well, there's more where that came from." Tammy smiled seductively. "It's getting late. We should get ready for bed."

Hansen laid Joshawa down on the pillows that served as his bed. Tammy was already under the blanket, dressed in only her panties and bra. She lifted the blanket, openly inviting Hansen to join her. He needed no further prodding. He stripped down to his boxers and lay beside Tammy. "Since we have Joshawa tonight, I just want to hold you in my arms all night. Feel you close to me. You're the most amazing woman I've ever met. I can't believe that I'm here with you, right now."

"Do you want me to pinch you?"

"Nope. But you can kiss me if you like."

Tammy obliged, and the two cuddled and kissed and talked into the early hours of the morning.

* * * *

Nathen looked up from the sleeping mat as Authia returned to their hut. She placed the plates of food next to the fire pit. "Are you not forgetting someone?"

"We have the night off. Tammy and Hansen are going to look after Joshawa."

Nathen grinned. "A whole night... all alone." Nathen ached with sexual tension as he watched his wife undress. Earlier he had started a small fire in the fire pit, and the light from it danced seductively on her naked body. "Hope you're not planning on eating or getting any sleep tonight. I have much to make up for." He lifted the blanket so Authia could crawl in beside him. Nathen's entire body pulsated with desire. He wrapped his arms around Authia and brought her tight against his own naked body.

* * * *

She felt his arousal as well as the passion building deep inside of her. Authia wanted him as desperately as she knew he wanted her. Nathen gently lay on top of her, kissing her lips and her neck before slowly making his way down to her breasts. He teased and tantalized, bringing her to the brink of ecstasy. Then he entered her, his own passion releasing deep inside of her. Throughout the night, Nathen fulfilled his promise to bring her to the heavens and back as often as her body could handle. The sun was rising when they finally fell asleep in each other's arms.

* * * *

It was noon when Nathen woke up. Authia was still sleeping. Gently he kissed her forehead, then got up and put his jeans on. He decided to forgo the shirt and left the hut. Sitting on the ground, right outside the hut, was Dena. She had put aside her ceremonial gown and was wearing a top that barely covered her breasts and a skirt like a loincloth, both made of animal skin. She stood and bowed as Nathen approached her. "There's no need to bow every time you see me."

"There is, my Lord. You have much to learn. Will you accompany me?"

"Where are we going?"

"To the falls. But not to enter them."

"If we're not entering the falls... then why go there?"

"Privacy, my Lord."

"All right. I'll just have to check on Joshawa first."

Nathen found Tammy and Hansen sitting outside their hut, with Joshawa cradled safely in Tammy's arms. "Good morning."

"Actually, it's good afternoon." Hansen smirked at Nathen. "Had yourself a late night?"

"You could say that. I hate to impose, but could you watch Joshawa a little longer."

Nathen stood next to Joshawa and held his tiny hand. Joshawa smiled up at his father, which took Nathen's breath away. How he loved his little man. "Authia's still sleeping, and Dena and I are heading out to the falls."

Tammy looked at Nathen in disbelief. "You're not

crossing without Authia... are you?"

"No. Just going for a walk."

"Then sure. Hansen and I will watch him."

"Thank you." Nathen tenderly kissed his son's forehead. "I'll be back soon."

Dena was quiet during their walk. Nathen spent the time wondering what was so important that it couldn't be discussed back at the village. He was soon to find out as the two of them reached their destination. "Please, my Lord, sit down." Dena motioned toward an outcrop of rocks that lined the pond. Nathen did as he was requested, with Dena sitting across from him. "I brought you here so that we could talk without interruption. You have no knowledge of our tribe or our ways. That could prove to be dangerous for both you and my Mistress. When we cross over, I'll no longer be in a position to help you."

"What do you mean?"

"My sister, Casandra, will take me prisoner. By seeking you out, I have turned my back on my family. She will show me no mercy."

"Do you mean she'll kill you?"

"No, I don't think so. However, she could take away my privileges as a priestess. Then you'll have to rely on Tamara to help you. When we cross over, we'll be met by Casandra's warriors. They'll try to take all of us as their prisoners. You must be assertive. The Lord of our tribe bows to no one. You must enter our village of your own free will. You must confront Casandra and defend your bloodline in front of the entire tribe. Authia must also stand up to Casandra. Show the tribe that she is gifted. That will go a long way to your acceptance. But be warned. Casandra's not to be trusted. She is evil and will stop at nothing to end the bloodline of Joshawa."

"And what if I fail to intimidate the warriors that wait for us on the other side of the falls?"

"You must allow Authia and me to be taken prisoner. You must escape and head north."

"That's not going to happen. I'll not leave Authia's side."

"You both will die if you don't do as I say. There's a band of warriors and scouts that are loyal to Lord Joshawa. To you. They've been banished for many years and live apart from the village. Find them. They'll help you regain your right to rule our tribe. Tamara will protect my Mistress. My Lord, you are our only hope. You must be strong. You must bring peace back to our village."

"Why should I risk my life and the life of the woman I love to help a tribe of people that, until recently, I didn't know even existed?"

Dena looked puzzled. "Have you not spent your entire life wondering who you were? Trying to fit into a world that you don't belong in. This is your destiny. You were meant to find us. It's your duty as the son of Joshawa to help your tribe."

Nathen closed his eyes and sought out Authia. *Can you hear me, my love?*

Yes. I've been eavesdropping on the entire conversation.

Then it's your decision. Do we venture forward or return to Burwood?

No. This is not just my decision. What does your heart tell you?

Nathen thought for a second. *To find my people.*

Then that settles it. We venture forward. Dena, when do we leave?

At first light. Have this day to spend with your son.

So, everything was set in place. Nathen was not pleased that Authia would be crossing through the falls with him. Tammy and Hansen would stay behind and take care of Joshawa while Nathen risked everything so that he might find himself.

* * * *

Meanwhile, Tamara awaited the arrival of her Lord. She foresaw the unrest and suffering yet to come. She prayed her Lord and his mate were strong enough for the battle to save her people.

CHAPTER TWENTY-FIVE

Casandra sat all alone by the fire pit in the priestesses' hut. The turmoil surrounded her like a heavy blanket being wrapped too tightly. It was time to get answers. For reasons she didn't understand, her visions were clouded. It was almost as if someone was blocking her ability to see beyond the obvious. But who? Who had the strength and the know-how to perform such a deep block? Then Casandra thought of Dena. Was Dena so powerful that she could block Casandra's visions from such a distance? Of course, it had to be Dena. Casandra placed six of her leaf-covered packets in the fire pit. She started chanting, waving her arms over the packets. She focused on Dena. Filling Dena's mind with her thoughts. Showing Dena just how inferior she was. The pit filled with smoke as Casandra concentrated on her sister. *You're a fool if you think you can prevent me from conjuring my visions. I'll show you, little sister. You'll pay for your treachery!*

* * * *

On the other side of the falls, Dena sat and watched her Lord interact with his family. Maybe, one day, she could have a family of her own. She closed her eyes to imagine her child, when her mind filled with her sister's thoughts. Did she answer? No. Dena sat quietly, listening to her sister. Listening to see just how much she knew.

* * * *

Casandra focused on the fire pit. The smoke cleared, and a vision was presented to her. It was Dena. But she was not alone. There, standing at Dena's side, was the exact image of Joshawa. She knew it was Joshawa's son. And, if he was with Dena, that meant he was on the other side of the falls. Casandra concentrated on the vision. There was more. She could sense it. Blurred images floated before her. Then the vision was gone. *Dena, you've gone too far! Be warned! If you cross into our valley with that bastard son of Joshawa's, you will secure his fate. He'll not live to see another day.*

You are mistaken, Casandra. Our Lord will cross into our valley and take his rightful place as Lord of our people.

Casandra stood. *We'll see about that.* She left the hut in search of Jamya, leader of the warriors. She found him by the gathering hut. He was tall for his people, standing a good five inches over the height of any of the other males in his village. He had wide shoulders, large biceps, muscular legs, and his fire-red hair cascaded past his shoulders. The fine hair that covered his body glistened in the sun. "You, come with me." Jamya obeyed and followed her to the outskirts of their village. "Go to the falls. Instruct your men that they're to kill anyone who crosses through the falls."

"Anyone, my Mistress?"

"Anyone! Including Dena and those that follow her. Go now! You don't have much time."

Jamya vanished into the jungle. Content that she had dealt with Dena and the son of Joshawa once and for all, Casandra left for the priestesses' hut. Upon Jamya's return, she would announce the passing of her sister and place the blame on Dena's Lord.

* * * *

Tamara had been observing her mother and shook her head.

She'd heard all that her mother had to say. Not only to Jamya but also her conversation with Dena. She closed her eyes and reached out to Dena. *You have no time. You must cross now. My mother has sent word that you are to be killed on sight. You must cross before Jamya reaches the falls. Be safe.*

* * * *

Dena approached Authia and Nathen. They were sitting outside their hut with Tammy and Hansen. "We must leave now, my Lord. Say your goodbyes."

Nathen looked up at Dena. "You said at first light. What's the hurry?"

"My Lord, Casandra knows that you're here. She means to kill you. We must leave now."

Authia handed Joshawa to Tammy. "Will we be safe if we leave now?"

"All I know is that if we don't leave now, all this could be for nothing."

Authia bent down and kissed Joshawa's forehead. "I love you. I promise you, we'll be back."

Hansen stood and shook Nathen's hand. "Tammy and I'll stay here as long as it takes. Your son will be safe with us."

Dena started walking away from the group. She stopped and turned around. "Please, my Lord, we must hurry." Dena broke out into a full run.

* * * *

Nathen scooped Authia up in his arms and took a last look at his son, then caught up with Dena. Fear began to envelop him as his powerful legs propelled him toward the falls. Minutes later they reached their objective. Gently Nathen placed Authia down.

"What now, Dena? Where do we go from here?"

"There's a passage just behind the falls. Follow me. Allow me to enter the valley first."

The trio, led by Dena, carefully made their way over the rocks that were their stepping stones to the entrance behind the falls. It was a narrow passage no more than two feet wide. Authia was right behind Dena, followed closely by Nathen. The spray from the falls not only saturated their clothing but made every step they took hazardous over the slimy rock. The thunderous roar of the falls reverberated all around them. Dena stopped and pointed to a small opening in the rock. She raised her voice as loud as she dared to be heard over the falls. "This is our way. Do not pass until I call you."

Nathen moved closer to Dena. "And what if they capture you?"

"Then send Authia out. She must accompany me to the village. When we're gone, you head north."

Before Nathen could argue, Dena disappeared through the opening. Nathen stood close so he could try to hear what was transpiring between Dena and those that were waiting for them.

* * * *

Dena stepped out onto the lush jungle floor of her valley. She had only taken a few steps when four men confronted her, bows raised and pulled back. They were warriors dressed only in animal skin. "What's the meaning of this. How dare you raise a weapon to me!"

Samin, the oldest of the warriors, respectfully addressed his priestess. "Your transgression has displeased our high priestess. It's under her orders that we take you."

"And what, may I ask, did she tell you that I was doing on the other side of the falls?"

Samin lowered his bow but instructed the other men to keep theirs raised. "Treachery! You have mingled with the outside world, which is strictly forbidden."

Dena smiled at Samin. "No, Samin, I went to the outside world in search of the son of Lord Joshawa."

The men all looked at each other, astonished. Samin took a step closer to Dena. "A son of Joshawa exists? Why do we not know of this? What proof do you have?"

"If I show you proof, will you put down your bows and accept the son of Joshawa as your Lord?"

Believing that she had no proof, the four men agreed. Without taking her eyes off them, Dena called out to Nathen. "Come out, my Lord. Your people await you."

The men lowered their bows as their jaws dropped. They watched as Nathen emerged from the falls and came to stand next to Dena. "I present to you Nathen, the son of Joshawa. The rightful leader of our tribe. Bow if you accept him, or stand and be heard."

All four men were about to bow when Jamya came out of the jungle right behind Dena and Nathen. His bow was drawn and aimed at Nathen's head. "Don't listen to her. She lies. Our High Priestess has ordered us to kill all who come from the falls."

Nathen turned to face Jamya. "Am I a lie? Am I not the image of my father? Is it not written that I have the opportunity to defend myself and my bloodline?"

"This must be trickery. The bloodline of Joshawa is long gone." Jamya slowly aimed his bow at the ground as he took a step back. "Yet here you stand before me. My high priestess demands that I kill you and Dena. I'm honour bound to follow her wishes even when it's to kill one of my own."

"You would kill innocent people. Your own people. I don't think so."

* * * *

The warrior whirled around to find Authia brandishing a large branch. With everything she had, she swung out and hit Jamya across the head. He dropped his bow and fell to his knees, then crumpled to the ground. Samin drew his bow, aimed it at Authia, and released the arrow. Nathen rushed to push Authia out of the way. As she fell, she saw the arrow as it entered his flesh and burrowed into his shoulder. Dena ran to his side. "You must leave. Head north." She grabbed Authia and placed the two of them between the archers and Nathen. "Take us to Casandra. This woman has the gift. Casandra will want to see her."

For a split second, the men's attention was diverted to the two women, as Authia watched Nathen from the corner of her eye. They did not notice Nathen slowly stand up. However, as Nathen made his way into the jungle, he must have caught Samin's attention, who let one more arrow fly. Authia screamed as she threw herself at Samin, knocking him off his feet. But it was too late. The arrow found its mark and was embedded in Nathen's right calf. Authia got up and tried to follow Nathen, but Dena held her back. Quickly she melded with Nathen and Authia. *Let him go, my Mistress. He'll be fine. His people are watching him.*

Authia looked off into the jungle, searching for any sign of Nathen, but none existed. The warrior she'd attacked with the branch slowly stood, rubbing the right side of his head. "You'll pay for that. Bind them. We'll take them to our high priestess."

"But I thought our orders were to kill any that cross from the falls?"

He shook his head at Samin. "That was before I saw him. Our high priestess will have to explain his existence." Authia and Dena were bound and led to the village.

* * * *

From his hiding place, Nathen could hear what transpired and felt powerless as he watched Authia being taken away. *You better be right, Dena. No harm can come to Authia.*

She'll be fine, my Lord. I intend to make a very public appearance. One that Casandra cannot deny. Head north quickly, my Lord. Your people await you.

Authia, I'll be back, and I'll save you.

Run, Nathen. Save yourself, then save me.

Nathen hobbled deeper into the jungle. When he felt he was safe, he sat down on the jungle floor and examined his injuries. Both arrows had penetrated his flesh, just missing the bone. They were lodged in place, with the shaft of the arrow on either side of the wound. Nathen grabbed the shaft of the arrow that was protruding from the front of his shoulder and broke it off. Carefully he pulled the back half of the arrow out of his shoulder, grimacing in pain as he did. He tore his shirt to make a compress to slow down the bleeding. Nathen repeated the procedure with the arrow in his calf. When his wounds were bound, he stood, took the compass from his pocket, and headed north.

CHAPTER TWENTY-SIX

They were getting closer to the village. But then Jamya changed direction, leading them away from the main entrance and straight to the priestesses' hut. Dena stopped dead in her tracks. She knew that in order for her plan to work, they needed to make a public entrance. "Why are we going this way, Jamya?"

"I'm keeping you out of sight."

"Why? What are you afraid of?"

Jamya stepped closer to Dena. "I'm afraid of nothing."

"Then allow us to enter by the gathering hut. If you have nothing to be afraid of, then this shouldn't be a problem."

* * * *

Jamya weighed his options. He was already defying the High Priestess by not killing Dena and those that followed her. But the High Priestess failed to mention that one of the followers could very well be the son of Joshawa. "All right. Have it your way." Jamya turned away from the direction of the priestesses' hut and led them toward the gathering hut. He was very much interested in hearing his Mistress' explanation.

The villagers all gathered as Dena and Authia were led into the clearing in front of the gathering hut. They all looked shocked. Dena was back, and she'd brought an outsider with her.

* * * *

All the commotion attracted Casandra's attention. Dressed in her long ceremonial gown complete with mask, she approached the clearing, expecting to see the body of her sister. But, as her people moved aside, she found her sister standing tall and proud and very much alive. An outsider stood at her side and wore that same look of contempt that her sister was showing her. Casandra glared at Jamya and, as she walked past him, whispered, "I'll deal with you later."

"So, Dena, my sister. You've found your way back home. And it appears that you've brought an outsider with you. Is she your prisoner?"

The woman melded with Casandra. *No. It appears that I'm your prisoner.*

Casandra's eyes went wide. The outsider could communicate in only a way that the priestesses knew. "Why have you brought her here?"

Dena raised her hands, exposing the bindings that held them tight. "You're mistaken. I'm not the one that brought her here. She and I are both prisoners. Your prisoners. And the man that accompanied us. You know of whom I speak. He'll return and claim his rightful place." The whispers went wild amongst the crowd that had gathered to see the outsider.

Casandra thought for a moment, then addressed the crowd. "Dena has betrayed our trust by bringing this outsider into our home. She must be punished, and the outsider must be dealt with. Bow if you agree with me, or stand and be heard." To Casandra's astonishment, as all her people bowed before her, Jamya remained standing. "You wish to be heard?"

"Yes, my High Priestess."

"Then continue, but know this—I'll not stand for

treachery or lies. My punishment will be swift. Do you understand me?"

"Yes."

"Then speak."

"We found these two by the falls. There was a third. I respectfully request that we hold off punishing these two until we locate the third person."

"You saw the third person?"

"Yes."

"Then why is that person not here with you now?"

"He ran off. He has been struck by two arrows, so he should be easy to find."

Casandra was livid. If Jamya could produce the son of Joshawa, she could stand to lose everything. "Unbind the prisoners. You won't need to go hunting for the third person. He'll come to us. And when he does, he'll have to explain himself not only to me but also to the entire tribe." Casandra looked directly at Samin, who had remained quiet throughout the whole encounter. "Take Dena to the priestesses' hut and place a guard at the door. As for the outsider, find the smallest hut we have. Empty it and place her in it. Guard her day and night."

"Yes, my high priestess." After Samin had taken the two women, Casandra moved closer to Jamya. "I must say, I'm very disappointed in you."

"My Mistress. You failed to mention that a possible link to Joshawa's bloodline would be there. You know our laws. I could not kill him."

"Actually, yes you could. And if you don't want to suffer by my hand, then you'll return to the jungle and finish the job. You have to know that a son of Joshawa doesn't exist and this man is just a false Lord."

Jamya bowed to Casandra. "It will be done." Taking only his machete and bow, Jamya headed back into the jungle.

After Casandra had watched Jamya leave, she entered the hut where the woman was kept captive. "So, what other gifts do you possess?"

"I'm not telling you anything. You're just going to have to figure it for yourself."

Casandra raised her arm and slapped her face so hard that it left an imprint of her hand on the woman's cheek as well as three deep gouges from her fingernails. The woman stretched out her jaw and tenderly ran her fingers along the gouges. "Is that all you have? I don't fear you. In that very second that your hand touched me, I saw plenty. Your destiny, for starters."

"I don't believe you. No outsider possesses these gifts. You are nothing but a trickster."

"And I suppose I was tricking you when I melded with you? After you leave here, you're going to see Dena. You're going to take away her gift. That will be her punishment."

Casandra stared at her prisoner. The outsider was going to be trouble. "I'll deal with you later."

Casandra turned to leave, but the outsider was not quite finished with her. "Casandra. I'm more powerful than you can ever imagine. I learned much from Serena. Harm anyone that I care for, and you'll have me to deal with." Casandra left the hut, actually afraid of what she could do. She'd stood up to Serena. One of the most powerful priestesses of her time. And she'd been victorious! However, it was the son of Joshawa that landed the final blow. Casandra knew that under no circumstance could the outsider and the son of Joshawa join forces. Together they could be her undoing.

* * * *

Authia reached out to Nathen. *Nathen, I'm in the village. Where are you?*

Not sure. I'm heading north as Dena instructed.

How are your injuries?

I'm fine. How are you doing?

I bluffed with Casandra, and I think she bought it. Someone's coming. I'll talk to you later. Stay safe.

A guard entered Authia's hut and stood by the entrance. "Are you going to be my roommate?" He didn't answer. "Oh. The strong, silent type." Cautiously Authia approached him till she was close enough to lay a hand on his arm. The man did not move or look at Authia. He just stared straight ahead. But that didn't bother Authia. She got what she needed. He believed in the return of the Lord. He would be an ally.

* ** *

Casandra entered the priestesses' hut to find not only Dena waiting for her but also Tamara. "I'm surprised to see you here, daughter."

"I sensed that you would need me. If I am wrong, Mother, then I will leave."

"No. Stay. I want you to witness this."

"Witness what, Mother?"

"How we deal with traitors to our family. Especially those that are a part of our family."

Tamara's expression was that of confusion. "I am not sure I understand. Who is the traitor that you speak of?"

Casandra turned to face Tamara as she pointed to Dena. "Dena has gone against all our rules. She crossed over to the outsiders' world. And to compound her indiscretions, she returned with not only an outsider but also with the son of Joshawa. She will be punished."

"Should I go get the other priestesses?"

"No, child! This is between you, her, and me. We'll exact punishment ourselves. Both of you, sit by the fire pit." Dena and Tamara did as they were told as Casandra went to the table and produced a clay pot. "Dena, you know what's in this pot?"

"Yes, Casandra. It's my life essence. The original packet."

"Your other packets, the ones that I could find, have been destroyed." Casandra passed the pot to Dena. "You know what has to be done."

"You do realize that what you're asking me to do will not only take away my gifts, but it could also kill me."

"You should have thought of that before you left the village. Now inhale your essence!"

* * * *

Dena wanted so much to hug her niece. To tell her to stick to the plan. A meld could very easily be overheard by Casandra. Instead, she looked at Tamara and smiled. "You'll make a powerful High Priestess when your time comes. But remember with great power comes great responsibility. Learn from the mistakes of your mother." Before Casandra could react to that comment, Dena reached into the pot. She withdrew the packet, carefully opened it, and breathed in as much of the powder as she could. Dena began to feel faint. The room began to spin. She felt as though she were floating, like a cloud in the sky. Then everything went dark, and Dena fell to the ground.

CHAPTER TWENTY-SEVEN

Nathen trudged through the jungle. Without the aid of a machete, the going was arduous. And all the time he had that uneasy feeling that he was being watched. He walked for nearly an hour in the sweltering heat. Insects were swarming around his head, biting at any exposed skin they could find. His injuries were throbbing with every step he took. Blood was trickling down his arm and calf from the holes the arrows had made. Nathen stopped for a moment and checked his compass. He was heading in the right direction but, according to the compass, he didn't gain much ground.

Nathen surveyed the jungle that surrounded him. It felt as though it were trying to smother him. As if the jungle had a will of its own. Feeling slightly defeated, he leaned against a large palm tree and slowly sank to the ground. He rested his head on the trunk of the tree and stared up at the sky, though he could barely see it through the canopies of the larger trees.

What was he doing? His quest had barely begun, and he was already separated from Authia. He had to find her. He needed to protect her. But he had no idea where to look for her. Then Nathen thought of the rogue tribe that Dena spoke of. They were the answer. They would be able to help him find his Authia. But, if he was going to find the rogue tribe, he was going to need help. Nathen stood and calmly addressed those that chose to remain invisible to him. "I know that you're there. You've been watching me since I entered the jungle at the falls. I ask that you show yourselves."

The jungle remained silent. Then Nathen remembered what Dena had said on how a Lord should act. And he remembered what she had asked her captors to do. Once again, Nathen spoke to the surrounding jungle. "I am Nathen, son of Joshawa. I've come here to free my people from the tyrant that rules them. I demand that you show yourselves! Come forward and bow if you accept me, or stand and be heard."

Still, no one came forward and as Nathen was about to turn around and continue his battle through the unforgiving jungle, a solitary man approached him. He walked up to Nathen, stopped a few feet away, then slowly bowed. Nathen scanned the area, and sure enough, one man after another came forward. A total of ten men walked out of the jungle. They left behind the dense vegetation that concealed them to reveal themselves to a man who claimed to be their Lord.

All but one man bowed. He was a little shorter than Nathen, and his facial features were more pronounced than the other males that Nathen had encountered. With a spear in one hand a machete in the other, he slowly made his way to the front of the group. "You wish to be heard?"

"I am Arman, a descendant of Tamiel. He was a true and loyal follower of Lord Joshawa. That loyalty cost him his life." Arman motioned to the small gathering. "We live for only one purpose. To find a descendant of our Lord and help him regain his place as Lord of our people. Priestesses throughout the years have been helping us. It's Dena and Tamara that sensed your arrival. The fact that Dena entered this valley with you assures me that she believes that you are our Lord."

"And what do you believe?"

"You are here. You have an outsider for a mate. I don't question as to whether or not you're our Lord. I believe in my heart that you are. However, I stand here before you to ask one question. Are you prepared to fight for what's yours?"

"Yes, I am. My question to you is, will you stand by your Lord and help him in this fight?"

Arman bowed to Nathen and without raising his head, he answered his Lord. "We are all here to protect you and to help you regain your rightful place as Lord of our people."

"I appreciate that. First and foremost, I must find my mate, Authia."

"She's in the main village. We'll need more men if we're going to rescue her. My village is a three-day walk from here. There are men there willing to support you." Arman noticed Nathen's blood-soaked arm and leg. "We'll tend to your wounds when we rest for the night."

Nathen watched in awe as the ten men protectively encircled him, then continued to hack their way through the dense foliage. No one said a word.

Nathen wanted so much to meld with Authia, but he had no idea if it was safe to do so. He didn't know if Casandra would be listening or not. It was the plan to reveal Authia's gifts to Casandra. But when they were going to do that, he had no way of knowing. And, when they did, would Casandra dismiss Authia's ability or protect herself from it. Nathen's frustration ate away at him. To be so far from Authia and unable to protect her was more than he could bear. His only hope was that if anything went wrong, she would be in a position to let him know or he would sense it himself. As he followed Arman, the fact that he was going to be three days away from Authia hit him hard. That was too far. A lot could happen in three days.

Nathen called out to Arman, who was several feet ahead of him. "Arman."

"Yes, my Lord." Arman joined Nathen and walked side by side with him.

"Why's your village three days from the main village?"

"We keep to just outside of their hunting grounds. We remain hidden this way."

"Three days is too long. I fear for Authia. I fear that I would be too late if she required my help. Is there not any way we can camp closer and still have a tactical advantage?"

Arman stopped and signalled to the rest of the men. "We camp here tonight. Make sure that there are four guards posted at all times." Arman turned back to him. "Sit here while I attend to your wounds."

Nathen sat on the ground while Arman removed the bandaging. "They've become infected." He turned to one of his men. "Retrieve my satchel." A few minutes later, Arman was plastering the holes with a salve that had been made with herbs and a little tree sap.

"You still haven't answered my question. Is there not a closer place?"

"There is an area very close to the village. It used to be a place where the priestesses conjured. But evil things have happened there, and now the entire village, including the priestesses, are forbidden to enter the area."

"What kind of evil things are we talking about?"

* * * *

Arman finished binding Nathen's wounds. He looked at his Lord, sizing him up. He believed in his heart that the man sitting before him was the Lord they sought. But he had much to learn... about himself and his people. "Sorcery. There's a birthing hut there. Too many children have been born dead. People that hunt there disappear and are never heard from again. Is this the type of place that you want us to hide in?"

"I don't believe in witchcraft. If evil's happening there, then someone's behind it. Do you know when the last reported incident happened?"

"Yes, my Lord. The deaths and disappearances happened soon after your mother and father disappeared."

"Are you telling me that this place has been deserted for over two hundred years?"

"Yes. As far as I know. We keep a close watch on the main village. There's been no activity in that area. The jungle has reclaimed the path and the clearing around the birthing hut."

"My mother and father were not taken by evil spirits. They were murdered by Serena and her mother."

"How do you know this?"

"I have fought Serena and came out the victor. She gloated over the fact that she murdered my family and sent me to the outside world. I was never to see my home again. The only evil in that area lives in the main village. And hopefully, she no longer considers that area important. If what you tell me is true, then she has forgotten about it altogether. We'll use that to our advantage. That's where we'll hide."

"You'll have to convince your people. No one wants to anger the spirits."

"I have experience in angering the spirits. Believe me when I say, they can be defeated just like an ordinary man."

"I'll defend you, and I'll follow you. There is much you say that you can't prove. However, if you can answer the questions that have tormented our people for so many years, then maybe our people will follow you as well."

"I have the answers. I need my people to trust me. To

have faith in me."

"Over the years, we have grown twenty men strong. Do you think you can overcome the High Priestess with only twenty men?"

Nathen smiled at Arman. "Twenty-one men and one very motivated woman."

"Of whom do you speak?"

"I speak of Authia, my mate."

Chapter Twenty-Eight

Authia sat on the ground of the hut she was a prisoner in. It was completely bare, with no sleeping mats, no fire pit, and no windows. The ground was packed hard and, as she sat there, she stared at the only opening to her prison. It had been hours since she heard from anyone. She didn't attempt a meld with Tamara or Dena in case Casandra was listening. Another meld with Nathen was even more dangerous. It could give away his hiding place. And Authia wasn't ready to risk that. She had to keep her mind focused on the moment.

But that was not an easy task. All she could think about was Nathen. Knowing that he was injured, but not knowing how severe his injuries were, was tearing her apart. He had told her he was all right, but that didn't ease her concern for his well-being. Authia needed to gain control of the situation. She needed to find some way to contact Nathen. She needed to find out the extent of Casandra's gift. Maybe she could convince Casandra to let her read her. Maybe then she'd find out just how powerful Casandra was. A half hour later, Authia was given her opportunity as Casandra entered her hut. At first, Casandra remained standing at the entrance. To Authia, it appeared as if she was deciding whether she wanted to approach Authia or keep her distance. It was Authia who spoke first.

"You can come closer. I don't bite... much."

"Well, I do."

Authia gently rubbed her cheek. She was sure that it was

still red from the slap, and she could feel the blood that had dried on the edges of the three gouges. "Yes, I remember."

"I don't appreciate being threatened."

"And I don't appreciate being taken prisoner."

"You speak as if you share the same gifts as us priestesses. I want you to prove it. Then maybe I'll consider releasing you."

"Maybe consider. You're going to have to do better than that."

"You can meld with me. Can you foresee the future? Can you produce a vision of things past, present, and future?"

"Yes. But I need a vessel to obtain my vision from. Care to volunteer?"

Casandra stood there and stared at Authia, then turned to face the guard. "If at any time I'm in distress, I want you to shoot an arrow straight through her heart without hesitation." The guard leaned his spear against the wall of the hut, picked up his bow, and pulled it back. However, he aimed it at the ground by Authia's feet. Not where his Mistress instructed him to aim. A fact that did not escape Authia. Casandra sat next to Authia. "Tell me, how do you wish to accomplish this?"

"Well, I could use a strand of your hair. Holding hands produces a stronger vision."

Casandra held out her hands, which Authia readily accepted. As most times, the vision came to her in a blur, swirling in a pool of mist. Authia closed her eyes and concentrated on Casandra. The vision began to take shape, and when it finally cleared, Authia could see Dena lying on the ground, motionless. Tamara was trying to meld with Dena. How was it that Casandra didn't see or hear the meld? The vision dissipated, but just as Authia was going to let go of Casandra's hands, another vision came forth. It was of herself, bound and gagged, lying in a strange hut. Then the vision left and Authia opened her eyes and let go of Casandra's hands. "What have you done to Dena?"

"Why do you ask?"

"I saw her lying on the ground. Is she dead?"

"No. She'll be fine. She just will no longer be part of my family. Her powers have left her. Did you see anything else?"

"I saw that you won't be keeping your word. Where are you planning to take me?"

* * * *

Casandra was taken aback. She told no one of her plan to move Authia. So, the outsider did possess the power of sight. All the more reason to dispose of her. But she must be careful. There was no telling how strong her gift was. Could she remain in the spirit world? Did she have the power to inflict punishment when she was in spirit form? Casandra could not be certain. Maybe killing her was not the best way to deal with the situation. No, she'd have to keep her alive, imprisoned in the hut. At least until she learned the extent of the outsider's powers. As far as the tribe was concerned... she would tell them that the prisoner was dangerous and would remain in the hut until such time that the third person revealed himself.

Casandra smiled at Authia. "That is none of your concern. Now it's my turn."

Before Authia realized what was happening, Casandra had grabbed a handful of her hair.

* * * *

Authia grasped at Casandra's hands, desperately trying to pull her away, but Casandra grip was too tight. *Block her,* she thought to herself. *She can't find out the truth.* Authia used all the skills that her mother taught her. She flooded her mind, her thoughts, with memories of her battle with Serena. That was what she would show Casandra. Nothing more... she hoped. Five minutes later, Casandra stepped back and looked apprehensively at Authia.

"You are strong. You were able to block me." Casandra took a deep breath. "I've decided that you are a threat to me and to everything I stand for. You'll be dealt with."

"I didn't see death in the visions I retrieved from you. So, what are you planning to do with me?"

Casandra just laughed as she left the hut. "You'll see. Very soon."

* * * *

Waiting outside of the hut for Casandra was Tamara. "So, Mother, does she possess the gift?"

"Walk with me. We will talk in privacy. By the way, is Dena awake?"

"No. She still sleeps. Can she ever regain her gift?"

"No. The transfer only works once. I don't know why, but once a priestess decides to become one with the tribe, she can never take it back. I know this, for a priestess tried it once before. She fell in love with a warrior. It didn't work out and she couldn't regain her gift. No matter what she tried."

"That is sad. Have you decided what we will be doing with the outsider?"

"Yes. And I'll need your assistance."

"I will help however you need me."

They entered the priestesses' hut to find Dena awake and sitting up. "You're free to go."

"And where should I go, sister? Am I still welcomed in

the family hut?"

Casandra snorted. "Of course not. You disgraced your family. We want nothing to do with you. Find your own way in the village." Casandra thought for a second. "And stay away from the prisoner. If I find you anywhere near her, you'll share her fate. Do I make myself clear?"

"Perfectly."

* * * *

Dena did exactly what she wasn't supposed to do. She headed straight for the hut that Authia was held a prisoner in. The guard on the outside of the hut blocked her way to the entrance.

"I can't let you pass. You know the rules."

"And rules are made to be broken. As the entire tribe probably knows by now, I no longer have my powers. So, tell me. How am I a threat to you?"

"You're no threat. But I must obey the High Priestess' orders."

"I'm going in whether you like it or not. You'll have to use force to keep me out." The guard grasped Dena's arm as she tried to enter the hut.

"I'm sorry, Dena. You may not be a threat, but my Mistress is. I can't let you pass."

"I knew you'd be loyal. So, I'm going to make it easy for you." She took a packet from her waistband. One of many that she'd hidden before she'd left for the outside world. Carefully she unwrapped it, then blew its contents into the guard's face. Within seconds he was on the ground, motionless. "I may not have my powers, but my potions still work." She stepped over the guard and entered the hut. The guard within the hut immediately raised his bow and placed himself between Dena and Authia. Dena looked at him, puzzled. "Why do you protect the prisoner?"

He did not lower his bow, but instead, stared deep into Dena's eyes. "I've made my choice. I'll protect my Lord's mate to my death."

"Good. Now lower your bow, for we're on the same side."

Authia stepped from behind her protector. She ran to Dena and threw her arms around Dena's neck. "Dena, I thought you were dead!"

"Well, that still could come to pass. Casandra made it very clear that I wasn't to see you. When she finds out I was here... well, her anger will know no bounds." Dena turned to the guard. "My stay will be longer if you replace the guard outside."

"Dena, his name is Cameron and he's loyal to Nathen." Authia turned to Cameron, who was waiting for her approval. "Go ahead and do as she says."

"Yes, my Mistress." Cameron dragged the unconscious guard into the hut, then went to stand guard himself.

"Please sit, Authia. There's much I have to tell you."

"Dena, is there any way I can find out how Nathen is doing?"

"Tamara is blocking her mother from seeing her melds. You'll be able to meld with Tamara. As far as melding with our Lord... only Tamara knows the answer to that."

"It's killing me not knowing how he's doing."

"Our Lord is strong, and he has his people to help him."

"But how's he going to find them?"

Dena smiled. "He's already with them, for they were at the falls when we were there."

"How do you know that?"

"Before I passed through the falls, I paid a visit to Arman. I told him what I was doing and suggested he wait by the falls to help me protect our Lord."

"Who's Arman?"

"He's the leader of the outcasts. Don't waste time with concern about our Lord. You must find a way to protect yourself. Casandra believes that you're a threat to her. However, she doesn't know the true extent of your gift. That's what's going to keep you alive. Tell her things that only she will know. Infer that you'll get your revenge if anything should happen to yourself or to our Lord."

"And how am I to tell her things that only she'd know?"

Tamara's thoughts came alive in Authia's and Dena's mind. *You will be my puppet and I the puppeteer. I will meld with you when you are with my mother. I will tell you things that only my mother knows. I have been listening to her conversations. Even those she has within herself. It saddens me that my mother is so full of hate and evil. It saddens me more that I must go through you to stop her. Do as I say, speak as I would, and we will keep you alive. I am working on a way to take away my mother's gift so that she becomes as Dena. She will no longer be a threat then.*

How are you going to accomplish that?

By locating her original essence. Once I have that in my possession, we can control my mother. Tamara went quiet for just a second, then frantically melded with Dena. *Dena... leave... my mother is on her way.*

* * * *

As Dena left the hut, Authia reached out to Tamara. *Wait! How can I reach Nathen?*

He is fine and with his people. Do not try to meld with him now. It is too dangerous. And with that, Tamara was gone.

Authia could hear Casandra yelling at Cameron. "Why are you here? Where's the man that's supposed to be guarding this hut?"

"He's in the hut, my Mistress. I heard nothing from outside, so I checked on him and found him on the ground. I brought him into the hut and took his place."

It became quite, and Authia strained to hear anything she could. Then Casandra spoke again. "You did well. Have you seen Dena?"

"No, my Mistress. Do you expect her?"

"Oh yes, I do." Casandra left Cameron to enter the hut.

"Miss me?" Authia's tone dripped heavy with sarcasm.

Casandra examined the guard and found traces of white powder on his face. "Did Dena come visit you?"

"I thought she was laying on the floor of your hut?"

"You don't fool me. You know more than what you're telling."

Authia just smiled. Then Tamara came to her. *She is carrying one of her packets in the folds of her gown. She is deciding if she should use it on you. The packet is meant to vanquish you from our existence.*

Authia stepped a little closer to Casandra. "You know, I've always wanted to know what kind of spell you put on your packets. Take the one that you carry with you now." Casandra's face went pale. "You mean to destroy me with it. I saw Serena use one once, in a dream. But I'm not dreaming now. Go ahead, use your packet. And then wait and see what I can do."

* * * *

Casandra did not utter one word. She left Authia and headed straight for the priestesses' hut. Once there she paced, continually walking around the fire pit, her mind racing with the new knowledge that the outsider could see events that were about to transpire. She was about to send for her daughter when Tamara entered the hut.

"You wish to see me, Mother?"

"Your gift to sense when I need you is getting stronger."

"Does that please you?"

"It'll serve you well when you are high priestess."

"How can I help you, Mother?"

"I have decided that we can't kill the outsider. She's strong. Her powers may be greater than I originally anticipated."

"So, what do you want to do with her?"

"The birthing hut. She will live out her remaining years in the birthing hut."

"The birthing hut actually exists? I have heard stories of strong magic and evil that exists in the jungle to the south of us. It is said that the birthing hut exists in the centre of the darkest of all evil. If that is where you are sending her, how will you get her there?"

Casandra turned her back to Tamara and grinned ever so wickedly. "You, my daughter, are going to take her there."

CHAPTER TWENTY-NINE

Night fell upon the jungle, encasing Nathen's camp in total darkness. They dared not start a fire at the risk of alerting the main village of their whereabouts. Nathen remained on the outskirts of the camp, alone. He sat on the ground, with his back resting against a large palm tree. He missed Authia and he missed his son. He worried for Authia, for there was no telling what Casandra was doing to her. The only comfort he could allow himself was the knowledge that she wasn't hurt. Nathen would sense her pain if Casandra had seriously injured her. He rested his head against the tree and closed his eyes. *Please, someone, meld with me. Assure me that my love is not suffering at the hands of Casandra.*

It took a few minutes, but Nathen's prayer was answered. *My Lord, it is Tamara. My Mistress tells me you were injured. How are you?*

Nathen's eyes flew open. *Tamara! How's Authia? Is she safe?*

She is fine, my Lord, and under my care. Do not meld with her. At least not now. I can block my melds from my mother mostly because she does not suspect what I am doing. However, she is focused on my Mistress. She will hear any meld that you two share. Again, I respectfully ask, my Lord... how are you?

I'm fine. Please tell Authia that I'm all right and I've found Arman.

Arman! He is with you?

Yes. You know of him?

You will be well taken care of. Trust Arman, for his heart only know kindness.

Tamara ended the meld, and Nathen felt at peace. What was his next move? He had to try to convince twenty grown men not to be afraid of a place that they'd heard so many stories about. Stories of the evil that resonated from the very area he wanted to hide in. Convince them that, in fact, there was no evil. At least not at the birthing hut. The only evil that existed for them was Casandra. Nathen thought of Charles. He could use his wisdom, his insight into the many decisions he had to make.

"You look deep in thought." Arman sat on the ground in front of Nathen. He passed him a container of water and a stick that was covered in cooked meat.

"I'm trying to decide on how I'm going to approach your men."

"Well, for one thing, you can start by referring to them as your men. If you're truly our Lord, then we're your servants, ready to do your bidding. Why not try talking to the eight that are here right now."

"Eight? What happened to the other two?"

"My Lord, I know it pains you to be separated from your mate. I know you worry about her. And I know the high priestess. We'll remain here, close by, in case we're needed. Meanwhile, the two men I sent will bring the remaining ten men to us. Then it's all up to you, my Lord."

"Not an easy task." Nathen took a bite of the meat and washed it down with the water. "I'm going to the birthing hut. If my people see me there, then maybe it'll be enough to trust that evil doesn't exist there. However, I need you to show me the way."

"It'd be my honour." Arman caught the attention of two of his men and motioned for them to join him. "I'm taking our Lord to the birthing hut." The two men looked at each other, then back at Arman. They were panic-stricken by what they were hearing. Nathen could see the fear in their eyes. "Our Lord believes that evil doesn't reside there, and he's prepared to prove it by staying at the birthing hut. It's my intention to stay with our Lord. To protect him. I want you two to take care of the camp. Send word when the rest of the men arrive."

The two men bowed, then left to join the rest of the men.

"There's no need for you to stay with me."

"There is every need. My purpose, what I've lived my life for, is to accomplish one thing. And that one thing is that if a son of Joshawa should return, it's my duty to keep him safe. To keep you, my Lord, safe. I'll stay by your side as long as you'll have me."

Nathen was overwhelmed by the loyalty that Arman gave to him. He didn't know Nathen. He didn't know what kind of man he was. For that matter, Arman didn't know with any certainty that Nathen was the son of Joshawa. He trusted in a parchment that was centuries old. Dena and Tamara could see Nathen for who he was through their gift. Arman put all his faith into those two women. He believed because they believed. "I'm grateful for your loyalty, and I welcome your company. When did you want to leave?"

"In the morning, my Lord. It's too dangerous to risk moving at night." Arman stood. "Come, we'll sleep as a group." Nathen followed Arman to the inner circle of the camp. He lay down on the ground without the benefit of a sleeping bag or blanket. Four men sat around him, protecting him. They would alternate halfway through the night so that the guards would be fresh and awake. Nathen closed his eyes and envisioned Authia. How he longed to see her. Tamara had assured him that Authia was all right. But, under the circumstances, Nathen would have preferred to see for himself. As he fell asleep, he tried thinking of a way to get closer to the village. Closer to Authia.

* * * *

It was the dead of night when Tamara left the family hut and silently made her way to the priestesses' hut. In the family hut, Casandra and the rest of her family were fast asleep. Tamara knew that there was only one way to defeat her mother. She had to find her mother's essence. The original packet. All priestesses hid their original packets for fear of them being used against them. Tamara stood in the middle of the priestesses' hut, surveying her surroundings. The packet was in the hut, somewhere. It had to be. Her mother would have it hidden in plain sight. Some mundane item that would normally not attract attention.

Tamara began her search sifting through the shelves and the table, looking for anything that could possibly be the vessel that held her mother's essence. But after two hours of intense searching, she came up with nothing. Her mother would keep it close to her, so if it was not in the priestesses' hut, where else could it be? There were only two other places that she could think of. The family hut or the gathering hut. It was getting late. She had to return before she was missed. She would continue her search another day and, she hoped, find what her Mistress needed to put an end to her mother's tyranny.

* * * *

Authia sat on the ground of her hut, tenderly touching her swollen cheek. With only a slap, Casandra managed to bruise and swell the left side of Authia's face. Not to mention leaving three gouges that ran from her temple to just below her cheekbone. Since she had no mirror, she could only examine the gouges by touch. They didn't seem to be too deep and had already stopped bleeding. *I owe you one.* Cameron knelt beside her. "You've been injured. Is there something I can get you?"

Authia smiled at her protector. "No. If my injury is tended to, then Casandra will know you helped me. I need to keep you here to protect me."

"And that's what I'll do. You should get some sleep." Cameron looked around but saw no blanket or sleeping mat. He stood and went to talk to the man guarding the outside of the hut. A few minutes later, Authia was given a sleeping mat and blanket.

"Thank you, Cameron. Could you get me something to drink and maybe something to eat? I promise, I won't leave the hut."

Cameron returned with water and a piece of bread. Authia thanked Cameron, ate her meagre meal, then crawled under her blanket and stared up at the roof.

She wanted to be with Nathen so badly. She wanted to know that he was all right. But she knew that melding with Nathen would only put him in danger. So, she lay there, alone, trying to figure a way to overthrow a priestess as powerful as Casandra.

Chapter Thirty

Nathen stirred in his sleep. Visions of Authia bound and gagged, lying on the ground, filled his mind. She was not alone, for a priestess was there dressed in her ceremonial gown. She was chanting while leaning over Authia's body. Authia started to convulse, desperately trying to breathe. Nathen roared in his sleep, which not only woke him but also the four men camped around him. Nathen sat up, sweat running down his face, his breathing laboured.

Arman immediately came to his side. He stood, machete in hand, ready to protect his Lord. "What troubles you, my Lord?"

"Nothing. Just a bad dream. Actually, I think my dream was a premonition. I believe that Casandra plans to hurt Authia. We have no time. We must leave for the birthing hut now."

"Yes, my Lord." Arman turned to face the seven men who were all waiting for instructions. "Stay here. Wait for the rest of our men. Tuval, you'll come with us. Once we reach the birthing hut, you'll return here to assure our men that it's safe." Tuval did not say a word. He walked over to where he'd been sleeping and retrieved his bow and spear.

Nathen watched in awe as his men were prepared to dutifully follow his every command. He stood, ignoring the pain in his shoulder and calf, and surveyed the eight men that made up the small group whose only objective was to protect him. They were not your ordinary men. They were part of the village of the Lion people. With these people,

Nathen was no longer different. He belonged to the tribe. He was one of them. It didn't take long for Nathen to find the words that needed to be said.

"I want each of you to know that I'm honoured to have such loyal companions. I want you to believe me when I say that where we're going is a safe place. Evil doesn't attach itself to inanimate objects. It comes from a living, breathing soul. One that's filled with hatred, jealousy, and contempt. The evil that we'll be fighting isn't at the birthing hut. It's in the village, and it has a name... Casandra. Evil did happen at the birthing hut, for that's where my mother and father were murdered. But evil doesn't live there. The birthing hut will be a perfect place for us to regroup and decide what our next plan of action will be. And, if we work together, we'll be able to vanquish the evil that plagues our village. We'll be able to defeat Casandra. I know this to be possible, for I recently defeated a priestess named Serena." The men all looked at each other in disbelief, for they knew that name. "She was a priestess that lived in the main village centuries ago, and since her time her family has been ruling you, our people, based on lies and deception. Their rule ends now, with me. I'll see to the destruction of Casandra and all the evil that surrounds her. Bow if you agree with me, if you are unafraid to follow me. Or stand and be heard." Nathen drew a breath of relief as each of his men bowed to their Lord.

* * * *

Authia awoke and, for a minute, she was unaware of her surroundings. Then slowly it all came back. *Right... Casandra... that's why I am here.* She looked up to find Cameron standing over her. "Good morning. How long have you been standing there?"

"Just a few minutes. Can I get you anything?"

"Yes." Authia threw her blanket off and stood. "I want to see Casandra."

"The High Priestess? All right, my Mistress, but I don't understand."

Authia smiled at her protector. "You will. Now go get her, please."

Cameron went to speak to the guard standing outside. After a short conversation, the guard left, supposedly in search of Casandra. Cameron returned to his post. "I hope my Mistress knows what she's doing. The High Priestess is very angry when she's disturbed."

"She's already disturbed." Cameron appeared to be confused by the comment. "You know, good, I want her upset. I want her to see that she doesn't frighten me."

"But she should. She is capable of the dark arts. She could harm you in ways that would torment your very soul."

Authia remained standing as Casandra barged into the hut. She was dressed in only her animal skins. Unlike the other women in the village, Casandra's top, tanned a soft brown, completely covered her breasts. The loincloth that wrapped around her waist fell to just above her knees. "What, you don't know how to knock? Just because I summoned you doesn't mean that you have to forget your manners."

Authia could tell that Casandra was livid. "You summon no one. You have no power here."

"Says you."

"You are a mere insignificant nuisance. One that I plan to deal with... soon!"

Tamara came to Authia. *She plans to take you to the birthing hut. It is far from the village. No one has gone there in many years. They say evil lives there.*

"Let me guess." Authia slowly circled Casandra as if sizing her up. When she was face to face with her, she stopped. Authia smiled at Casandra like the cat that ate the canary. "You plan to take me away from the village." Authia reached out and touched Casandra's arm. Casandra immediately pulled away. "To a place far from here... but not too far. Evil lives there, though it used to be a place of joy... of bringing in the new... of birth."

* * * *

Casandra was shaking she was so scared and angered. How could the outsider know of things that had not yet come to pass? How could she, a mere outsider, be no different than herself? If the village knew about her gifts, Casandra would have to present her to the entire tribe, and they would decide her fate. Casandra could not let that happen. "You know nothing. You're a mere trickster, nothing more."

"If I'm just a mere trickster, then why do you fear me?"

"I don't fear you!"

Authia laughed. "Oh, but you do. You're hoping that whatever evil possesses the place you're taking me to, that it'll deal with me. Keeping your hands clean, so to speak. If you don't fear me, then present me at the gathering hut."

"Do you honestly think that my people would accept you? Embrace you as one of them?"

"Maybe not your people, but Nathen's people will." Casandra looked dumbfounded. "Yes, that's his name. Nathen, son of Joshawa. The rightful ruler of this tribe."

Casandra went to strike Authia, but Authia caught her wrist before she made contact. "Once is all you get. Try it again, and I'll fight back." She let go of Casandra's hand. Casandra backed up. "Smart move. Look, Casandra, I don't want to make an enemy of you. I'm not here to take your rule away from you."

Casandra knew that Authia was lying. Why else would she be here if not to pave the way for the son of Joshawa?

Authia continued. "All I want is for you to share it with Nathen. He'll need your wisdom and your guidance."

"I'm not sharing anything with anyone." Casandra went to turn around but stopped and looked back at Authia. "You have no idea who you're dealing with. I'm tired of playing games with you. You'll remain here, and I'll deal with you in ways that you could never dream of."

Casandra stormed out of the hut, and as she made her way to the priestesses' hut, she smiled, a smile of hatred and contempt. Casandra had an idea on how to deal with the outsider. Something more permanent than the birthing hut. An idea that involved the darkest of spells.

* * * *

Nathen, Arman, and Tuval began their hike toward the birthing hut. Tuval led the way, cutting through the dense foliage with his machete. Arman stayed in back, protecting his Lord. Nathen turned to Arman. "How far is this birthing hut?"

"Not far, my Lord. We'll reach it fairly soon. If your mother and father were killed at the birthing hut, does that mean you were born there?"

"Yes. My parents were killed the minute I was born."

"I don't understand. You're saying that Lord Joshawa is your father. That your bloodline ends with you. There are no others. How is that possible? How can you be the blood son of Joshawa?"

"Serena cursed my father and me. For the past two centuries, I lived for twenty-nine years in the outside world. Then, before I turn thirty, Serena would kill me. She would then summon my spirit, and I'd be reborn to an outsider."

"Then you're truly our Lord. How old are you, my Lord?"

"I just turned thirty a few months ago."

Arman smiled as he nodded. "This is good news. There's a ritual we must perform. You're of age, and it's time for you to become a man. Only then can you rule as our Lord."

"We can perform this ritual once Casandra is defeated. And only if the tribe excepts Authia as my mate." Nathen was focused on Arman as he spoke and didn't see Tuval stop until he ran into the back of him. Arman grabbed Nathen's arm and pulled him back. He then stood in front of Nathen, his machete raised and ready.

"Why have you stopped?"

"We're being followed." Tuval pointed to his right. "There. He has been following us since we left our camp."

Arman scanned the jungle but saw no one. "Why are you just telling me of this now?"

"Because he has kept his distance." Tuval raised his bow, pulled it back, and aimed. "But now he chooses to come closer."

Arman shouted to the vastness of the jungle. "We know that you're there. Come forward, and you'll not be harmed." To the astonishment of Nathen, Jamya came forth.

Nathen walked around Arman and stood in front of Jamya. "Why are you here? You do realize that you can't harm me without jeopardizing your own life?"

"I've come to speak to you. To discover on my own if you are truly the son of Joshawa."

"I am. Your priestesses know that as fact."

"Dena's no longer a priestess, and the high priestess isn't admitting to anything."

The fact that Jamya didn't mention Tamara did not go unnoticed by Nathen. He shot a warning glance toward Arman. If Jamya didn't know of Tamara's involvement, Nathen wanted to keep it that way. "Look at me, Jamya. Do I not resemble your people? You know I came from the outside world. You know that Dena believes that I'm who I claim to be. Whether she's a priestess or not, deceit doesn't rule her heart. She has sacrificed everything not only for me but also for you and every person in your village. Casandra thinks of only herself. She doesn't care about her people. Tell me, Jamya, is your village a place of peace and contentment?"

Jamya slowly shook his head. "There has been no peace and contentment for many years. The people live in fear. Fear of the high priestess and what she can do. I want to believe in you, but I must know. Will you do everything in your power to combat the evil that lives in our village?"

"Yes. But I can't do it alone. I need strong, determined men that are loyal to me. That will fight by my side. Are you one of those men? Bow if you are, or stand and be heard."

Jamya immediately bowed to his Lord.

Chapter Thirty-One

Casandra, dressed in her ceremonial gown, sat on the ground in the priestesses' hut. In front of her was a parchment rolled out revealing the incantations for a very old and treacherous spell. The parchment was weathered, its edging yellowed from age, though the writing was as bold as the day it was written. The spell, written in a language as old as time itself, came from the darkest of all spells and hadn't been used since Serena's time. Casandra was at odds with herself. Part of her would use the spell without hesitation. It was a perfect way to deal with the outsider. But, part of her was leery. The spell had not been used because the high priestesses of centuries ago deemed it unsafe. For once it was put in force, it could never be undone. Not without killing the victim of the spell and possibly the person who conjured it. But was that not what she wanted. The outsider gone, disposed of. It would cost Casandra, for she would have to incorporate part of her essence, her original essence, in order for the spell to work. Doing so put her at risk as well. She had to decide and soon. The outsider was becoming more combative. She was challenging Casandra. How long before she got the upper hand? Just how powerful was she? There was no way of telling without exposing her. Casandra stood and gently rolled the parchment up. She placed it on the table and retrieved two small clay vials. She thought of her daughter. "Come see me, my daughter. I've a job for you."

* * * *

Arman wasn't totally convinced of Jamya's loyalty to his Lord. "Do you know where the birthing hut is?"

"Yes. It's not far from here. Why do you ask?"

Arman passed Jamya his machete. Tuval immediately raised his bow. "Because that's where we're headed. You'll lead, but know this—Tuval's arrow will pierce your heart if you but try to attack our Lord."

"I know you have no reason to trust me. I'm the leader of the warriors. I can prove my trust by giving you the high priestess."

Nathen stepped forward. "And how can you give us Casandra?"

"She sent me into the jungle to kill you. If I return and tell her you're dead, she'll be at ease. She'll be off her guard and you, my Lord, can enter the village unchallenged."

"And how do you plan on accomplishing that?"

"Many of us warriors dream of protecting the Lord of our tribe. Of protecting a Lord that rules with kindness and strength. For years we've been forced to protect priestesses that rule with greed, hatred, and anger. Allow me to return to the village, and I'll bring to you the strength of the warriors!"

* * * *

Nathen listened to what Jamya had to say. If he was truthful, it could bring about the end of Casandra's rule far sooner than Nathen surmised. But if he was lying, Jamya could return with a force greater than what protected Nathen. It would seal his fate and Authia's. "Lead us to the birthing hut, and then we'll decide how truthful you actually are."

"If that's your wish." Jamya turned and started hacking

his way toward the birthing hut. Tuval followed, his bow at his side, pulled back, ready to release the arrow at a moment's notice. Arman took up the rear, protecting Nathen all the while keeping a watchful eye on Jamya.

* * * *

Tamara, dressed in animal skin, was heading toward Authia's hut when her mind filled with her mother's thoughts. She stood still and listened to what her mother had to say. *How strange.* She wondered why her mother would be seeking her out. She had never attempted that before. Tamara turned and headed back toward the priestesses' hut. She entered the hut to find her mother waiting, a small clay vial in each hand.

"Good, you heard me."

"Of course. What can I do for you, Mother?"

Casandra moved closer to her so what she had to say would go no further. "I've decided to vanquish the outsider."

Tamara looked at her mother, puzzled by what she said. "I thought that I was to bring her to the birthing hut. Have you changed your mind?"

"I believe that it would be too dangerous. The outsider's gifts are strong. She may harm you on the way, then escape. I can't permit her to join with Joshawa's son. If that were to happen, then my rule could be jeopardized."

The fact that Casandra was more worried about herself than her own daughter did not escape Tamara's notice. "And how do you plan to vanquish her?"

"With your help and an age-old spell."

"What spell is that, Mother?"

Casandra handed Tamara the two clay vials. "As far as the spell is concerned, you'll find out when it's time.

Meanwhile, I need you to fill those two vials."

Tamara examined the clay vials that she held in her hands, then looked up to face her mother. "With what shall I fill them?"

Casandra melded with Tamara. *In one vial, you must place strands of the outsider's hair. In the other her blood. You're to tell no one of what you're doing. Do you understand?*

Not really, Mother. How are you going to vanquish her with only strands of hair and blood?

You'll find out soon enough. Now leave me. Find a way to accomplish what I've asked you to do.

Are you going to tell the other priestesses? You will need their help, will you not?

I said no one!

Tamara knew not to push her mother further, so she turned and left the hut, lingering outside the entrance just long enough to witness her mother hiding a parchment behind the shelves that held the clay pots. Quietly she slipped away and headed straight to Authia's hut.

* * * *

Authia was bored out of her mind. She lay on the sleeping mat just staring up at the roof. It had been hours since anyone checked in on her. Tamara had not melded with her, and she had no idea how Nathen was doing. Maybe it was time to show her hand. The hut was only made with sapling trees. How hard could it be to escape? Especially with Cameron as her guard. Authia sat up so that she could face Cameron and was about to express her desire to break out when she heard Tamara's voice. Cautiously Authia stood and moved closer to the entrance. She listened to see if she could hear Casandra's as well. But it was only Tamara speaking to the guard.

Tamara entered the hut and looked questioningly at

Authia. "Is there something you need, my Mistress? Why are you so close to the entrance? My mother would not like that."

"Like I care what your mother likes or dislikes." Authia went back to her sleeping mat, sitting on it cross-legged as she faced Tamara.

"You should care. Angered, my mother is capable of horrible things." Tamara went to join Authia on her mat while Cameron moved to stand in front of the entrance. "My mother is afraid of you. Of what you are capable of doing."

"Good. Maybe we can use that to our advantage. How would she react if I escaped from this hut and just showed up at her door?"

Tamara looked wide-eyed at Authia. "You must not. If you escape, she will punish the men that guard you. She will be ruthless."

"What would she do?"

"My mother does not inflict usual forms of punishment. She keeps her people loyal to her because they are afraid of what she can do. She is gifted in the dark arts. And she is not afraid to use them. She uses spells and curses to cause her victims great pain and suffering. That is the reason I am here." Tamara held out the two clay vials.

"What are those?"

"My mother has requested that I collect your hair and your blood."

"What would she want those for?"

"My mother believes that if she hurts you herself that you will exact revenge on her. However, if she uses a method that does not directly involve her, then maybe she will be immune to your sorcery."

"So, she's going to use my hair and blood to hurt me indirectly. What's she going to do? Make a voodoo doll of me."

"I do not understand. What is voodoo?"

"Witchcraft. You make a doll with the strands of the person's hair, and you can inflict pain on them by hurting the doll."

Tamara thought for a moment. "I saw my mother hide a parchment before I came here. If what you say is true, then maybe that parchment contains a spell that will create this doll that you speak of. I must read this parchment. I need you to distract my mother."

"That won't be a problem. But what about the vials. Isn't she expecting you back with those filled?"

"Yes, but I am afraid to do so. My mother is determined to kill you. Apparently, she requires these vials to complete her spell. However, if I choose not to fill these vials, she will."

"Okay, so you take some of my hair. She would know right away if it was my hair or not. But what about the blood. What if we give her someone else's blood?"

"Then, depending on the spell, they could be cursed as well."

Cameron stepped forward. "Take my blood. It would be my honour."

Authia looked up at Cameron. "I couldn't put you in that much danger."

"I'm here to protect you." Cameron offered his hand to Tamara. "Take my blood. I accept the consequences."

Tamara laid the clay vials on the ground, then stood and held out her hand to Cameron. "Your spear, please." Cameron passed his spear to Tamara, then held his hand out for her to extract the blood. "No, I will not take it from your hand." She turned the spearhead toward the ground and nicked Cameron's ankle. Authia immediately picked up one of the vials, removed the stopper, and held it tight against the cut so that the blood flowed into the vial. Once the vial was almost full, she replaced the stopper.

Authia focused on Cameron. "Are you sure? There's no guarantee that you'll not be inflicted by whatever curse Casandra's planning on."

"I understand, and I accept whatever path lies ahead."

Authia smiled at Cameron, then yanked out a couple of her own hairs, placing them in the second vial. "There is one thing left to do." With that, Tamara sliced Authia's palm, then passed the spear back to Cameron. "If the spell does not work and my mother inspects you, she will see where I cut you to retrieve the blood." Tamara looked over to Cameron. "A cut on your ankle has a good chance of going unnoticed. I hope that our deception will counteract whatever evil my mother is planning. I will go to her now and tell her that you insist on seeing her."

Authia handed both vials to Tamara, who secured them in the waistband of her loincloth. "I'll keep her busy. How much time do you need?"

"A few minutes. I know where the parchment is. Cameron, bind her wound and clean off yours." Tamara bowed to Authia. "I will protect you... with my life..."

Chapter Thirty-two

Jamya swung at the dense vegetation as he made his way to the birthing hut. He had mixed feelings when it came to the birthing hut and the land that surrounded it. He'd grown up on the stories of the evil that resided there. But as he forged closer, a single thought came to him. The stories were all told to the village by the high priestesses of the time. Those stories were kept alive by the high priestesses that ruled the tribe over the many years. He glanced back at Nathen, which resulted in an arrow aimed directly at his chest. He turned back, his mind running wild with questions, uncertainties. If the high priestesses were lying about the existence of a son of Joshawa, the tribe's rightful Lord, maybe, just maybe, they were lying about the birthing hut as well. Jamya was about to find out, for as he cleared a section of vegetation, just a few feet away, he could see one of the walls of the birthing hut.

* * * *

Tamara entered the priestesses' hut and laid the clay vials down on the table next to all the clay pots. "I have done what you requested, Mother." She smiled innocently at her mother.

Casandra, on the other hand, looked at Tamara with skepticism. "She allowed you to fill these vials with no hesitation."

"She was adamant about seeing you. She requested that I

bring her to you. She paid no attention to what I was doing. Her focus was all on you. Shall I bring her to you?"

"Think, child. If you bring her to me, then more of our people will see her. What if she displays one or more of her gifts? I don't want the entire village demanding that she be brought forth. I'll go see her." Casandra took a couple of steps toward the entrance, then hesitated as she turned to face her daughter. "Are you not coming with me?"

"No, Mother. The outsider made it quite clear that she wants to see you and only you. I will stay here and wait for your return."

* * * *

Casandra was leery of leaving her daughter alone in the hut. But really, what did she have to fear. Her daughter knew nothing of the parchment or what those vials were for. Casandra dismissed the deep-seated warning that something wasn't right. It had nothing to do with her daughter. It had everything to do with the outsider. All the more reason to destroy her as quickly as possible. "Suit yourself. I won't be long."

* * * *

Tamara stood at the entrance and waited until her mother disappeared into the hut which held her Mistress prisoner. Then she smiled at the guard standing next to the entrance. The guard nodded, moving over so that he was completely blocking the entrance. Knowing that it was safe, Tamara went in search of the parchment. She reached behind the shelving unit that contained the clay pots. At first, she felt nothing, but as she reached in as far as her arm would allow, her fingers touched what felt like rolled-up paper. Gingerly she pulled at the parchment until it was free from its hiding place. Tamara took the parchment, sat down on the ground, and gently unrolled it. What she read took her breath away. It was as her Mistress said... witchcraft. A spell that would take the very life of the person whose hair and blood were mixed with the essence of the priestess. The three had to be combined in a specific order for the spell to work.

Tamara read on in the hope of finding a counterspell, but instead, she found so much more. At the very bottom of the parchment, it was written that the priestess that relinquished a portion of her original essence for the spell may lose a portion of her gift. It was also written that if the ingredients were not pure or if the spell wasn't carried out precisely as it was inscribed, the life of the priestess could be forfeited as well as the person who contributed the blood and hair. Tamara's mind was reeling with the newfound information. She rolled up the parchment and returned it to its hiding place. Did her mother not know the consequences of the spell? She was notorious for seeing or hearing only what she wanted. Possibly, she hadn't read to the end of the parchment. Possibly, she had only read what she needed to know in order to destroy the outsider. Tamara had to act quickly. Her mother must not, under any circumstance, perform the spell.

* * * *

The four men gathered in what little clearing that was afforded to them by the jungle. The yard and the birthing hut were overrun with vegetation. Nathen separated himself from the group and started to walk the perimeter. The path surrounding the hut was clogged with ferns, vines, and young sapling trees. Nathen pulled apart the vines and sapling trees, pushing his way through until he came upon the entrance.

Inside, in the middle of the hut, grew a large tree. Its canopy reached high above the birthing hut through a hole in the roof. Nathen walked up to the tree and placed his hand on its massive trunk. Visions exploded around him. As he closed his eyes, he was brought back in time to when he was born. He watched as the entire scenario of his parents' death played out before him. Nathen opened his eyes and stared at the ground. He knew that beneath the tree were the remains of his parents. He looked around the hut. Very little remained of the original structure. There was just enough to keep the roof from falling to the ground. The birthing bed had rotted away along with anything else that was contained within the hut.

Arman joined Nathen. "Well, my Lord, what's your bidding?"

"The hut is too dangerous to stay in." Nathen turned to face Arman. "And by that, I mean the structure is unsafe. I don't sense any danger here. The aura of this place is of sadness and loneliness. There's no evil here."

"How is it that you, a Lord, can sense an aura? Only our priestesses have that ability."

"It's a gift I have possessed since I was a child. Send Tuval to our men. Have him tell them that it's safe to hide here. In the meantime, we'll clear an area to set up camp." Nathen and Arman left the birthing hut to join Jamya and Tuval. Nathen turned to Jamya. "How far are we from the village?"

"Far enough that we'll be safe. Close enough to execute any plan you may have."

"Will a fire be seen from the village?"

"Only if my warriors are paying attention to the southern border of our village. If I leave now, I can instruct my warriors to watch the western borders. I can also tell the High Priestess that you are dead. Which will give you a favourable advantage."

Nathen thought for a moment. Should he trust a man that only a couple of days ago had tried to kill him? "How will you prove that I am dead without a body?"

Jamya thought for a moment. "One of my warriors was recently killed in an animal attack. He stands as tall as you and is as big as you. He is buried along the western border. His grave is marked with a warrior shield. Take him and drop his body into the ravine that's to the east of us."

Arman interjected. "I know that ravine. It'll be rough going."

"That's what I am hoping on. When I tell the High Priestess that your body is at the bottom of that ravine, she may not want to venture out. However, if she does, she'll see what she wants to see and you, my Lord, will be free to do as you please."

"I'm putting a lot of faith in you, Jamya. There's one thing I want you to do for me to prove your loyalty."

"Anything, my Lord."

"After you inform Casandra of my death, you'll go visit my mate, Authia. Tell her that I've asked that she reads you. When she's finished, she'll know what to do." Jamya went to turn around but was stopped when Nathen grabbed his shoulder.

"Harm Authia, and I'll know. Harm Authia, and I'll kill you myself."

"Understood, my Lord. Believe me when I say that she'll be well protected." Jamya left, disappearing into the jungle.

* * * *

Authia was sitting cross-legged on her mat when Casandra entered. She was drawing shapes into the ground with her finger. "What's this that you are drawing?"

Authia looked up at Casandra with a smile of contempt. "You don't recognize a spell when you see one?"

Casandra eyed Authia cautiously. "What do you know of spells?"

Authia melded with Casandra. *As much if not more than you do.*

"When you're in my presence, you will speak to me."

Again, Authia melded with Casandra. *I thought that's what I was doing.*

"I demand that you stand before me."

Authia spoke directly to Casandra. "No pretty please with that?" Casandra stared at Authia, her anger clearly defined in her expression. "Guess not." Authia stood, wiped the dirt off her jeans, then approached Casandra until they were only a couple of feet apart. "Look, I've been in these clothes far too long. You want to make demands? Here are some of my own. I demand that I'm given clean clothes to wear. I demand that I get a proper meal. I demand that I'm allowed to bathe. I demand that you set me free from this hut and allow me to walk amongst your people."

Casandra took a step back. "You're in no position to make demands. We have no outsider clothes, and you're not permitted to dress as one of us. I'll have some food and a basin of water brought to you. You will not be bathing in the same waters that my people do. And under no circumstance are you allowed to leave this hut."

As Casandra spouted off, Tamara melded with Authia. *I have what I need. You no longer need to distract her.* Authia snickered at Casandra. "Well, I guess agreeing to half of my demands will have to do. You can leave now. I no longer need you or for that matter want your company."

* * * *

Casandra stormed out and headed straight for the

priestesses' hut. It was time to end the life of the outsider. However, when she reached the hut, she was met by Jamya.

"I trust you have good news for me."

"The best, my Mistress."

"Follow me." Casandra led Jamya into the priestesses' hut to find her daughter waiting for her. "Leave us. I must speak to Jamya in private."

"But, Mother, if I am to learn from you, should I not witness how you handle your warriors?"

"Yes, you're right. But not in this instance. Leave! I'll summon you when I need you."

* * * *

Tamara bowed to Casandra and left the hut. She stood next to the communal fire pit and addressed her mother, though Casandra would not hear her. "My mind is open, Mother. I will hear your words." Tamara felt the blood drain from her face as she heard her mother rejoice with the news that the Lord was dead!

CHAPTER THIRTY-THREE

How was Tamara to tell Authia that her mate was dead? All hope of regaining peace to the tribe was gone. Tamara gazed in the direction of the hut that imprisoned Authia. Maybe, if it was the priestesses that were destined to rule, Authia could take her place as the rightful ruler of the tribe. Tamara's mind began to race with the question of how she was to prove Authia's lineage. As she stood there desperately trying to fight back the tears, Jamya passed her and headed straight for Authia's hut. He spoke to the guard, then entered the hut. Tamara quickly checked behind her toward the priestesses' hut. Her mother was still inside rejoicing in the news of her Lord's death. Without giving it much thought, Tamara also headed for Authia's hut. As she entered, she overhead Jamya saying that it was the request of his Lord. Authia looked up to Tamara.

"What's wrong, Tamara?"

Tamara stared directly at Jamya. "What is your business here?"

"I'm making sure that this prisoner is secure."

Tamara slightly tilted her head. "I do not believe you."

"No disrespect, but it's not your place to question me. However, it is my place to question as to why you're here."

Authia raised her hand. "Okay, you two, stop it." She looked toward Jamya. "Give me your hands." Jamya obeyed, placing his hands in hers. Tamara watched as Authia closed her eyes. Within a couple of minutes, she was smiling. She opened her eyes and nodded toward Jamya.

"Tamara, please tell Nathen that Jamya is pure of heart. That he's loyal only to him."

Tamara could not believe what she was hearing. "I do not understand. I thought that our Lord... You told my mother that our Lord was dead."

"I gather that you serve our Lord as I do."

"Yes. Now explain yourself."

"Our Lord is alive and well. I told the High Priestess what she wanted to hear. She'll be vulnerable now." Jamya headed for the entrance. "I have to instruct my men to guard the western border. Make them blind to what's happening to the south."

He left the hut to Tamara shaking her head. "I feared the worst." She closed her eyes and melded with Nathen. *My Lord, you are to know that Jamya is pure of heart. That he is loyal to you.*

Thank you, Tamara. How's my wife?

She is well. She has many protectors.

Tell her that I love her dearly, and I'll see her soon.

Yes, my Lord. Tamara opened her eyes and smiled at Authia. "Our Lord misses his mate. He loves you very much."

"And I love him. I'd do anything to keep him safe."

Tamara went to leave, then reconsidered. She turned back to face Authia. "I have read the parchment that contains the spell that my mother wishes to use on you."

"And?"

"It is as you said... witchcraft. And it is very dangerous. Not only to you but also to Cameron and my mother."

"So, how do we keep her from conjuring the spell?"

"The easiest way would be to find where she hides her original essence. Without it, she is no longer a threat, and you can overpower her. The only other way is to make sure that I am there when she attempts the spell."

"And how would that help us?"

"By being there, I could create a situation that would cause my mother to question the safety of performing the spell. I will do anything to protect you. Do not worry, my Mistress."

Tamara left Authia, knowing that her plan had no guarantee. Her mother was unpredictable and so determined to see Authia die that she might risk anything to achieve her goal.

* * * *

Casandra was in her glory. The bastard son of Joshawa was dead. All she had left to do was deal with the outsider. Casandra left for the gathering hut, and on her way, she noticed that Jamya was repositioning his warriors. She stopped in the middle of the clearing and glared at him. What was he up to? He'd challenged her when she'd ordered the death of Dena and her Lord. Why the sudden change of heart? She approached Jamya, startling him as she came up behind him.

"May I help you, my Mistress?"

"What are you doing?"

"I have learned that a group that's loyal to Joshawa's bloodline lies in wait to the west of us. They're unaware of the death of this man claiming to be our Lord. They're also unaware that I know of them."

"And tell me, Jamya, how did you find out about them?"

* * * *

Jamya realized that Casandra was beginning to doubt him. He had to convince her. Everything depended on it. "I captured one of the men guarding this imposter. I persuaded him to tell me everything he knew."

"And where's this man now?"

"He rests with his false Lord."

Casandra thought for a moment. "I would like to see this resting place."

"It's treacherous, my Mistress. He's at the bottom of the ravine just to the east of us. I'd be honoured to show you."

* * * *

Where Jamya was anxious to have Casandra alone, Casandra knew better. She would send someone in her place. But whom could she trust? As she stood there thinking of that one person, Tamara came from the gathering hut. Casandra smiled. Yes, she would do.

* * * *

Nathen was at peace. Jamya could be trusted, and he would be a welcome addition to their group. For with him came the strength of the warriors. Nathen also knew that his beloved Authia was safe and unharmed. And to him that meant everything. Arman had built a small fire. The sun was beginning its descent, blanketing the area around the birthing hut in darkness. Nathen sensed Arman's uneasiness. He sat on the ground across the fire from Arman. "You're not totally convinced that we're safe here?"

"Sorry, my Lord, but you're right. I don't feel safe here."

Nathen looked around at his surroundings, his gaze coming to rest on the large tree that grew from inside the hut. "My life began here. I don't believe it'll end here. This place of birth cries out to be useful again. I feel its aura. It's saddened by what it has become. We'll give this place a purpose and it, in turn, will protect us."

"How do you know this? How will it protect us?"

"Look at the fire, Arman. Its glow doesn't penetrate the darkness that surrounds us. Trust me. Trust in your Lord. We'll be safe here. We should eat, but I know nothing of how to hunt in the jungle."

Arman grabbed his spear and stood. "I'll trust in you and this place. Let us see if it'll provide dinner for us."

Arman had only been gone ten minutes when he returned with a small animal skewered on a pole. He smiled at Nathen as he sat cross-legged on the ground, holding the animal over the fire.

* * * *

Casandra had Tamara follow her to the priestesses' hut, leaving Jamya to deal with his warriors. "I have a duty for you to perform."

"What is it, Mother?"

"You're to follow Jamya to the ravine east of here and confirm that the son of Joshawa is dead."

Tamara pretended to be surprised by the announcement. "He is dead? How did this happen?"

"Jamya killed him. He believes that the man he killed is a false Lord. Make sure that he continues this belief."

"Darkness is coming upon us. Shall we leave in the morning?"

"Of course. Oh, and make sure there are two bodies at the bottom of this ravine."

"Yes, Mother. I will be gone for some time. I trust that you will wait for me before you vanquish the outsider. I truly want to learn from you." Tamara smiled at her mother. "I think it is time that you teach me all I need to learn about the dark arts. Only then can I rule as you would wish."

Casandra embraced her daughter. "Yes, I'll wait for you." She stood back and gazed deep into her daughter's eyes, her hands resting on Tamara's shoulders. "I'll wait, for it will be your essence that we'll use to perform this spell. You, my daughter, will have the honour to vanquish the outsider yourself."

Chapter Thirty-Four

The sun rose over the horizon, its rays bathing the birthing hut in a warm, comforting light. Nathen awoke to find himself cradled in the roots of the tree that grew there. He looked around at his surroundings. How did he get there? He had no recollection of entering the hut during the night, never mind curling up in the roots of the tree to sleep. As he stood to leave, the aura of the birthing hut surrounded him, not unlike a blanket being wrapped around a small child. It called out to him in a voice he easily recognized. *You've done well, my son. You've found your way home. Know that I'm here to protect you and to help you in your fight. I can't leave the birthing hut, but I can keep you and your men safe while you're here. This tree marks your mother's and my resting place. As long as this tree stands, I'll be with you.*

How's this possible, Father? How is it that you are here?

That's not important. What is important is that I'm here. Now go to your men. Be patient, my son. You'll know when the time is right. Your beautiful bride will show you the way.

The aura dissipated before Nathen could question his father as to what part Authia played in the quest. For it was not just his father but Tamara and Dena who also believed that Authia was the key. After everything he'd been through at the hand of Serena, his melding with his father left Nathen with a profound sense that justice had not yet been served. The rule of the priestesses, Serena's bloodline, had to end. Only then would justice prevail.

Nathen left the birthing hut to find twenty men standing

tall and proud in the clearing that he and Arman had made earlier. As Nathen approached them, each and every one bowed to him. "Arman, I wasn't expecting our men so soon."

"They were motivated, my Lord. What's your bidding?"

"We wait here until we hear from Tamara. Apparently, my mate plays an integral part in defeating Casandra. She'll make the first move."

* * * *

Tamara awoke to find her mother's sleeping mat empty. Quickly she dressed, choosing the animal skin over her long robe. Tamara headed straight for the priestesses' hut. She entered to find her mother reading the parchment that was meant to vanquish her Mistress. "What parchment are you reading, Mother?"

Startled, Casandra looked up. She smiled every so smugly. "I didn't hear you enter. Come and see." Casandra moved to one side so Tamara could read the parchment. Before she reached the end, Casandra started rolling up the parchment. "Mother, I did not finish."

"That's of no consequence. We can't perform the spell until we retrieve your essence. Which we'll do once you have seen the body of the son of Joshawa."

"As you wish. I will seek out Jamya. The sun has risen. We can leave now."

Casandra placed an arm around her shoulders, lowered her voice, then whispered into Tamara's ear. "If there are not two bodies in that ravine, then you're to punish Jamya."

Tamara melded with her mother. *How do you wish me to punish him?*

Push him into the ravine. Put an end to his lies and deception.

And if there are two bodies?

Then Jamya will be rewarded for his loyalty. Casandra gave her daughter a gentle squeeze, then let go of her shoulders and left the hut. Tamara shook her head. Her mother's vindictiveness was becoming harsher. There wasn't much time. They were going to have to make a stand and make it soon.

* * * *

Dena had joined Authia in her hut. She brought her Mistress breakfast, which consisted of bread and fruit wrapped in a palm leaf. Dena risked everything being there, for if Casandra discovered her, Dena's punishment would be severe. "Is there anything else I can do for you, my Mistress?"

"Short of a clean pair of jeans and t-shirt, I can't think of anything. Are you privy to anything Casandra's doing?"

"No. I've been banished from the family hut. My family will no longer have anything to do with me." Dena placed the palm leaf in front of her Mistress, then sat down across from her. "I miss my family. Do you miss your son?"

"Immensely! I would give anything to hold him close to me. But I know it's not safe for him here. Tammy and Hansen will take good care of him. Keep him safe until I can return. For that matter, the entire village has promised that they will protect him with their lives."

* * * *

Unknown to Authia and Dena, Casandra was listening at the entrance. So, there was a child. Finally, she had what she needed to control the outsider. If Jamya proved to be faithful, she would send him to find the child. It was a day for revelations. She would find out just how loyal Jamya was. And she was going to have what she needed to defeat her enemy. To conquer the outsider. To finally put the bloodline of Joshawa to rest!

* * * *

The guard standing outside Authia's hut quietly called for Cameron. After a short conversation, Cameron returned inside the hut, his face heavy with concern. Authia took one look at him and frowned. "What's the problem, Cameron?"

"The High Priestess stood outside the entrance while you spoke of your son. The guard heard what you were saying, and if he heard you, then the High Priestess heard you as well."

Authia went white as a ghost.

* * * *

Jamya and Tamara met behind the gathering hut. Tamara was still wearing the animal skin instead of her robe. Jamya looked at her questioningly. "My priestess, I was hoping you'd be wearing your ceremonial robe. It would be the proper attire to greet our Lord, which I'm hoping to do after we see the ravine."

"First I must see the ravine. I know of this ravine, for I played there as a child. My robe would not be appropriate for such a perilous climb. I assume you have two bodies there?"

"Actually, my priestess, there's only one. But why must you see the ravine for yourself? You know our Lord is not dead."

"I must see it in order to appease my mother. I will meld with her when I am there. She will see what I see."

"I'll take you there, but there is but one body."

Tamara smiled at Jamya. "The ravine is deep. Bodies

could go unnoticed."

She and Jamya were about to leave when Dena came up to them. "We have a problem, Tamara."

"What problem could have you so upset, Dena?"

"Your mother. She knows of our Lord's child. She knows he's under the protection of a village. However, I don't know if she knows where the village is."

Tamara thought quickly. "Dena, can you make it to the outsiders' village and back before anyone notices you are gone?"

"Yes. But why wouldn't I stay at the outsiders' village and protect the child."

"Because, if you disappear, my mother may come to the conclusion that you have gone to protect the child. If you are missing, she will know where to look for the village. Go to the outsiders' village. My mother no longer has anyone patrolling the entrance to our valley. Warn the guardians of the child and return as quickly as possible. Our Mistress and I will cover for you if need be. Now go!"

Tamara watched as Dena casually walked toward the border of the village. She glanced over her shoulder at Tamara, then broke out in a full run, heading in the direction of the waterfall.

Tamara kept a close eye on Casandra as she returned to the priestesses' hut. Then Tamara melded with Authia. *My Mistress, know that Dena is on her way to warn the guardians of your child. Cover for her if you must. My mother will not find him.*

Can you guarantee me that, Tamara?

No. But I give you my word that there are many of us that are prepared to give their lives to save the life of your child. And with that, Tamara ended the meld.

The path to the ravine was as treacherous as Tamara recalled. No grass or vegetation of any sort grew on the barren rocks. Jamya, being as large as he was, turned out to be quite agile on his feet as he easily scaled the jagged face of the ravine. Tamara was not so fortunate. She found herself constantly losing her step, with Jamya, more than once, saving her from losing her balance altogether. When they finally reached the edge of the ravine, Tamara looked down into its depths and saw, lying on an outcrop of rock, a solitary body. It was a male lying face down. His hair, falling to the side, effectively concealed his face. Tamara took a deep breath, then melded with her mother. *Mother, are you with me?*

Yes, my daughter. What do you see?

Tamara peered over the edge of the ravine. *The ravine is very deep. I cannot see to the bottom.*

Are there two bodies! I feel as though you only see one.

I see one body barely caught on the edge of some rocks. He is tall, broad in the shoulders. Strange, Mother, but his hair is not like ours. The colouring is off. Does that mean anything to you? Tamara knew full well that the observation, as untruthful as it was, would appease her mother. For her mother knew that the Lord's hair was a golden red and not the fiery red of the tribe's hair.

I sense a second lying at the bottom. There are two auras here. Two distinct auras. Tamara stepped back from the ravine's edge. *Can you sense them also, Mother?* Tamara knew her mother was not capable of sensing auras. At least not to the degree that she could.

You'd have me believe that Jamya is worthy of our trust and our gratitude.

Is that not why you sent me here, Mother? To determine his worthiness?

Yes, my child. However, I would be more convinced if you had actually seen two bodies. That being said, I'll trust in your decision. Return home. Speak with Jamya. Learn what he knows. I have plans for him... and his family.

CHAPTER THIRTY-FIVE

Dena made it back to the outsiders' village in record time. The villagers were surprised to see her. But no one more so than Tammy and Hansen. Dena purposely ignored the villagers and headed straight for Joshawa's guardians. Tammy, dressed in cut-off jeans and a tank top, was cradling Joshawa in her arms. Hansen, shirtless and in shorts as well, was by her side. Dena's breath was laboured as she spoke to them. "You're in danger. Casandra knows that there's a child."

Tammy instinctively held Joshawa closer to her body. "What do you mean we're in danger, and who's Casandra?"

"She's my sister. The High Priestess of our tribe. She's trying to prevent the return of our Lord. And now she's aware of the child. She'll stop at nothing to use the child against our Lord and Mistress. You must leave the village and hide. And you must do that now. I have to return to avoid suspicion." Dena turned to leave only to have Hansen detain her by placing a hand on her arm.

"Not so fast. How do we hide from her? Where do you suggest we hide?"

"As far away as you can. And let no one know. I find it highly unlikely that my sister will search for the child herself but, if she does, no secret shall be safe. I must leave. Stay safe." Dena left the village and headed back toward the falls.

* * * *

Hansen looked over to Tammy, who could not hide her fear. He smiled at her, wrapping his arms around her and drawing her close. "Now don't worry, sweetheart. We'll keep Joshawa safe. I have an idea." Hansen kissed Tammy's forehead, then went in search of Sam.

* * * *

Jamya stood, patiently waiting for Tamara to finish melding with her mother. He tried to get a feel for how the conversation was going, but Tamara showed no expression on her face. She just stared out toward the ravine, her head slightly tilted to one side. Finally, she smiled as she turned to face Jamya. "My mother says she has plans for you."

"I'm not sure how I should take that."

"My mother believes the son of Joshawa lies dead in the depths of the ravine. It has been the wish of my family for many years that a strong, loyal warrior clan be named the successor to Joshawa's family line. I believe it is your family whom she has in mind for that honour."

Jamya shook his head. "I guess she's in for a surprise. If we've time, we should meet our Lord at the birthing hut. We need to start working on a plan."

"The birthing hut? My mother spoke of this place. She was going to leave our Mistress there to be killed by whatever evil lives there. Why would our Lord choose such a dangerous place in which to hide?"

"Apparently, the only danger that awaits us there is what we bring with us. Do we have time to go there? When does your mother expect us back?"

"Time... it is so very precious." Tamara gazed in the direction of the village. "My time with my mother is coming to an end." She looked back at Jamya. "It saddens me, for only one of us will survive this ordeal. In order for our village to prosper, that one cannot be my mother. Time is not our friend. For as each minute passes by, my mother becomes even more ruthless. We have to return, now. My mother is suspicious of everything and everyone, including myself. We cannot give her a reason to question us."

"I need to speak to our Lord. When do you suggest I go there?"

"Tonight, under cover of darkness. You and I together will venture to the birthing hut. I will see to it that my mother sleeps the night."

* * * *

Hansen found Sam sitting around a fire pit with several other men. Hansen caught his attention, nodded, then walked away. Sam got up and followed. The two walked in silence until they reached Hansen's hut. When they entered, they found Tammy sitting on the sleeping mat, feeding Joshawa.

Hansen sat on the ground and motioned for Sam to join him. "Please sit, I have a favour to ask." Sam sat cross-legged on the dirt floor, facing Hansen and Tammy. "Joshawa's in danger. The high priestess of the Lion people knows of his existence. She'll try to harm him or use him as leverage against Nathen and Authia. I need you to help me hide him."

"Where do you wish to hide him?"

"With any luck, the Free Spirit hasn't left Cabinda yet. We need to get back to the freighter."

Tammy looked over to Hansen. "Are you suggesting that we take Joshawa back to Vancouver?"

"No." Hansen took a deep breath. "If the freighter is still there, then I'll see to it that it remains there for as long as we need. We'll hide on the freighter." Hansen turned to Sam. "I need you to help us find our way back to the road, and hopefully the truck will still be there. Then I need you to get word to me when it's safe to return. You can't tell anyone of where we're going."

"I can do this for you. Your secret will be safe with me."

Tammy knelt as she laid Joshawa down on his bed of pillows, then tenderly brushed the hair away from his face. Content that he would fall asleep, she stood, directing her attention to Hansen. "Dena specifically said that we are to tell no one of where we're hiding. That if the high priestess comes looking for Joshawa herself and someone knows where we are, she has a way of finding out."

"I know, sweetheart. But we need Sam to find the road. I'm trusting that the Lion people will not follow us to a populated area where they could be discovered. The freighter is the safest place for us to hide."

"I agree with Hansen. When I return, I'll keep my distance from the village. I'll watch for anyone coming from the falls." Sam stood and headed for the entrance. He paused for a second. "If you can leave now, we can make the campsite before dark. Bring nothing with you. The jungle will provide for us. Do you remember where you came out of the jungle?" Tammy nodded. "Good, I'll join you on the path." Sam turned to leave only to be stopped by Tammy.

"Sam, wait a minute. What about Joshawa? How will the jungle provide for him? He's just a baby."

Sam smiled. "The jungle is our mother, and she'll take care of us. All of us." Sam left the hut as Tammy turned to face Hansen. The fear he felt deep within him was evident on Tammy's face. She was scared and, for that matter, so was he.

* * * *

Tamara and Jamya returned to the village moments before Dena. Jamya went to check on his warriors. Tamara purposely stalled while she waited for Dena. She didn't want her mother to see her going out of her way to speak to Dena. As Dena walked by, she stopped for only a second. "It has been done. They have been warned." Dena continued on her way while Tamara watched as her mother left the gathering hut and headed toward the priestesses' hut. Tamara drew a deep breath and slowly let it out. So much was happening. Her world was spiralling out of control. She needed to stop her mother from performing the spell from the parchment. She had to find her mother's essence and, most importantly, she had to stall her mother from taking her own essence. Her essence in her mother's hands would be her undoing. She'd no longer be of any use to her Lord and Mistress. Tamara squared her shoulders and headed for the priestesses' hut. *If everything goes well, it'll be over... soon.*

Tamara entered the priestesses' hut to find her mother placing packets in the fire pit. "Are you planning to conjure a vision, Mother?"

Casandra looked up at her and smiled. "Ah, you're back. Where's Jamya?"

"He went to see to his warriors. Do you need him?"

Casandra smirked. "Possibly. Come sit with me." Casandra sat in front of the fire pit and motioned Tamara to sit across from her. "Today's a wondrous day. It has seen the demise of the son of Joshawa. And it has given me a way to control the outsider."

Tamara sat across from her mother. "How, Mother?"

"The outsider has a child. We'll conjure a vision and find the child. Then I'll send Jamya to retrieve the child and bring it to me."

"Are we not going to use the spell from the parchment?"

Casandra was taken aback. "You're not surprised to hear

that there's a child. Why is that?"

Tamara realized her mistake. She could jeopardize everything if she was not careful. Sheepishly she lowered her head and stared into the fire pit. "I ask your forgiveness, Mother."

"And what am I forgiving you for?"

Tamara looked up at her mother. "When I melded with you at the ravine, I could sense that you were hiding something. That you knew something that pleased you. I thought it was the death of Joshawa's son, so I joined my thoughts with yours. I wanted to share in your happiness. That is when I learned about the child. I should have told you earlier. Are you displeased with me?"

"Your gift is truly amazing. How is it that I don't sense you when you're reading my thoughts?"

Tamara was digging herself a hole that would be her grave if she could not appease her mother. "I cannot actually read your thoughts. It is more of a sense of what you are thinking or feeling."

A bold-faced lie that she hoped her mother would not see through. "I want so much to please you, Mother. You must understand that." Tamara lowered her head, her eyes focused on the ground.

* * * *

Casandra was quiet for several minutes. She trusted her daughter with her life. But Tamara needed to be mindful of her boundaries. "You are never to read me again. If I find out that you have, even though I love you dearly, you'll be punished, severely. And I'll know."

* * * *

Tamara, still looking upon the ground, closed her eyes in relief. She needed her mother to trust her. Everything hinged on her remaining close. Slowly she raised her head and gazed deep into her mother's eyes. "I will never disappoint you again, Mother. Now let us conjure a vision and see where this child is hiding."

CHAPTER THIRTY-SIX

Nathen sat at the base of the tree that grew inside the birthing hut. He lost all sense of time. How many days had it been? Three... maybe four. It didn't matter how many days had gone by. He was no closer to winning the battle than he had been when he'd begun the venture. And, for that matter, he had no idea on how he was supposed to overpower a priestess whose abilities were not that much different from Serena's. *Trust in yourself.* That was what his father told him. Patience, something he was in short supply of.

He drew his legs to his chest, wrapping his massive arms around them. He closed his eyes and rested his head on his knees. He felt for these people. They were his people, and he was obligated to help them. But at what cost? His family had been separated. He had no guarantee that Authia would remain safe. There was nothing he could do but wait. Wait for Jamya and Tamara.

Nathen remained in the hut until day became night. His men built a fire on which to cook their dinner. The light from the fire danced on the walls of the hut. From where Nathen sat, he could see the fire pit. As he watched the brilliant reds, oranges, and yellows of the flames, he envisioned his people as free as the flames that reached high above the fire pit. They danced in celebration of their newfound freedom. So many people, his people, were relying on him to set them free. To heal their tribe... his tribe. Nathen stood and placed his hand on the trunk of the tree. "I will do this for you,

Father. I will see this to the end."

* * * *

Tamara and Casandra sat cross-legged on the ground in front of the fire pit. Casandra was about to place her leaf-covered packets in the pit when Dena entered the hut. Casandra looked up at her, annoyed by her presence. "What are you doing here?"

"I came for a visit. How are you, Tamara?"

"I am well." Before Casandra could interrupt, Tamara told all she knew to Dena. "Did you know that the outsider has a child? We were just going to conjure a vision to tell us where the child is hiding. Would you care to join us?"

"Tamara!" Casandra screeched Tamara's name. "She's not welcome here. Mind your place."

"But, Mother, would our search not be stronger if we had a vessel other than the packets? We could conjure together through Dena."

Casandra thought for a moment. Her daughter was right. With pure contempt, she addressed Dena. "If you wish, you may join us. Place yourself in the pit."

Dena did as she was told and sat in the middle of the pit. Casandra then placed the packets around her.

* * * *

Tamara sat there hoping that by using Dena as the vessel, it would leave her free to block any vision that her mother could conjure. But Tamara was wrong. Her mother's desire to conjure a vision was so strong that for just a moment a vision appeared. It was of two outsiders holding the child. They were surrounded by jungle, and in the distance, there was the outline of a large vessel.

* * * *

Hansen and Tammy entered the same camp they had stayed at just a few days ago. Sometime during the next day, they would reach the road, and they hoped the truck would still be there. Sam went in search of their dinner while Hansen built a fire. Tammy went down to the pond to bathe Joshawa. She laid him on the ground, knelt next to him, and was starting to undress him when she heard a buzzing in her head. She tried to shake it off, but it only got louder. Slowly she sank to the ground as she covered her face with her hands. She felt as though her head were about to explode. Then suddenly the buzzing cleared. The sounds within her head became more lucid, and she thought she could hear voices. They were garbled, incoherent. Tammy looked up and focused on what she was hearing. *Is this what melding is? Is this what Authia spoke about?* She focused on Authia, but instead, she heard a voice that was unfamiliar to her. It was a female voice, and she was laughing. The words she spoke sent shivers down Tammy's spine...

"I found you..."

* * * *

Casandra opened her eyes and smiled at her daughter. "They're hiding in the jungle. Two outsiders and the child."

"Are you sure, Mother?"

"Did you not see the vision? The guardians are outsiders. Of course it's her child!"

"You are right, Mother. But all I could see was the jungle. Do you know where they are hiding?"

"If the guardians are outsiders, then I know they're on the other side of the falls."

Dena snorted at Casandra. "You think you know so much. They could be anywhere."

Casandra glared at Dena. "Not that it's any of your concern, but if they were on this side of the falls, my warriors would have found them days ago. No, they're on the other side. And I intend to send Jamya in search of them."

Dena shook her head. "But Jamya would be in great danger. Why would you risk your best warrior, your best tracker, on a mission that's so perilous?"

Casandra stood, took one look at Dena, then turned her back to her. "Your opinions are neither required or welcomed. Leave this hut, now!"

"Mother, since you are focused on the child, does that mean you will no longer require my essence?"

Dena swung around and stared at Tamara, wide-eyed. "What are you talking about? What do you mean your essence?"

"Mother is going to conjure a spell that requires the essence of a priestess. She is going to use my essence. I am so fortunate to have a mother who includes me even when she is performing the darkest of spells."

Cassandra turned to face Tamara. She needed to shut her up! But before she could even utter one word, Dena was in her face. "What do you think you're doing? You can't take her essence. She's not of age! And what's this spell that she speaks of?"

"You have no right to be here. What spells I conjure are none of your business."

"That might be so, sister, but it is the business of the other priestesses. If you so much as attempt to take Tamara's essence before her time, then you'll have to answer to all of us." Dena stormed out of the hut.

"Did I speak out of turn, Mother?"

"When don't you?"

"My apologies. Does this mean we will not be conjuring the spell?"

Casandra thought for a moment. "It's secondary to finding the child. I'll have much more power over the outsider if I have her child. Don't get me wrong, daughter, if it comes down to it, we will be conjuring the spell. There just might be much more at stake."

* * * *

Tamara wasn't sure what her mother meant by that. She stood and walked over to Casandra, taking her hand in hers. "It has been a difficult day. Let us go to the family hut, and I will prepare you a soothing broth. You need to rest, Mother."

"Yes, let's do that. And hopefully tomorrow the spirits will look kindly on us, and we'll have that child."

Two hours later, dressed in her ceremonial gown, Tamara was entering Authia's hut. Sitting next to Authia was Jamya. Tamara bowed to her Mistress. "I am sure it has been a long day for you. We have the night. Let us go visit our Lord and plan our freedom."

Authia gazed up to Tamara with a puzzled expression on her face. "Are you including me in this little outing of yours?"

"Yes, my Mistress. But you must be back here before my mother wakes."

"Why? If she doesn't know where I am and if Cameron comes with us, who's she going to hurt?"

"If she finds you missing, she will be on her guard. Presenting you to the village will be much more difficult. Now come, we must not waste a moment."

* * * *

Tammy sat on the ground, staring into the fire pit as she protectively cradled Joshawa in her arms. "It was so real. I could hear her as if she was standing right there."

Hansen sat next to her, tenderly wrapping his arm around her shoulders. "Do you know who it was? Could it have been Authia?"

Tammy turned to look at Hansen. "No, it wasn't Authia. But maybe it was that Casandra woman that Dena told us about." She turned her gaze to Sam. "I'm scared. Scared to death! Can't we leave now? You said the jungle would provide for us."

"Yes, she will and has provided for us. But she'll not protect us. It's too dangerous to travel at night. We'll leave at first light."

Once again, Tammy focused on Hansen. "What if they follow us? What if they find us?"

"That's a lot of what ifs, sweetheart. Look, we got a good head start. All we need to do is to get to Cabinda, and then we should be safe. I doubt that they'll follow us into the open."

Tammy gazed thoughtfully upon the sleeping face of Joshawa. "I hope you're right for all our sakes."

CHAPTER THIRTY-SEVEN

Nathen joined his men around the fire and watched as the flames licked at the bush pig that was placed over the pit. Nathen was standing in front of the fire, his back to the jungle, when all his men suddenly stood and bowed before him. Puzzled by their actions, he turned to see if someone was behind him. That was when he was nearly caught off balance as Authia ran up to him, throwing herself into his arms. She wrapped her arms around his neck and passionately kissed him. A kiss he eagerly returned.

"Oh my God, Nathen! I've missed you so much. I've been so worried about you."

Nathen drew her tight against his body. "And I've missed you. It's tearing me apart not being close to protect you." He kissed the top of her head, then gently pulled her away from him. One look at her face caused his blood to boil. "What happened to you? Who hurt you?" Tenderly he ran his fingers along the side of her face.

"Casandra. It's nothing. She just slapped me. I'm fine, Nathen."

"Are you here to stay?"

Tamara approached Nathen, bowed, then looked deep into his eyes. "I am Tamara, my Lord. I see you. I feel your aura. You are truly the son of Joshawa. To answer you, my Lord, my Mistress is not here to stay." Tamara gestured toward the fire pit. "Come and sit with me. We have a lot to discuss."

Nathen, Arman, Jamya, Tamara, and Authia all sat on the

ground around the fire pit. Nathen's men stood guard around the perimeter of the clearing. The flames in the fire pit lit up the clearing, but the light did not penetrate the jungle. Jamya looked quizzically at Nathen. "How is it, my Lord, that we didn't see your fire as we approached the birthing hut?" Both Nathen and Arman smiled at Jamya. "Am I missing something?"

Tamara was the one who answered. "I do not sense evil here." She tilted her head as she examined the hut. "The birthing hut is alive with the souls of your parents. They protect you and all who follow you."

"Yes, but only here, at the birthing hut. Their protection doesn't extend beyond this clearing."

Jamya spoke up. "Too bad. We could use the help of spirits in our battle with Casandra."

"Speaking of Casandra." Authia sat a little further back from the heat of the fire. "Tamara."

"Yes, my Mistress."

"How do you know that your mother won't wake up and discover both you and me missing."

Tamara smiled. "I made her a broth. And in that broth, I added a potion to make her sleep. She will not wake till the morning."

"Wait a minute, you slipped her a potion? If it's that easy, why don't you slip her a potion that takes away her gift? Wouldn't that be simpler than trying to find her essence?" Authia asked.

"Unfortunately, that would not solve our problem. If my mother loses her gift, then she will just be replaced by one of the other priestesses. And they would rule as she has."

Nathen's frustration was evident to everyone. "How am I supposed to gain control of the village? You speak of me defeating Casandra. In what way am I to defeat her?"

"You need to be presented to the village. Prove to your

people who you are. The village must choose you as their Lord."

"And how am I supposed to do that?"

Tamara sighed. "My mother will stop at nothing to keep you and my Mistress from being presented at the gathering hut. To stop her, I need to find her original essence. If I do, then I can control her and present you and my Mistress at the gathering hut without fear of reprisal. Failing that, then you, my Lord, will have to fight your way into the village. Be seen by our people before my mother can conjure a spell to stop you." Tamara leaned closer to Nathen and placed a hand on his knee. "I ask for your patience. Give me time to find her essence. Give me time to safely introduce my Mistress to the other priestesses, to our people. If I fail, then those who are loyal to you will fight. As our Lord, do you not want a peaceful solution?"

"Of course, Tamara. I don't want a fight if it can be avoided. But I fear for my wife. I can't protect her while she's a prisoner in the village."

Jamya spoke up. "With my life, I'll protect my Mistress. Know that the men that guard her are loyal to you both."

"And I will shadow my mother. Keep watch over her."

* * * *

Authia listened as everyone pledged their willingness to protect her. However, they forgot one important person. "And what about my son? Can you protect him as well?"

Nathen drew a sharp breath as he focused his gaze on Authia. "What's happening to our son?" He turned his attention to Tamara. "Is my son in danger?"

"I will not lie to you, my Lord. My mother knows of his existence. She knows that he is protected by two outsiders and that they hide in the jungle. We conjured a vision. In that vision, I saw the same vessel that brought you here. I do not believe that my mother knows what the vessel is or of its importance. Your son's guardians are heading back to that vessel. If they can reach the openness of the outside world before my mother reaches them, then they will be safe."

Authia could tell that Nathen wasn't totally convinced of his son's well-being. "What are the chances that your mother will find them before they reach Cabinda?"

"My mother will not put herself in danger. If she sends Jamya in search of the child, then they will be safe."

Nathen's voice was laced with anger. "And if she sends someone else?"

Tamara stood and looked apprehensively at her Lord. "That is a problem that we will deal with when it arises. Come, my Mistress. We must get you back."

Nathen stood, then helped Authia to her feet. He drew her close to him. Authia rested her head on his chest. "I don't want to leave you." She gazed up into his emerald eyes. "My place is by your side."

"I know, my love, but we have to trust Tamara. I'll be by your side soon." Nathen glanced over to Tamara. "Is that a safe assumption?"

"I cannot promise you what I do not know. I can tell you what I do know. What I have seen in my visions. My Mistress will be presented at the gathering hut. She will win the hearts of our people. My Mistress will be the one to open the door for you."

* * * *

Casandra felt as if she were in a dense fog. She was dreaming of the outsider. The outsider was being presented at the gathering hut. Casandra tried to open her eyes, but they would not corporate. In her sleep-induced stupor, she reached for her daughter only to find the sleeping mat empty. At that point, Casandra lost the battle and fell into a deep sleep. A sleep filled with dreams of the outsider.

* * * *

Tammy lay on the ground, holding Joshawa close to her side. Hansen and Sam stayed by the fire, keeping a watch on their surroundings. Tammy could not sleep. Every sound the jungle made caused her to jump. She knew in her heart that Casandra was on her way. Silently she prayed that they would reach the road and the truck before Casandra caught up to them.

* * * *

Nathen sat by the fire, mulling over everything Tamara had told him. According to Tamara and his father, Authia would be the key to permit him to enter the village. Nathen was not very good at sitting back and waiting while others paved the way for him. While others risked their lives for him. But unfortunately, that was exactly what he had to do. He was not a participant in the quest to prove his lineage. At least, not yet.

* * * *

Authia lay on her sleeping mat in the hut that served as her prison. She rolled onto her back, staring up at the roof of the hut. The village was quiet. Even the sounds of the jungle were quieter than usual, as if the jungle held its breath... waiting for something to happen. And Authia could do nothing. Like Nathen, she had to wait. Wait for Tamara to find a peaceful solution.

CHAPTER THIRTY-EIGHT

Casandra awoke, the grogginess lifting from her as if she were removing a heavy veil. Something was gnawing at her, warning her. She looked beside her to find her daughter sleeping on her mat. Something was not as it should be. Casandra got up and chose her animal skins to dress in. Quietly, she left the family hut and headed for the priestesses' hut.

She didn't acknowledge the guard standing next to the entrance as she entered the hut and walked over to the shelves that held all the clay pots. From one pot, she withdrew three leaf-covered packets. These packets contained the gift of sight. She placed them in the fire pit, sat cross-legged on the ground, and closed her eyes as she waved her hands over the packets. One by one they burst into flames, producing a fog-like mist. Casandra opened her eyes, then leaned closer to the fire pit. Once, twice, three times she took a deep breath, filling her lungs and her mind. Slowly she sat back, resting her arms on her legs. As she opened her eyes, she spoke to the spirits that would be listening. "Show me what there is to see. Show me what is hidden in the depths of my mind."

Once again, she closed her eyes while she searched her mind for a vision. Something that would put her uneasiness to rest. Then the vision came to her as clearly as if it were a memory. The outsider was at the back of the gathering hut, standing on the platform. Her own people were there, and they were bowing to the outsider. She searched her vision for herself, but she was nowhere to be seen. Then something caught her eye. There was an amulet around the outsider's neck. Casandra's head shot up. The vision vanished as she frantically reached for her neck. The amulet was still there. It was a vision of things yet to come. But how could it happen? How could the outsider be at the gathering hut and how did she gain possession of the amulet? Casandra stood and stared into the fire pit. She had to find the child. She had to control the outsider. Then her gaze fell upon the hiding place for the parchment. If all else failed, she would have to use the parchment. *The outsider must be stopped!*

* * * *

Tammy didn't fall asleep till the early hours of the morning. At six, Hansen gently nudged her awake. "Sorry, sweetheart, but we have to leave. I want to reach the road before dark."

Tammy stretched her arms above her head as she yawned. "Did you sleep?"

"A little. We'll have plenty of time to sleep once we're on the freighter."

Tammy was distracted as Joshawa cried to be fed. She had brought two bottles of formula for him, but he had already finished them. She got up, grabbed the empty bottles, and walked over to Sam. "Okay, Sam." She held out the bottles for him to take. "How's the jungle going to provide for Joshawa?"

Sam didn't take the bottles but instead turned and headed for a large palm tree. With the agility of a monkey, he scaled the tree till he reached the top. Seconds later, two coconuts fell to the ground. Using his machete, he skinned the coconuts, and before too long, Joshawa was feeding on coconut milk. As Tammy fed Joshawa, she looked up at Sam and smiled. "I guess you're right. Thank you."

The group left minutes later, ever so conscious of their surroundings. It was a long hike to the road, and they were mindful of every movement, of every noise.

* * * *

Casandra returned to the family hut and changed into her ceremonial gown. She then returned to the priestesses' hut, only this time she acknowledged the guard. "Bring Jamya to me." She thought for a second. "And bring me Dena and Tamara." Casandra dismissed the guard and entered the hut. The son of Joshawa hadn't been in her vision, so Casandra felt comfortable that Jamya had killed him. He could be trusted. Not that she questioned her daughter's observation at the ravine. Her daughter's ability to sense auras was unsurpassed. However, Casandra would have been happier if two bodies had been visible. She went over to the table and started mixing a potion. Carefully, she added various powders and herbs to a clay bowl. As she mixed the concoction together, she chanted in an age-old language that only a priestess could understand. She was just finishing filling a packet when Jamya, Tamara, and Dena entered the hut. Casandra ignored them while she finished wrapping the packet. She placed it in the folds of her gown, then turned to face her visitors.

"I have a job for you, Jamya."

"What does my Mistress wish of me?"

"The outsider has a child. I want you to bring me that child."

"Where's the child?"

Casandra grinned ever so wickedly as she gazed upon Dena. "Dena will tell us."

"Child? What child? I know nothing of what you speak

of."

"We'll see. Jamya, bind her and place her in the fire pit."

"Mother, what are you doing?" Tamara stood between Jamya and Dena. "Do you plan to injure her?"

"Tamara! Step out of the way and allow Jamya to do his job."

* * * *

Tamara bowed her head and moved aside. Her heart was pounding in her chest. She knew exactly what her mother was planning on doing. Jamya did as he was told and bound Dena's wrists and ankles, then placed her in the middle of the fire pit.

Dena knelt there staring up at Casandra. "Well, sister, I know what you plan to do. It's a waste of your time. I know nothing of the child. You'll get nothing from me."

"We shall see." To Tamara's horror, Casandra reached into the folds of her gown and produced a packet, which she placed in front of Dena. She then sat on the ground, facing her. Tamara risked everything and melded with Dena.

Do not seek me out. Think of the child. That is what is important to my mother. Give her what she wants as far as the child is concerned, and maybe she will be blinded to everything else. Tamara knew that the child was safe, especially if it was Jamya that went in search of him.

* * * *

Casandra closed her eyes and began chanting as she waved her hands over the packet. The packet began to smolder and the smoke it produced slowly engulfed Dena. The potion was designed to open Dena's mind. Make her susceptible to Casandra's probing. Casandra entered Dena's mind, ripping it apart while she searched for the child. The pain was excruciating as Casandra delved deeper into Dena's subconscious. Dena bit her lower lip as she struggled to focus only on the child. She didn't cry out in pain. She wouldn't give her sister the satisfaction. Casandra moved about Dena's mind until she came upon a memory. Dena was looking upon the child. She was thinking of her own child. A child that was yet to be. Casandra pushed harder as Dena's face contorted in pain. Tears ran down her cheeks, but still, no sound came from her. Then Casandra found what she was looking for. Dena, speaking to the outsiders that cared for the child. Warning them of her. Telling them to hide but tell no one where they were going. Casandra laughed. She knew where they were going. They were outsiders. They would hide where they would be comfortable. Casandra left Dena's mind, and as she did, Dena crumpled to the ground.

* * * *

Casandra smiled at Jamya. Victory was hers. "Jamya, the outsiders are taking the child back to their world. You must stop them. And you must do this alone. Procure the child, kill the guardians. Bring it to me, but let no one see you or the child."

Jamya bowed to her and left the hut.

* * * *

Tamara was nervous. What all had her mother seen? Had she been in any of the visions? "Mother, did you see all that there was to see?"

"I am confident that Dena gave me all there is. The pain I inflicted was unbearable. She wouldn't have been able to hide anything from me."

Tamara drew a breath of relief. Her mother's arrogance was impeding her better judgment. Something she'd accused Serena of not so long ago. "May I tend to Dena?"

"Suit yourself. Remove her from my hut. I want her out of my sight."

"As you wish, Mother." Tamara removed the binding from Dena's wrists and ankles. As she helped her to her feet, she whispered into her ear. "You did well."

* * * *

Jamya, machete and bow in hand, headed out into the jungle. Should he actually cross through the falls? What would he tell his Mistress when he returned without the child? Maybe he could tell her that the outsiders killed the child rather than seeing it in her hands. She would want proof. Jamya decided that he would wait two days before his return. In the meantime, he would head for the birthing hut. Perhaps his Lord would have the answer on how to pacify the High Priestess.

* * * *

Casandra watched as Tamara struggled to help Dena to her feet. Then Tamara looked toward her mother. "Where would you like me to take Dena? She still has not been allotted a hut."

Casandra thought for a moment. Dena was not to be trusted. And as far as her daughter was concerned, it would be best if she separated the two of them. "Take her to the outsider's hut. She'll be treated as our prisoner. She deserves no better. And, as far as you are concerned, my daughter, you're never to approach their hut. You're never to see or speak to Dena again. Do you understand?"

****

Tamara allowed Dena to place her left arm around her shoulders, using Tamara to keep herself from sinking to the ground. Tamara did her best to hold her up by wrapping her arms around Dena's waist. Tamara shook her head. "Yes, of course, Mother."

Tamara turned and exited the hut. As she headed toward Authia's hut, she noticed that the people of the village had stopped what they were doing and were gawking at her and Dena. The fear that possessed them was clearly evident in their shocked expressions. Dena was pale and could barely keep her head up. Tamara was doing her best to support most of Dena's weight. As she looked from one villager to the next, there was no doubt in her mind that the villagers knew Dena's condition was a direct result of her mother's wrath. She also knew that the villagers were aware that something was terribly wrong. There were too many secrets.

Whispers floated throughout the village. Whispers that the son of Joshawa had returned. But, unfortunately, Tamara could not rely on support from the village, for no one dared voice their suspicions aloud. No one dared to stand and be heard. The punishment would be too severe.

Chapter Thirty-nine

Tamara entered Authia's hut, supporting Dena, who was obviously struggling with what little strength she had left. Authia looked up and immediately went to Dena's side. She put Dena's free arm around her shoulders to help support her weight. Then she and Tamara gently guided Dena to the sleeping mat and laid her down on it.

Authia stood back, taking in all that she saw. "Oh my God, Tamara. What happened?"

"My mother." Tamara sat beside Dena then leaned closer, and kissed her on her forehead. As she sat back up, she placed a hand on Dena's head. "You did well. My mother saw only what you wanted her to see. Our secret is still safe." Tamara stood and bowed to her. "I must leave you now. I will no longer be able to see you unless under cover of darkness. But I will meld with you. I will keep you informed of what is happening outside of your hut."

"Wait a minute. What's going on here? What happened to Dena? And why can't you see me?"

"Take care of Dena. She will explain everything when she regains her strength." With that, Tamara left. Authia stood in the middle of the hut, feeling bewildered and exasperated.

* * * *

Jamya made his way to the birthing hut. His Lord would want to know what was transpiring in the village. He arrived just as the group of men were finishing their noonday meal. He searched the group for his Lord, but he was nowhere to be found. Quickly he sought out Arman, finding him by the fire pit. He was kneeling on his haunches, chewing on a piece of meat that he'd ripped off the animal that was skewered and placed over the fire in front of him. Without turning around, he addressed Jamya. "Join me, Jamya. There's plenty."

Jamya sat on the ground next to Arman. He looked at him quizzically. "How did you know that it was I that was standing behind you?"

Arman turned to face Jamya, smiling at him. "My men wouldn't be doing their job if I did not."

"True. Where's our Lord? I must speak with him."

Arman motioned toward the birthing hut. "He has been in there for several hours. He'll join us when he's ready. What do you need to speak to him about?"

"I have news of his son."

"And what news do you have for me?" Both men turned to find Nathen towering over them. Jamya quickly stood and bowed to his Lord.

"As you know, our high priestess has discovered that you have a child."

"Yes, I'm aware of that."

"Just today she tortured Dena to find all she could about your child."

Jamya could see the anger as it began to take control of Nathen. "She tortured her? How's Dena?"

"She survived and is resting. The High Priestess placed her in the hut with our Mistress."

"And what did Casandra learn from Dena?"

"That your child and his guardians are heading for the outside world. She has sent me to retrieve the child and bring him to her."

"That places you in a precarious position. Do you know

how you're going to handle it?"

"No, my Lord. I ask for your guidance. I will have to tell the High Priestess why I didn't return with the child."

* * * *

Nathen stared off into the jungle. He had to control his anger. He needed to think with a clear head. There was only one way Jamya could return to the village and not jeopardize his position with Casandra. He sighed as he turned his attention to Jamya. "Where are your scouts?"

"To the west of us. They're scouting for a group of men that don't exist."

Nathen looked at Jamya, emerald eyes locking with steel blue. "There are three choices for you, Jamya. Return with the child, remain here, or be found by your scouts. Do you understand what I'm saying?"

"Yes, my Lord." Jamya bowed to Nathen.

"You are a valuable asset inside the village. That being said, I'll completely understand if you choose to remain with us."

"My Lord. Returning with the child isn't an option. If I remain here, I'll be unable to control my scouts and warriors. Left on their own, they will find us. No. There is but one option for me."

Nathen rested his hand on Jamya's shoulder. "It causes me great pain to even consider this. Are you sure, Jamya? There's no dishonour in remaining here. The birthing hut will protect us."

Jamya smiled at Nathen. "I'm sorry to say that I don't hold as much trust in the sorcery that lives here as you do. I'll return to the village. If I go back injured, then I have a chance of appeasing the high priestess. I'll say I was attacked by the outsiders and left for dead." Jamya focused his attention to Arman. "If you follow me to the western border, you can leave me there, and I'll be found."

"If I'm to injure you, I would choose a machete. The chances are that the outsiders are not in possession of a bow. I can cause an injury that appears serious but not be life threating. It should be enough to convince the high priestess."

"I thank you, Arman. We'll wait here until sunrise. That should give enough time for the guardians to reach their world. We'll head for the western border at first light. I'll be found sooner that way."

* * * *

Arman had to admit to himself that he'd been wrong about Jamya. He was a true warrior worthy of his respect. "You've proven to me that you have earned your place as leader of the warriors, and I'll be honoured to follow you when our Lord takes his place." Arman offered his hand to Jamya, who readily accepted it.

Nathen placed his hand on top of Jamya's. "We're one united together in this cause. Jamya, I will not forget what you are prepared to do in order to protect my son. I'm in your debt."

* * * *

Authia paced the confines of her hut while Dena slept off the remaining effects of Casandra's probing. Finally, a couple of hours later, Dena began to stir. Slowly she sat up. When she saw Authia, she tried to bow, which only resulted in her losing her balance and almost falling backward onto the ground. Authia rushed to her side, knelt beside her, and held her tenderly in her arms. "My God, Dena! What happened to you?"

Dena looked up into her eyes. She smiled. "My sister foolishly believes that I'm weak. She entered my mind but not as in a meld. She desperately wants your child. But she doesn't know with any certainty where your child hides. And now she has sent Jamya in search of him. Jamya would rather die than return with your child. You've nothing to fear."

Authia's anger welled up inside of her. If Casandra wanted a fight, she was going to get one! Gently, Authia laid Dena back down on the sleeping mat. Then she melded with Casandra. *You're nothing but a coward! You have no honour, no self-respect. You hide behind Dena, your daughter, and all those that support you. Well, I'm done with you and the games you play. Your days of ruling this tribe are over!* Authia headed for the entrance to the hut. Before she reached it, Tamara's thoughts flooded her mind.

My Mistress! What are you doing? You are not in a position to confront my mother.

I'm tired of being held up in this hut. I'm tired of sitting back and doing nothing. I'm tired of standing by while your mother hurts the ones I care about. I'm sorry, Tamara, but I'm going to confront your mother. It was mid-afternoon when Authia stormed out of the hut that was her prison. The guard standing outside the hut pointed out the priestesses' hut to her. Authia marched through the village, her anger growing with every step she took. Anger because at Casandra's hand, Nathen was injured. Anger because Casandra almost killed Dena. But most of all, anger because Casandra was a threat to her son. Authia was so focused on her destination that she barely noticed the crowd that was following her.

* * * *

Cameron left the hut and stood in the clearing, watching

his people, the Lion people, gather in awe of his Mistress. She was heading for the priestesses' hut, and Cameron, as well as everyone else, knew that what she was doing was not a good thing. She marched past the crowd. Fear did not guide her. What he saw in her was strength and courage. There were whispers amongst the crowd. Could she be the one? Was she the outsider that the parchments spoke of? Cameron held his breath as she entered the priestesses' hut and everyone dispersed. For no one wanted to be accused of siding with an outsider. Dena, her own sister, was the example of what would happen if the high priestess even suspected as much. No one would be immune to her wrath, no matter what their station was in the village.

* * * *

Authia barged into the hut, startling Casandra. She whirled around to face Authia just as Tamara entered the hut. "What are you doing here? Tamara, did you bring her here?"

Authia walked closer to Casandra, making sure the fire pit stood between them. "I brought myself here. You've gone too far. It's time to end this. I warned you what would happen if you hurt anyone that I cared about."

Casandra appeared to be puzzled. "You are concerned for Dena?"

"Yes, but that's not what I'm here for." It was time to see how convincing Authia could be. "I've been unable to meld with Nathen. Just now, he came to me, in a vision. You killed him!"

Casandra gazed upon Authia with a smug look of condescension. "You're mistaken. I didn't kill him."

"Don't mince words with me. I know you sent your warrior Jamya to kill him. My husband lies at the bottom of a ravine because of you."

* * * *

Casandra was taken aback. How could she know? Had Dena told her? Did Dena even know? Did the outsider have the ability to speak with the spirits? "I have no idea what you're talking about."

"Oh yes, you do. I can read you as easily as I could a child. Not only do I know that you killed him, but I also know that you plan to use my son against me. Failing that, you'll have your daughter perform a spell that will kill me. Does she know that it can also kill her too?"

Casandra stared wide-eyed at Authia. Only herself and Tamara knew of the spell and only she knew what it was capable of doing. How could the outsider possibly learn of the spell? Did she really have the gift of sight? Casandra was about to respond to Authia when Tamara interrupted her. "Mother, what does she speak of? How can the spell kill me?"

"She knows nothing. She is trying to confuse you. To turn you against me."

Authia snickered. "I know nothing? Really. I know that you are afraid of me. I know that you are afraid to present me at the gathering hut. I know where you hide your essence... your original essence."

Instinctively, Casandra's hand went to cover her throat, but she stopped midway. She realized her mistake. Instead, she raised her hand as if she intended to slap Authia but then thought better of it. Slowly she lowered her hand and brought it down to her side.

* * * *

The mistake did not go unnoticed by Authia. The essence

was on her person. That was why Tamara couldn't find it. "You're a quick learner. If you even try to lay a hand me, you'll regret it. I promise you that."

As Authia spoke, she discreetly looked about Casandra's body. It was there. It had to be. That was when she noticed the thin leather string around Casandra's neck. The collar of her ceremonial gown was concealing most of the string. Authia averted her gaze. "It would be a real bonus if I possessed your essence. You would be powerless, and I could present myself to the village."

"You are bluffing. You know nothing of my essence."

Authia walked past Casandra and headed to the shelves that held all the clay pots. "You have quite the assortment here. Is this where you keep all your potions?"

"You are supposed to be all-seeing. You tell me."

Authia turned to face Casandra. "I'll tell you something. I know all about your essence. I learned it from Serena. She was arrogant and spoke too much for her good. Much like yourself."

"You know nothing of me."

"I know more than you would like. But, to be honest, I have no idea where your essence is. Nor do I care."

Authia was sure that Casandra's essence was around her neck. She hoped to convince Casandra that she didn't know where it was, and in achieving that, Casandra would not change her hiding place. "Tell me one thing. If your people are so loyal to you, why would you fear to present me?"

"My people are loyal to me. I fear nothing."

"Tamara. If I am presented, and your people choose your mother, what happens to me?"

Tamara lowered her eyes, as if ashamed of the answer. When she looked up, there were tears in her eyes. "You would be put to death."

"Wow! Put to death." Authia grinned as an idea formed.

"I have a proposal for you, Casandra. Present me at the gathering hut. You win, and I die."

"And if you should win?"

"Then you will willingly hand over your essence... your original essence."

* * * *

Casandra remained quiet while she mulled over the ramifications of the outsider's proposal. What were the chances that her people would choose the outsider? Without the son of Joshawa present, the chances were slim. Casandra snickered to herself as she also formulated a plan. "I accept your proposal. You'll be presented at the gathering hut tomorrow. As the sun sets, you'll be given the opportunity to speak."

"You must feel very confident that you'll win. Honesty and trust versus deception and lies. Which will be the victor?" Authia turned to leave only to be stopped by Casandra.

"Not so fast." Authia turned to face her. "Don't think for one moment that you'll walk out of this hut unscathed." Casandra reached into her gown, retrieved a packet, and threw it at Authia's feet. Before Authia could move, the smoke from the packet encased her. She inhaled two breaths of the sweet-smelling fog, then fell to the ground, unconscious.

Chapter Forty

It was late afternoon as Nathen sat around the fire with his men. He was listening to stories of his people when Authia flashed through his mind. She was in trouble, but he only sensed her for a second. Then she was gone. Nathen jumped to his feet. He tried desperately to concentrate on Authia. But there was nothing. Just emptiness. Jamya and Arman stood next to him. Arman placed a hand on Nathen's shoulder. "My Lord. What troubles you?"

"There's something wrong. Authia's in danger. But I can't reach her."

Nathen was at a loss. What was he to do? He couldn't meld with Authia without risking her safety. Could he meld with Tamara without Casandra knowing? In desperation, Nathen turned to Jamya. "I need to get to the village, now!"

Before Jamya could answer, Tamara melded with Nathen. *Do not fear, my Lord. My Mistress is all right. We will come when the village sleeps.*

Nathen remained standing, staring into the depths of the jungle. Cautiously Jamya approached Nathen. "What is your bidding, my Lord?"

Nathen closed his eyes and drew a deep breath, then slowly released it. He opened his eyes and faced Arman and Jamya. "Apparently, we're to wait here. Tamara is bringing Authia to me tonight. I don't like this. There's something wrong with Authia, and there's nothing I can do to help her." Nathen left his men and went to spend his time waiting for Authia in the birthing hut.

* * * *

Casandra stood over the motionless body of the outsider. It would be so easy to dispose of her while she slept. Be done with her. But Casandra still was not confident that the outsider could not inflict some sort of punishment on her. She still had to be careful. Casandra smiled as she gently moved Authia's limp arm with her foot. So much for the presentation. Casandra tuned her attention to her daughter. "Bind her. She'll remain here until I have the child in my possession."

"What if she wakes? Should we not gag her as well?"

* * * *

Tamara had a very good idea what was contained in the packet that her mother had used on her Mistress. She just needed her mother to confirm her suspicion.

"That won't be necessary." Casandra giggled as she walked over to the table that held her clay pots. "The outsider will remain silent. She'll have no choice." Casandra took a large clay pot and started mixing herbs and powders from the smaller clay pots.

"What did you do, Mother?"

"I took her voice."

"I have heard of that. It is a very complicated spell. But, of course, not for you. Are you not concerned about retaliation?"

"It'll be days before she regains her voice, and by that time I'll have her child. In the meantime..." Casandra turned and handed Tamara the clay pot she had been working on.

"What is this?"

"I'm trusting the outsider into your care. You'll feed this

potion to her whenever she begins to regain consciousness. She'll remain asleep until I have the child." Casandra headed for the entrance.

"Where are you going, Mother?"

"To see the men that guard her. They have much to explain."

Tamara stood by the entrance of the hut and watched as her mother screamed at the guard who stood outside of her Mistress' hut. He followed her inside, and Tamara could no longer hear her mother's ranting. She looked up at the guard standing outside her door. "Please let me know when my mother leaves the hut."

"Yes, my Mistress." The guard moved closer to the entrance, keeping her out of view from anyone that should pass by.

Tamara knew what she needed to do. Her mother greatly underestimated her talents. Tamara observed her mother and the other priestesses closely. She had learned a great deal. Standing in front of the table that held all the clay pots, Tamara began mixing her own concoction. It took her ten minutes to finish and another five minutes to clean up. She had to leave the table exactly as she'd found it. When she was satisfied that nothing was amiss, she placed the two packets she'd created in her waistband. Then she went to inform the guard that he no longer had to keep an eye open for Casandra. "I am done now. Has my mother left the hut?"

"No, my Mistress."

"Those poor men. I hope that my mother does not punish them too severely." Tamara left the guard and went back inside the hut to sit by her Mistress. Gently she stroked Authia's head, looking upon her with great admiration. Her Mistress was very brave and at the same time very foolish. Confronting her mother was a risk she shouldn't have taken. Yet, she did sense that her Mistress knew something. That she'd discovered something during the confrontation. "It will wait, my Mistress. Rest, for tonight we go to the birthing hut."

* * * *

Casandra's anger knew no bounds. Cameron stood in front of her, fearful of what she could do but willing to take any punishment in the name of his Mistress. The second guard, Dameon, stood tall and proud. Cameron knew that he also was prepared to accept any punishment Casandra would inflict on him. "You have not given me a satisfactory answer as to why that outsider ended up in my hut."

Dena pushed herself up to a sitting position and laughed at her sister. "You think yourself so clever. Did the outsider give you a hard time, sister?"

Casandra ignored Dena and concentrated on him and the other warrior standing in front of her. "Why did you release her?"

"Because, sister, I told them to."

Casandra whirled around. "What right do you have to make any decision concerning the outsider?" She returned her focus to them. "Speak. Explain to me why you would listen to someone that has been stripped of all her rights."

Cameron took the lead. "But, my Mistress, we were unaware that she had no rights. We knew she had been punished, but you neglected to inform us that she had no place with the priestesses. When she told us that you wanted to see the outsider immediately, we had no reason to doubt her."

Casandra's anger seemed to be at the boiling point. "It didn't occur to you to accompany her to my hut?"

"I told them it wouldn't be necessary. They're not to blame. If you are going to punish anyone, make that person me."

Casandra glanced over her shoulder to her sister. "Oh, don't worry, my sister. I'm not nearly finished with you." She turned her attention back to Cameron. "Let me make this perfectly clear. Dena is a prisoner of this tribe. She is to be treated as such. She has no more rights than the outsider has. No one, and I mean no one, is to enter this hut with the exception of myself."

Cameron spoke up. "What about your daughter, my Mistress?"

"Especially not Tamara. If you fail me again, I'll see to it that not only you are punished, but your entire family will suffer my wrath. And it won't be pleasant. Do I make myself abundantly clear?"

Both men nodded, then bowed to the High Priestess as she left the hut.

* * * *

Darkness had fallen on the Jelani village. Authia was starting to stir. She felt disorientated. As if she were not part of her own body. As she lay on her back, she looked up to find someone staring down at her. Authia tried to focus, but the person appeared to be more of an apparition rather than something real. Her eyelids were heavy, her mind swimming in a fog. Authia fought to stay awake. She concentrated on the person looming above her. But the potion that she'd inhaled still had a firm grasp on her, and Authia fell back to sleep.

* * * *

Tamara left the priestesses' hut and joined her mother in the family hut. "The outsider still sleeps, Mother. Did you want me to stay the night with her?"

Casandra shook her head in annoyance. "Of course. I don't want her roaming the village if she wakes. Now fix me some broth."

"Yes, Mother." Tamara prepared the broth, complete with the sleeping potion. Within half an hour, Casandra was on her sleeping mat, deep in a drug-induced slumber. Tamara took full advantage and headed for the hut that contained Dena. When she reached the hut, Dameon would not let her pass. Tamara looked up at the guard, puzzled by his reaction to her. "Why are you preventing me from entering the hut?"

"It's the high priestess' order that no one other than herself is allowed to enter the hut."

"You have nothing to fear. She is sleeping and will be unaware of what transpires this night."

"Sorry, but your mother has threatened my family. I can't let you pass."

Tamara smiled at the guard. "I understand. Are you still loyal to our Lord?"

"Of course. But I also have to protect my family."

"Our Lord will understand. Please ask Cameron to come out and see me."

The guard bowed to Tamara, entered the hut, and returned with Cameron.

"What is your bidding, my Mistress?"

"We are going to the birthing hut, but our Mistress is in need of your help."

Cameron bowed to Tamara. "Anything."

Tamara spoke to Dameon. "Will you be all right if I take Cameron with me?"

"If the High Priestess sleeps and is unaware... then yes. But please do not stay long."

"We shall return before first light. Cameron, please follow

me." Tamara and Cameron walked over to the priestesses' hut. When they entered, they found Authia slowly waking up. Though, when she tried to sit up, her strength left her and she fell back onto the ground.

Cameron hastened to her side. "What's wrong with our Mistress?"

"I am afraid my mother put a spell on her. But not to worry, for every spell, there is a counterspell." Tamara smiled at Cameron. "She is too weak to walk. Will you carry her to the birthing hut?"

Cameron scooped Authia into his arms, holding her tight to his chest. Neither Tamara nor Cameron said a word. They just left the hut together and headed into the jungle.

CHAPTER FORTY-ONE

Hansen, Tammy, and Sam battled the dense vegetation of the jungle. Their goal was to be at the truck by nightfall. The sun was already sinking into the horizon. It wouldn't be long before they would be engulfed in the darkest of the night. Half an hour later, as the sun was making its final appearance, they walked onto the road, but to their horror, the truck was not there.

Hansen and Tammy stared in disbelief at the empty road. All their hopes of saving Joshawa were gone. Then Sam started walking down the road in the direction of Cabinda. Hansen ran up to him and grabbed his arm to stop him. "Where do you think you're going? The truck's not here. We can't possibly walk to Cabinda."

Sam glanced down at Hansen's hand, which had a firm grip on his forearm. With no facial expression, he looked back up at Hansen. Hansen sighed as he let go of Sam's arm. "I'm sorry. It's just that we really need that truck."

"And you'll have it. Follow me."

"What are you talking about, Sam? It's not here."

* * * *

Sam ignored Hansen and continued to walk down the road. Reluctantly Hansen and Tammy followed him. For over fifteen minutes they walked in silence. Then, as they rounded yet another bend in the road, the truck came into view. Hansen was ecstatic. "Yes! What's it doing here?"

"It's exactly where we left it. I didn't bring you back the same way that we came. A good tracker could have easily recognized the path we made coming here. Even more so if we had shown it to him. I came a different way, keeping whoever is following always behind us. Now go. I'll come get you when it's safe." Hansen threw his arms around Sam, then stepped back and shook his hand. "I can't thank you enough, Sam."

"Keep Joshawa safe and that'll be all the thanks I need." Sam watched as Hansen and Tammy, cradling Joshawa, climbed into the truck. He remained where he stood until the truck rounded another bend and was out of sight. As the truck disappeared from view, so did the sun. While Sam concentrated on building a fire, Tomas came out of the jungle. "So, Tomas. Did anyone follow us?"

"No, there was no one."

"Strange. The female of the Lion people was certain that Joshawa was in danger. We'll camp here tonight, then head back to the falls in the morning."

"If they weren't followed, would it not be safe for us to return to the village?"

"No. The fear in both Tammy and Hansen's face was real. The danger is real. We'll wait by the falls. We'll be their ears and their eyes."

* * * *

Nathen paced the confines of the birthing hut as he impatiently waited for news on Authia. A few hours later, he noticed the men that Arman sent into the jungle returning. They were pointing back into the jungle, and they spoke of Authia. Nathen came out of the birthing hut. "I heard you speak Authia's name. Where is she?"

Arman faced him. "Not far, my Lord. But you should

know. It looks as though our Mistress has been injured. She's being carried by one of your men, Cameron, from the village."

Nathen's roar of anger could be heard throughout the jungle. "Show me where she is!"

Nathen and Arman left the camp to meet up with Authia. They did not have to go far before they ran into Tamara and Cameron. Nathen walked up to Cameron and looked at his precious Authia. She appeared to be asleep in Cameron's arms. Carefully Nathen took her from Cameron and held her close. Tears formed in his eyes as he leaned down and kissed Authia on her forehead. "Tamara, what's happened here? What's wrong with her?"

"My mother cast a spell on her. It was mixed in with a potion to make her sleep. She should be waking soon."

"What spell?"

"One that will take her voice. My Mistress wanted to be presented at the gathering hut. However, if she cannot speak, she will be unable to defend herself."

Authia started to move in Nathen's arms. She opened her eyes, then raised her hand to Nathen's face to wipe away the tears. But when she tried to speak, no sound came forth. Authia's eyes went wide. Her hand went to her throat. Desperately, she tried to make a sound. Nathen set her down, then cupped her chin in his hand. "Don't try to speak, my love. Casandra has cast a spell on you." Nathen turned to Tamara. "How do we undo this spell? There must be a way."

"Yes, my Lord, there is. I will need the fire pit."

The group made their way into the clearing. Nathen held Authia close. She still seemed weak and not sure of her footing. However, she refused to be carried. He led her to the fire pit as Arman cleared his men away. Then he and Jamya took their place standing close enough to be there if he needed them but far enough back so they wouldn't be in the way.

Tamara took Authia's hands in hers. "I want you to sit close to the fire pit." Authia did as she was told. Tamara sat next to her. Nathen stayed standing directly behind Authia. "My Mistress, I have conjured a counterspell that should give you back your voice." Tamara pulled one of the packets from her waistband. "I am going to place this in the fire. It will produce a fog-like mist. You must inhale the mist. As much as you can. It will make you dizzy and you will feel sick, but you must not stop inhaling the mist until I say. Do you understand?"

Authia nodded. "Now, everyone, please step away from the fire pit." Nathen did not budge. Tamara looked up at him, her eyes pleading. "Please, my Lord, it is important that you do not inhale the mist. You must step back."

Nathen took a few steps back, then stood there with his arms folded across his chest. "Will this work, Tamara? Will this give Authia her voice back?"

"If done properly, yes, my Lord, it will work." Tamara turned to face the fire pit. Carefully, she positioned the packet at the edge of the flames just in front of Authia. She closed her eyes, placed her hands on her knees and started chanting in the language of the priestesses. The packet smoldered and, as Tamara predicted, a fine fog-like mist escaped the confines of the packet. Tamara put her hand on the back of Authia's head and gently pushed her face over the mist.

* * * *

Authia breathed in the sour-smelling mist. After three deep breaths, her head began to spin. She felt like she was going to be sick. Authia tried to move away from the mist, but

Tamara held her head firmly and would not allow her to move. Several minutes later, the mist began to dissipate, and Tamara let go.

"Someone bring our Mistress some water and something to eat. Do not try to speak, my Mistress. It will take time."

"How much time?" Nathen passed Authia a container of water.

"Not long, my Lord."

Authia's head was spinning. The water helped. The meat she was given actually settled her stomach. Ten minutes later, her voice raspy, Authia spoke. "I know where Casandra's essence is."

CHAPTER FORTY-TWO

Tammy and Hansen negotiated the badly rutted road in the pitch dark of night. The truck's headlights could barely pierce the darkened shroud that encased them. It took them half a day to travel the road in the daylight. Hansen knew that they would not reach the main road till late morning. From there, they would continue their journey to the Free Spirit. He prayed that it would still be berthed at the pier.

* * * *

Tamara stared wide-eyed at her. "You know where my mother hides her original essence? How is it that you know this?"

Authia cleared her throat. It hurt to swallow. Her throat felt as though it were on fire. She took another couple of swigs of the water. Nathen sat on the ground behind her, then lifted her into his lap. "Take your time, my love. There's no rush."

"But, my Lord..." Nathen shot Tamara a warning glance. She bowed her head. "My apologies, my Lord." Tamara looked back up to Nathen. "But time is not our friend. If my Mistress knows where my mother's essence is, she must tell us."

"And she will. Just give her a few minutes."

Authia curled up in Nathen's arms. If felt so good to be held by him. To feel his breath on her face. To feel the warmth of his body against hers. She knew how important it was to tell everyone what she knew. But she was still very tired. Maybe she could shut her eyes for a moment. Authia nestled her head against Nathen's chest and immediately fell back asleep.

* * * *

Tamara sighed. "We may afford her an hour to sleep, but then we must wake her and find out what she knows. We do not have much time, my Lord. We must return before daylight."

Nathen drew Authia closer to his body. If felt good holding her in his arms. He didn't care how long she slept. "She's been through a lot. She needs her rest. That being said, we do need to find out what she knows. I'll wake her in an hour. In the meantime, tell me, Tamara. If she knows where the essence is, where do we go from there?"

Tamara smiled with delight. "My Lord. If my Mistress possesses the original essence, then she can present herself at the gathering hut with no fear of reprisal. But most importantly, she can present you."

"I still don't understand why I can't just enter the village, let my people see me, and present myself."

"You underestimate my mother. She could cast any numbers of spells on you, on our people. Have them see you as she wishes. The only reason that my Mistress is still alive is because my mother believes that she could harm her. By silencing her and keeping her asleep, Mother believes that my Mistress will be in no condition to cast a spell on her."

Authia stirred in Nathen's arms. He looked down upon his sleeping beauty. He had missed her so much. The last thing he wanted to do was to let her go back with Tamara. But, if she did have access to Casandra's original essence, maybe it would all be over soon.

An hour later, Nathen gently nudged Authia awake. It was several minutes before she was totally coherent. "My love, how do you feel?"

Authia sat up on Nathen's lap, yawned, and stretched her arms above her head. "Like I've been hit by a bus. What did Casandra do to me?"

"It is not so much what my mother did to you but rather what I did to you to counteract her spell. I am sorry, my Mistress, but at times the counterspell can have significant side effects."

"No problem. Thank you, Tamara, for whatever you did." Authia tried to move off Nathen's lap and sit on the ground next to him, but Nathen made no attempt to remove his arms from around her. "I think I know where Casandra keeps her essence. How small can the container be?"

"Very small." Tamara picked up a large pebble from the ground. "Something this size would work."

Authia laughed. "She's wearing it around her neck. I know she is."

"How do you know this? I find it hard to believe that my mother would keep it on her person."

"Yes. But you said yourself it would be inside a mundane object, out in the open. An amulet couldn't be more mundane. And it's right out in the open. Question is, how do we get it?"

"It will not be easy. I am probably the only one that my mother would allow to get that close and even then, I would have but one chance."

"Can't we take it from her as she sleeps. She's drugged, isn't she?"

"Yes. But my mother is very powerful and her natural instinct to protect the amulet could overpower the sleep potion."

"Nathen, even though I love being held by you, I need to think. And, right now, you're a distraction... if you know what I mean." Authia smiled seductively at Nathen, who reluctantly lowered his arms.

He knew exactly what Authia was referring to. Just holding her in his lap caused his manhood to bulge as though it were trying to burst the seams of his pants. Authia tenderly kissed Nathen, then stood and began to pace. "So, what do we know?"

* * * *

Authia was not expecting a response. She was thinking out loud. Somewhere, in all her knowledge of Casandra, there was the answer. She just needed to find it. "Casandra believes that Nathen's dead. She also believes that I'm silenced and in a drug-induced sleep. As far as she's concerned, Jamya's on his way with our child. Failing that, she has a spell that she can use that has the power to kill all those involved with the spell. So, everything is to our advantage with the exception of the spell. What we need to do is steal the parchment. No parchment, no spell. And then there's her essence. How do we get a hold of that? First things first." Authia directed her conversation to the group. "We need to take that parchment out of the equation."

Tamara looked curiously at her. "And how do you plan to accomplish this?"

Authia stopped her pacing and smiled at the group. "I think I've a plan that will put an end to Casandra's rule."

CHAPTER FORTY-THREE

Casandra started to stir. Her mind felt as if it were swimming in a pool of fog. She tried to open her eyes, but her eyelids would not cooperate. Slowly she sat up, resting on her right elbow. Again, she tried to open her eyes, focusing on the room around her. Someone was there. She could make out the silhouette of a person sitting at the end of her sleeping mat. She smiled, closed her eyes, and took a deep breath, hoping to clear her head. "Please fetch me some broth, Tamara. I'm having difficulty waking."

"Good morning to you too. And, no, I will not fetch you any broth."

Casandra's eyes flew open. She sat straight up. In that instant, all became clear. Sitting at the end of her mat was the outsider. "How could you possibly be here?"

Authia laughed. "Do you actually think that your childish spells would have any effect on me? You have much to learn."

"Where is Tamara?"

"Probably just waking up from the effects of the sleeping potion I gave her. The one that you were going to give me." Authia stood up, looming over Casandra. "I think we'll do the presentation as soon as the village is awake. And before you think that you may have the slightest chance of overpowering me... know this." Authia produced the parchment that she had tucked in the back of her jeans. Casandra's eyes went wide. She tried to speak, but no sound came. "Judging from your reaction, you know exactly which parchment this is."

"That could be any parchment!"

"I told you that I could read you like a child. You hid this parchment behind the shelves. You were going to use it on me if Jamya failed in bringing you my child. Well... he has failed. My child is far out of his—and for that matter, your—reach. Get dressed. I'll wait for you at the gathering hut."

Casandra watched in utter disbelief as Authia left her hut. She had the parchment and she knew of Jamya. Casandra sat there frightened of what was to transpire. She dared not try to stop the outsider with sorcery. Her only hope would be to discredit her at the presentation. She was an outsider without the Lord at her side. Her chances were slim. As Casandra threw the blanket off her, she was already planning a way to sway the odds in her favour. But she couldn't do it alone. She needed help, someone expendable. She thought of Samin. Quickly, Casandra dressed in her ceremonial gown, and as she left her hut, she gave orders to the guard to find Samin.

* * * *

As the sun rose above the horizon, Hansen drove the last few miles on the rutted road. Both he and Tammy drew a breath of relief as they left the jungle behind and headed toward the Free Spirit. Joshawa smiled as he reached out to Hansen with his tiny hands, as if he too knew that they were safe. Once they were clear of the jungle, the two-way radio in the truck started to work. Hansen keyed the mic and called Morris. He was ecstatic when he was told that the Free Spirit was still in her berth and would be there for several more days. Their safe harbour was only a few hours away.

* * * *

Nathen and his twenty-one men were preparing to leave the safety of the birthing hut and head to the village. They waited for Tamara to give them the signal. Once they knew the plan was in motion, Jamya would lead them to the village, following a route where they could arrive unnoticed. They would wait just outside the gathering hut while Authia paved the way to present herself and, more importantly, Nathen.

* * * *

Head held high, Authia walked through the centre of the village, heading toward the gathering hut. Cameron stayed in the shadows, keeping an eye on his Mistress. He noticed that some of the villagers were already awake and they watched on in wonderment and puzzlement. Cameron remembered that the last time they'd seen his Mistress was when she'd entered the priestesses' hut. By rights, she shouldn't have been allowed to live after confronting Casandra. Cameron smiled to himself, for there she was, alive and ready to take on the high priestess. Two minutes later, Cameron noticed Casandra as she left her family hut, dressed in her ceremonial gown complete with mask. She was heading for the gathering hut as well, stopping only once to speak with Samin.

* * * *

Tamara started to wake up. She was still lying on the ground of the priestesses' hut. Desperately she tried to shake off the remnants of the potion she had taken earlier. How long had she been asleep? Part of Authia's plan was to dose Tamara with the sleeping potion. That way, if Casandra came upon her, she would think that Authia dosed Tamara. Tamara looked about the hut but could not see Authia. She could only assume that her Mistress was already in the family hut.

Tamara closed her eyes and tried to focus on her Mistress. It was difficult, for her mind was still swimming in a fog so thick that it was effectively blocking her gift of sight. Tamara sat up, crossed her legs in front of her, then reached into her waistband and produced the second leaf packet. She placed it by her feet and closed her eyes. With her hands on her knees, she began chanting. Slowly the packet smoldered, releasing a fog-like mist not unlike what had been used on Authia. Tamara leaned in and inhaled three good breaths of the mist. Then sat up and allowed the potion to do its job.

Within minutes, Tamara's mind was clear. Once again, she could focus on her Mistress. She was just in time to catch the tail end of her Mistress' encounter with her mother. Tamara then switched her focus to her Lord. *The plan is in motion, my Lord. It is time for you to come.*

* * * *

Authia entered the gathering hut to find it empty. No villagers were present, and the only furniture was a large platform positioned at the very back of the hut. Authia walked over to it, examining the clay pots that surrounded it. "Is this really what you want?" Authia whirled around to find Casandra standing at the entrance of the hut. "You will not be accepted. No matter what powers you have, you're still just an outsider. You will lose and you will be put to death."

"You're rather confident. I'll take my chances." Authia walked around the platform until she came upon a set of stairs. She climbed, then sat cross-legged on the platform floor. "I'm ready when you are."

* * * *

Casandra eyed Authia cautiously. She was risking everything allowing the outsider to be presented. Unfortunately, it was out of her hands. Too many of her people had seen her. Without taking her attention off Authia, she called out for Samin. He was at her side in seconds. "Wake the village. Have everyone attend this presentation. And bring me my daughter."

Samin bowed to his Mistress and left to carry out her demands. "I don't wish to share the platform with you."

"Too bad. I'm not leaving."

"You have not earned the right to be raised above my people. You'll present yourself on the ground. Only when you are accepted are you permitted to stand on the platform."

"Why do I believe that you are making the rules up as we go. I'm not leaving this platform. We will state our cause on equal ground."

In order for Casandra's plan to work, Authia had to be on the ground. Authia was not budging and Casandra had to mind her manners. She couldn't have her people see her being cruel or unjust toward the outsider. That would definitely work against her.

Tamara entered the hut, looking upset with herself. "Mother, I do not know what to say. I am so sorry."

"Care to tell me what happened?"

"I thought she was asleep. I turned my back but for a moment. The next thing I remember is waking up, and the outsider was gone." Tamara lowered her head. "What will be my punishment, Mother?"

"That depends."

Tamara frowned. "I do not understand."

"It depends on the outcome of this presentation. Go. You'll take your place with me on the platform. You'll stand between the outsider and me at all times. Do I make myself clear?"

Tamara nodded and silently went to take her place on the platform. Casandra, however, remained standing ten feet from the platform until Samin returned. Quietly she whispered something in Samin's ear. Samin left, and Casandra smiled smugly at Authia. There was more than one way to get what she wanted. And what she wanted was the outsider dead!

CHAPTER FORTY-FOUR

The hut began to fill with villagers. And those that had not witnessed Authia entering the hut looked on in shocked bewilderment. When the hut was nearly full, Casandra squared her shoulders and, like a regal queen, made her way to the platform. Slowly, she climbed the steps, then took her place on the far right, keeping Tamara between them. Authia stood up as she gazed out at the crowd. She was in awe at the sheer number of people that were attending the presentation. All through her captivity it never occurred to her as to how many people were actually a part of the tribe.

* * * *

Also in awe of the size of his tribe was Nathen. He watched in the shadows of the jungle as the gathering hut filled to overcapacity. All were there to witness the presentation. Jamya took advantage of the large attendance and the fact that everyone's attention was riveted on Authia. Slowly he led the group to just outside of the gathering hut. Nathen remained at the back of the group as Jamya stood in the entrance. Nathen knew Jamya was waiting for the right opportunity to present him to his people.

Nathen stood with his back against the hut wall. The village that lay before him was unnervingly quiet. Behind him was the whispered hum of people wondering who the outsider was. He needed to see what was happening. He turned around and carefully pulled apart a very small section of the sapling trees. Just enough to give him sight into the hut. There, standing on a platform, was his beloved Authia. She looked confident as she stood facing her jury... the people that were going to decide her fate. Nathen was relieved. He didn't know what he would do if she had been frightened. Cautiously, Nathen watched on as Casandra raised her hand to silence the crowd.

"We're here today because this outsider feels that she has the right to be presented to our tribe as a possible leader. She feels that she has more power, more knowledge, than the priestesses that have ruled this tribe since the time of Joshawa." The crowd came alive, voicing their displeasure with the outsider. Who was she to think she was better than any of their priestesses.

* * * *

Casandra smirked at Authia. As far as she was concerned, Authia already had one foot in the grave. "You've every right to be disturbed by this outsider. She came to us claiming to have powers not unlike my own. She claimed that she could produce the son of Joshawa." The crowd gasped, whispers running wild amongst them. Once again, Casandra raised her hand to silence them. "I must admit that this outsider does possess the ability to meld with me, to read my mind. However, she has failed in producing the son of Joshawa. And why has she failed? Because he doesn't exist!" The crowd became more vocal, some calling for the death of the trickster and some fixated on the fact that she promised to produce the son of Joshawa. Casandra looked over to Authia, who seemed unaffected by the jeers from the crowd.

She just smiled back at Casandra, then melded with her. *Keep talking. Then I'll have my turn.*

Casandra turned back to the crowd. "It's written that one day when the son of Joshawa returns home, he'll do so with an outsider at his side. It's written that he'll be given the opportunity to defend his ancestor for abandoning his people. But the son of Joshawa isn't here, only the outsider. And an outsider on her own has no rights. No place amongst us. We don't care what powers she claims to have. She isn't a priestess and shouldn't be treated as one. She has, on more than one occasion, threatened me, your High Priestess. Just last night she attacked Tamara, rendering her unconscious and unable to defend herself. Who knows what sorcery she spoke while my daughter lay helpless. To listen to her is like speaking with the devil himself. This outsider is nothing but a liar, a trickster, and should be sentenced with a penalty fitting her crimes to our tribe. As your high priestess, I advise you not to listen to her lies and deception. Don't let her corrupt our ways, our life. I demand that she be put to death for her crimes. Bow if you agree, or stand if you wish for this trickster to be heard." To Cassandra's horror, a good number of people bowed, but still, a large portion of the gathering remained standing. She would be heard. *Now, before she speaks.*

* * * *

Jamya was observing the crowd and especially the guards. That was when he noticed Samin making his way to the front of the crowd. What was he up to? As a guard, he was to remain at his post. Jamya's gut started churning. Something wasn't right. Cautiously, he followed Samin, at the same time trying to remain invisible to the crowd around him.

* * * *

Casandra drew a deep breath and slowly let it out. "So, you wish to hear the outsider speak. Are you prepared for the lies that you will hear? Are you prepared to put our tribe, our home, at risk?" Those comments gave second thought to some of the people that remained standing but not all of them. "Fine. The outsider will have her chance to defend herself."

Casandra scanned the crowd and was pleased to see Samin at the base of the platform. Discreetly, she nodded. Samin jumped onto the platform and raised his machete high above his head. Screaming out the words, "Die sorceress," he plunged the machete at Authia.

* * * *

Jamya stood not a breath away from Samin. He saw the machete and knew what was happening. As Samin jumped onto the platform, Jamya was right behind him. He dove between Samin and Authia, knocking Authia off her feet. He felt the cold steel as Samin's blade penetrated his back, piercing his heart. Jamya fell to the ground, the blood running freely from his mouth.

* * * *

Arman and his men fell into action. Two men stayed behind, having to wrestle Nathen to keep him on the outside of the hut. Nathen shook the men free, then watched on as Arman, Tuval, and two other men jumped onto the platform. Arman tackled Samin to the ground while Tuval held his spear at Casandra's throat. Authia crawled over to Jamya, sat next to him, and placed his head on her lap. Her eyes welled up with tears that ran freely down her cheeks as Jamya took his last breath. The rest of Arman's men encircled the platform so that no other could try an attack.

Tamara stood by her mother, shaking her head. "What have you done, Mother? Jamya was a good man. A loyal warrior."

"I didn't kill him."

"Oh yes, you did, Mother. I have a confession to make. I can hear your words, your thoughts, and I heard you order Samin to kill the outsider. To kill my Mistress."

Casandra looked at her daughter in utter disbelief. "Your Mistress? What are you saying?"

"I am saying that your rule, the rule of our family, is over. Now will you willingly hand over your essence, or do I need to take it from you? Please, Mother, do not make me take it from you."

* * * *

Casandra looked at the crowd and saw in their faces hatred and contempt. She was done. She had gone too far. Slowly she reached up and untied the leather string that held her essence in place. Reluctantly, she handed to her daughter. "How did you know it was on me."

"I did not. My Mistress did." Tamara passed the amulet to Authia, then turned to face the crowd. "You, as well as myself, have all been deceived. Not just by my mother but by all the priestesses since the time of Serena. To the time that Lord Joshawa disappeared. I know the truth, for I have seen it in the eyes of this outsider. I have witnessed it myself. Lord Joshawa and Julia never left. Their bones lay resting beneath the birthing hut." The entire tribe went so quiet that she could have heard a pin drop. They could not believe what they were hearing.

Then one voice spoke out. "My priestess, how do you know this? How do we know that what you speak is not a lie?"

Tamara smiled. "Do you wish to speak the truth, Mother? Or shall I?"

Casandra started to step forward but hesitated when Tuval did not lower his spear. He glanced to his Mistress. Authia nodded. "It's all right. Let her pass." The crowd looked on, wide-eyed. Casandra closed her eyes in defeat. Her people had just witnessed one of their own actually taking orders from the outsider. When Tuval lowered his spear, Casandra stepped forward.

She stood next to her daughter. "And what would you have me say?"

"The truth. The truth about Joshawa's son."

Casandra scrutinized the crowd. This was not going to end well for her. "My daughter's speaking the truth. The bodies of Lord Joshawa and Julia lay beneath the birthing hut. They were placed there by Serena and her mother." The crowd vocally displayed their anger. They called for Casandra's blood.

"And what else, Mother?"

Casandra drew a deep breath. "Myself and the high priestesses before me have kept this secret so that we could rule the tribe. My daughter wasn't part of this conspiracy. Neither was Dena or the rest of my family, for that matter." Casandra hesitated for a moment, knowing what she was about to reveal would seal her fate. "The son of Joshawa does exist... or rather did exist. He's dead and, if you must know, it is I who ordered his death."

The crowd pushed forward, trying to get to Casandra. They were almost to the point of being out of control. Arman's men held them back as Tamara raised her hand to silence the unruly crowd. "Please do not do this. If you exact punishment on my mother, you will be no different than she is. It is up to the Lord and his mate to exact punishment."

Casandra watched as Tamara held her hand out for Authia to take. Authia gently laid Jamya's head on the platform, then stood and accepted Tamara's hand. The two stood side by side staring out at the crowd. "I present Authia. A priestess in her own right and the mate to our Lord, the son of Joshawa. And now I present to you, my people, the direct descendant of Lord Joshawa."

Everyone in the crowd looked at each, wondering what was happening.

Casandra shook her head. "No... he's dead." She turned to face her daughter. "You saw him!"

"I saw what you wanted to see, nothing more. Arman, if you would be so kind and bring in our Lord."

Arman's men cleared a path and, as Nathen entered the hut, each and every villager grew quiet. They stared at the stranger in total disbelief. A stranger whose appearance was not unlike their own. Nathen joined Authia on the platform, placed his arms around her, and tenderly kissed her.

Tamara respectfully stepped back. "Your people wait to hear from their Lord."

* * * *

Nathen looked out at the crowd... his people. "I am Nathen, son of Joshawa, and I've come here to liberate you from the evil that has ruled this village for so long. I bring with me my mate, Authia. Like my father, I have chosen an outsider for my wife. For too long you've lived in fear. Lived on lies and deceit. That ends now. With me. I'm sorry that I didn't come sooner, but for the past two centuries, I've been cursed. Living my life in the outside world, oblivious to the existence of my people. I'm no longer cursed, due mostly to my wife. And I'm no longer oblivious to your existence. I will not demand my right as the son of Joshawa to be your

Lord. But instead, I ask that you permit me to rule and become your Lord. I ask that you accept my wife as one of us. Bow if you approve, or stand and be heard." Nathen and Authia watched as one by one Nathen's people bowed to their Lord. All except Casandra.

CHAPTER FORTY-FIVE

An elaborate ceremony was held and Jamya was buried with all the rights and privileges of a great warrior. According to the Jelani tribe, in order to become Lord of the tribe, you must be ushered into manhood first. A rite of passage that involves a ceremony that had not been performed for over two hundred years. The tribe was a bustle of activity while they prepared for the ceremony. Dena had recovered from her ordeal with Casandra and was given the honour to retrieve Nathen and Authia's child. She left for the outsiders' village and was met by Sam and Tomas. Five days later, Hansen and Tammy stood by the falls. Safely cradled in Tammy's arms was Joshawa. Dena offered Hansen and Tammy, as well as Sam and Tomas, the opportunity to cross through the falls and enter the valley of the Lion people. They accepted and made the journey to the village.

* * * *

In the gathering hut, Casandra stood before Nathen and Authia. She looked upon Authia with extreme malice, for around Authia's neck was her essence. Her displeasure did not go unnoticed by Nathen. "I'd be a little more appreciative of Authia. It's because of her that you still live. The tribe wants vengeance and retribution. I believe the punishment for your crime is death."

"So, I'm to be grateful for my existence. Such as it is. I

wait every day for your decision as to what you're going to do to me. I'm a prisoner in that tiny hut, with no access to anyone."

Authia snorted. "That sounds familiar. That tiny hut is the same hut you kept me in. Casandra, make me believe that you're truly upset about what you've done. Give me a reason not to lock you up for the rest of your life."

Casandra appeared puzzled. "You're not planning to kill me?"

Nathen shook his head. "That's not what we do. You'll not be killed. I understand that your family used to be healers. Is that right?"

"Yes, and we still are. Why do you ask?"

"Here are your options. We are rebuilding the birthing hut as we speak. It'll become our medical hut. You may spend the rest of your days living there, tending to our sick and wounded. Helping to bring life into our world. Giving the birthing hut a purpose. Or, you can spend the remainder of your days in that tiny hut. Your choice."

"You would trust me to heal others? That would require my essence. I'll need it to summon the healing spirits."

Authia took the amulet from around her neck. "You'll have to earn our trust. Tamara is now high priestess. She has taken half of your original essence and placed it in safe keeping. You may become our healer, but step one foot out of line and your essence will be used against you. Do I make myself clear?" Authia passed the amulet to Casandra.

She held the amulet in her hand, obviously taken aback by what was happening. "Why would you do this? After everything I put you through. What I put everyone through."

Authia took a step closer to Casandra. "For Tamara. She loves you, and I owe her my life. If you love your daughter, you'll take our offer and make a better life for yourself."

Casandra bowed to Nathen and Authia. "I serve my Lord and Mistress."

Nathen's family was whole again. Hansen and Tammy had decided to stay on and live with the Jelani tribe. Sam and Tomas stayed on long enough to witness Nathen's ceremony into manhood, then returned to their own village. The months went by, and Nathen and Authia settled into their new life. Nathen had finally found himself. He finally knew who and what he was. The village thrived with their new Lord and Mistress.

* * * *

During their time of peace and contentment, Nathen was completely unaware of the conflict brewing in the outside world. Revolution had come to the Congo region, and soon it would find itself on the doorstep of the hidden valley. The fight was not yet over.

The End

ABOUT THE AUTHOR

Christine Frances was born July 29, 1958, in Halifax, Nova Scotia, Canada. She was born to a military family, her father being in the Royal Canadian Navy. Her passion for writing started at an early age with her seventh-grade teacher, Sister Lambert, playing an influential part in developing Christine's love for short stories. After a period in Christine's life when she put down her pen to run her own business, raise two boys and become a grandmother, the desire to write once again took over and the series Lord of His People was born.

77993622R00172

Made in the USA
Middletown, DE
29 June 2018